The Disharmonic Misadventures of David Stein

A Novel By

JONATHAN L. SEGAL

ISBN: 1466265426
ISBN 13: 9781466265424

To Noah.

After I wrote the first 60 pages and had basically put it aside for a very long time, he asked to read it and then said:

"Dad, this is good. I need to know what happens to this guy. You need to finish this." And so I did.

CHAPTER ONE

[NEAR THE END OF THE TWENTIETH CENTURY]

David Stein stood behind the "No Admittance" door wolfing down a hastily bought turkey and lettuce sandwich. No mayo, no frills. This had to be eaten quickly and quietly and there was no time for the pleasure of chewing. In fact, the minimally chewed mouthfuls were going down so fast that David knew he'd be in gut-wrenching pain soon enough.

Feeling ridiculous, like some perverse Clark Kent in a phone booth costume change, he opened the door and looked about furtively. Seeing nobody, he darted across the hall into the men's room. He brushed the crumbs off his tuxedo and studied his teeth in the mirror. Finding bits of lettuce tangled in his lower front teeth, he rinsed madly with cold water, swishing as violently as he could. After checking and finding no more crumbs he straightened his bow tie, combed what was left of his hair, and smiled his best headshot smile.

At forty-two, David Stein had the face of a much younger man. He had piercing blue eyes with sleepy lids. He liked it when women told him that he looked like Mikhail Baryshnikov, the great Russian dancer. True, he was thinner, but at five-foot-six and a half inches, about the right height. It was just too damn bad about his hair. All he could do was to keep it cut short.

Reaching into his pants pocket, he pulled out a cheap digital watch. The vinyl strap had broken long ago. Seeing that he had used up about seven minutes for food-stuffing and bathroom ablutions, he headed up the stairs. As he launched up this flight of stairs, two at a time, he began to scat sing. If you had been at the top of those stairs, you'd have thought that some sort of jazzed-out Freddy Kruger was coming. At the top of the flight of stairs, he entered the lobby. His all time favorite lobby. The Great Hall of New York's Metropolitan Museum Of Art, at Fifth Avenue at Eighty-second Street. He realized that as usual, he had rushed to be ready on time and was now a few minutes early. In a half hour he'd be singing and playing piano at a party in the Medieval Armor room.

Feeling a twinge of claustrophobia, he decided to take one last look at the outside world. He walked quickly and purposefully through the crowd, crossing the cavernous room. He stepped outside into the bright Spring sunshine.

Standing at the top of the Museum's legendary twenty-five step staircase, he gazed down and tried to study every face in the crowd. He had to make sure that he missed nothing. His friends thought that he knew more people than anyone they'd ever met, but in fact it was really because he studied every face in every crowd. He simply spotted people he knew when others might not have.

Tourists, yuppies and college students lounged on the great wide steps, basking in the sunlight and in their own successes. At the base of the steps, vendors sold pretzels and hot dogs. A cab pulled up, and a long haired young man with his face covered by white face makeup and wearing a black leotard and tights jumped out and strode quickly towards the steps. He stopped abruptly a few feet from the steps. He froze mid-stride in a walking position. A wave of recognition moved slowly through the crowd, starting with the people nearest the young man. As they realized that he was a mime, their reaction triggered the knowledge further back in the crowd that something was happening. New Yorkers have to get through that first moment when the worst is assumed; the moment when they think that violence is upon them. Only then could they go on happily to accept that entertainment had arrived instead.

David stopped to watch from the top of the steps. The mime was waiting for the right moment. That brief instant when all eyes were upon him, and boredom had not yet set in. David knew what the mime was thinking, and guessed correctly as to when the frozen stance would be abandoned. Get the audience's attention, but don't make them wait too long. Don't lose them, or it's all over.

Thawing from his stance, he started to imitate the first little toddler who approached him. His body became a two-year-old's, stiff-legged and slightly off-balance. Boris Karloff's Frankenstein with Robin Williams' baby face. The crowd laughed in recognition of the truth of his art. Like a two-legged chameleon, he now proceeded to become anyone who walked by. He became in succession, an elderly black man with a cane, a Japanese business man who took pictures of the mime as the mime mimed taking pictures of him, the pretzel vendor, an impossibly obese woman, and a beautiful girl in sunglasses. The crowd, enjoying being in on the joke every time, oohed and ah-hed, nodded their heads, clapped their hands, and fed the energy. David smiled.

Emboldened by the response, the young man stepped to the curb and stared uptown into the Fifth Avenue traffic. He stepped out into the street, even though the light was green for the oncoming downtown traffic. And now, to the gasps and excited whoops of the crowd, he became a traffic cop. In a wild mock semaphore, he used his arms to control the cabs and buses and cars that were whisked into his vortex. They were his hostages, and they were on stage now.

The first vehicle he stopped was a white stretch limousine. He extended his arms to stop the limo, and then, only when the limo driver had acquiesced, did he let him go on. The people on the museum steps whistled and cheered. Next, a city bus, half full of passengers just trying to get downtown, approached. The mime blocked its path, and the bus slowed down. He ran over to the front bumper of the bus. He jumped up on the bumper and stared eye to eye with the driver through the windshield. The crowd roared hysterically. Then he mimed tying a rope to the bumper and then proceeded to "pull" the bus with the great rope. He sweated and strained, and the bus driver played along. The bus moved slowly, looking to all as if the mime were actually towing it. The groaning of the bus seemed to David like a circus elephant trumpeting under the crack of the whip. The crowd on the stairs applauded for the young man.

A yellow taxi pulled up. The driver had been driving since 4:00 a.m. and it was now 4:00 p.m. He was exhausted but determined. He had just dropped a fare at Fifth Avenue and Eighty-sixth Street, and was hoping to head home to Queens. His intent was to take one last fare down Fifth, and then go east in the sixties and get on the Fifty-ninth Street Bridge to Queens and home. If he was lucky, he could still beat the heart of rush hour. He was not in the mood for a young man dressed like a demon to block his path in the middle of Fifth Avenue.

He hit his brakes and the cab screeched to a halt as the mime used his arms to signal him to do so. The driver leaned out his window and swore.

"You asshole! Get the fuck out of the way!"

The young man looked hurt. He rolled his shoulders into a slump and put his fists to his eyes in great big silent clown sobs. The people laughed and let out an "Awww!" to show their solidarity with the performer. The driver all but imploded and held his breath. His face turned red and beads of perspiration rolled down his stubbled cheek. The mime wagged his finger at the driver not to be a bad boy, and then he started to tow the car with his mime rope. The driver knew that he couldn't get through unless he played along. He knew that if he started to inch forward, the crowd would cheer for both of them. He really just wanted to get home to sleep, but it looked like the only way home was to join the show. But he was so damned angry! He meant to depress the accelerator just a bit. He meant for it to all turn out all right. He meant to. But in his pent up anger, he floored it. The cab shot forward catching the young man's foot.

To David, it reminded him of a toy he had had when he was a child. It was a small pair of rollers, like an old-fashioned clothes wringer. It was called a Magic Money Changer. You could put in a dollar bill and a preset ten dollar bill would come out the other side. This was what David saw when he saw the mime go under

5

the wheel. But what was different was that the white-faced head of the mime flew off. And it flew quite far, landing on the curb, amid the crowd.

After time stopped and total silence, they screamed. They screamed madness and blood and horror. The day was shaken and the birds flew away. People fainted. Some threw up. David stood staring in disbelief. He stood there for some time. To be honest with himself, he really wanted to get closer to the head, but he didn't dare. Not because of the horror of it, but because he didn't want anyone to know that he wanted to see such a thing close at hand. Reluctantly, as chaos smothered the crowd, David Stein turned around and walked into the Metropolitan Museum Of Art, to sing Gershwin at a cocktail party in the Medieval Armor Room.

What kind of person leaves a scene of carnage and goes off to entertain the wealthy? How could David reconcile these two worlds in the space of minutes? It seems that growing up in New York City necessitates an emotional makeup like that of a revolving door. Quick access into one world and quick access back out. David's psyche operated on many levels simultaneously. He could truly feel the pain of the mime's death, and yet he could instantly compartmentalize the feeling. The place where he stored that feeling was separated from the place where he bathed in the glitter of his musical performing life. And because of this compartmentalization, something usually rang false in his piano playing. While his skills and quick musical wit were always available to him on a moment's notice, truth was forever in a different part of his self than the part that was playing. He used that wit to mask the honesty that was lacking.

There were honest moments in his playing, but rarely was anyone around to hear them. The sound of chattering partygoers and clinking glasses had long ago overwhelmed his musical sense of integrity. If they weren't really listening, why struggle to release the truth? And again, if they did listen, he wasn't about to open up his feelings in front of these patrician snobs. Nobody understood who he was, if he understood it himself. At his best, he was a vehicle for the mysteries of the muse, but more often at his worst, he was a thoughtless regurgitator of musical patterns that he'd played thousands of times.

And what or who was this muse that we've heard so much about through the centuries? What world does the creative person enter while the crowd sees nothing? David's childhood friends who had become doctors, lawyers and Wall Street wizards were usually in the dark as to what David could do. While he despairingly envied them their affluence, he knew that something besides money separated them from him. He could enter that graceful world where the waters sing. All he had to do was place his hands on the keys when nobody was around, and he was in that door. The door was real, and he'd gone through for many years. His friends could not pass in. There was a a curtain between them and that world. They could not translate themselves into creators. He, on the other hand, could not seem to join their world of comfort, though he wished for it.

The artist tries to take others through that door. He may entice them, or he may drag them kicking and screaming, but to complete the artistic act, the others must pass through.

On the edge of this door stands David Stein. He walks carelessly along the edge of it, and his foot sometimes slips and he falls in a bit, and then he recovers himself and extricates the foot. His world is largely internal, and his outer persona is a misrepresentation of his own making. From within this vantage point he is safe from the probing stares of the mob. They see him sitting at the piano, rarely smiling. He is scared to death to smile, and that is one truth that shows.

Arriving in the museum's Medieval Room, he sees the knights on horseback that have been there his entire life. A blink of the mind ago he was a small child here, in the company of his Aunt Sonia. The knights towered above him, mid-joust. Now, in his black and white armor with bow tie, he has returned. Perhaps he is really the Court Jester. Maybe he is the King's Magician. Or is he a Troubadour? David feels that he fulfills all of these roles here.

A wealthy blond matron in a gown disturbs his reverie.

"Would you bring me some white wine."

It is not a question. It is an assumption. The assumption of class. In his mind David barks at her like an angry dog. She then lifts her gown to run away screaming in terror, and she runs directly into a knight's lance. Her face is skewered, neatly between the eyeballs. David thinks that this lance was waiting the many dusty centuries to do this one noble thing, here at the end of the twentieth century, on the East Side of New York City.

"I'm not the waiter, Madame. I am only the lowly pianist."

She covers her mouth with her diamond-studded hand, and with her other hand grabs his as if she had known him forever. He can smell her perfume and he can guess the price per ounce. She laughs good naturedly.

"I'm so sorry! Please forgive me."

"Of course, it's perfectly natural. After all, I am in uniform."

How many times he had been mistaken in his tuxedo for waiters and Maitre'd's, yet it still burned him.

"I believe that the bar is over there."

She presses his hand again, and apologizes once more. Though she follows his direction, rather than walk all the way to the bar, she stops a waiter and has him do it. She is only twenty feet from the bar, but she can't bring herself to serve herself. David wonders if she knows how to tie her own shoes.

A Steinway grand piano sits seductively in the middle of the room. Seeing it, David falls immediately under its spell. He walks up to the keyboard and looks it over before trying it. This is the moment for pianists that is so like the moment a man undresses a woman to see what's underneath. He lovingly caresses the keys without playing a note. They are smooth and they shine. He will not need to dust them off to prevent his fingers from turning black while playing. So many nice pianos in nice places and they haven't been touched and they're filthy. But not this one. She has become a virgin again through the magic of a piano tuner's craft. Right here in this room, in front of the very wealthy, David will possess her for a couple of hours. On a conscious level, it's a secret. But he knows that some people in the room will feel it. Music is mathematical, and also spiritual, but music is also very sexual. And when an adept jazz player performs a romantic ballad, he is really performing. When David plays a ballad, women in the room have a physiological reaction. They may be walking with their husbands, but they feel it. And David knows this. And not a word is said about it.

As people mill and mingle at this museum fundraiser, the effects of his playing vary. For some, it's an ambience that says that they have arrived at the top, and that they are as important as their inflated egos would have them believe. For others it is the thrill of New York at its most glamorous. Something to tell their friends about. For some it is the remembrance by song, of precious memories from other times. The song links these people to the events that passed when they first heard the song. But there are some out there, with a drink in their hand and a sudden glow in their eyes, for whom it is passion. And when he starts to sing, that passion burns. There is no mistaking the tone in his voice. It is a longing. And that longing awakens a response in many of the women in that room.

The knights clamber off their steeds and gather round the piano. David plays "Rule Britannia" and the knights laugh heartily. They have mugs of ale in their armored hands. They pry open their helmet visors and pour the ale into the emptiness within. They have no faces, of course. David plays Beatle songs for them. Then the James Bond theme. They sing lustily along to the score from "Camelot". One slaps David on the back so hard, that David almost goes flying. And now, they raise their mugs and bellow a British soccer song, to the tune of "My Bonnie Lies Over The Ocean."

Oh pour me a big glass of cider
Oh pour me a big glass of stout
Oh pour me a big glass of ale
And then watch me puke it all out
Puke it, Puke it,
Puke it all over yer mum, yer mum
Puke it, Puke it,
Puke it all over yer mum

As the song finishes, a pompous, overweight museum staffer comes over to the piano and speaks to the knights.

"Would you please get back on your horses? This is a cocktail party, not a fraternity beer bash! There are some very important people here who don't need to hear this crap!"

There is silence. The knights stand still like the statues they are. They don't answer.

"Well?" barks the red-faced staffer.

He is answered by a "whoosh" and a "kathonk" as his chest is pierced by an arrow. He gurgles in shock. He looks at David for an answer, but David just shrugs his shoulders. The man falls to the ground. The knight with the crossbow shakes his fist triumphantly and they all give each other clanging high-fives. David plays "God Save The Queen" and "We Are The Champions". They sing with great gusto. After this merry carousing, the knights return to their horses. David plays a slow blues.

CHAPTER TWO

David's apartment on West Eighty-sixth Street was a dark studio dominated by a black Mason-Hamlin grand piano. The darkness was the result of the studio's positioning in the back of the building. Out his only window was a brick wall that he could reach out and touch with his foot. He did this often. He'd hold on to either side of his window frame and stick out his foot 'til he made contact. Then he'd pull his leg back in, lean out and look up, hoping to catch a small square of blue sky.

He always felt trapped in his home and so hated being there. He was much more comfortable viewing Manhattan as his home. On the street he felt natural. His own nervousness matched the stuttering rhythms of the city. When he ran into friends on the street, it was justifiable to have short, artificial conversations and then move on. Nobody could dig too deep on the street and he liked that. His friends numbered few, and none really knew him. His aloofness and his tendency to brood kept many good people away. His heart was jammed like a stopped-up toilet and he badly needed a plumber named God. His veneer, perfected through endless appearances as a pianist, was slick and evasive. He had learned over and over not to warm to people that he'd only see once and never again. Except for his perfunctory politeness, the world, like his audience, was shunned.

Out in space among the stars, David stood in his tux, half a million miles tall. In his hand he held a giant pool cue. As he chalked it up, the Earth's people screamed in horrific anticipation. David whistled "We'll Take Manhattan" and calmly shot the moon into the Earth. As tidal waves destroyed civilization, the Earth careened into Venus and then rolled down into a black hole, never to be seen again. David lit a cigarette from the Sun, and inhaled deeply. He then exhaled a nebula that would eventually form a new world for him to control. He sighed a sigh of relief. He did not see God staring at him from behind an asteroid.

At midnight he sat with Saul at a small table in the Stage Deli on Seventh Avenue. Two men in tuxes with bow ties removed, eating giant bowls of chicken soup while they smoked cigarettes. At sixty, Saul was a role model for David. A violinist, he had always worked, he had invested wisely, and but for a hacking cough, was in relatively good health.

"Listen to me David, I'm going to tell you how I think things work."

He drew on his filterless camel, inhaled and coughed loudly in spasms till David had to reach across the table and put his hand on the older man's shoulder.

"Y'okay Saul?"

Saul nodded but kept coughing. He put up his finger to gain a minute's pause. Finally, his shoulders stopped heaving and the color returned to his cheeks.

"David, Bubby, this is how it is... I think. And you of all people will appreciate this if you're smart!"

Saul stared fiercely into his eyes unblinkingly.

"Life, David, is like a piano."

"I don't think I've heard this one, Saul."

"You haven't heard it because it's not a joke. Now listen for once in your life!"

David put down his cigarette in the ashtray, and with his palms flat on the table sat still.

"You have my attention."

"Life, David," Saul began, "is like a piano. Starting at the low end, each note is a year of our life. There are eighty-eight notes, and if we're really lucky, maybe we get eighty-eight years."

David laughed nervously. "Interesting concept. So how come Mozart only lived to thirty-five?"

Saul fixed his gaze upon David. "Mozart traveled with a little four-octave piano, so he was very lucky, actually. He almost outlived the length of his keyboard! Don't be a schmuck, David."

"You really believe this?"

"What's better to believe? David, how old were you when you and the piano became close friends?"

"Five," David remembered.

"So now, you're what, forty-two?"

David nodded and slurped his soup.

"So, let me see. If I'm correct, you are two notes short of half a piano. You are now at D above middle C. That's your note."

David's eyes lit up. He genuinely liked this. Why hadn't he ever thought of it before? All those years staring at the keys and never seeing the calendar of life before his eyes. D above middle C! In two years he would reach half-way.

"Saul, you're sixty. That puts you at ... high A Flat?"

"A good range for a tenor, don't you think?"

Saul sang a high note in a soft squeak of a voice. Both men laughed.

"I'm singing my life, David!"

They shook uncontrollably from the laughter till tears were in their eyes.

"And then, David, and then, you get older and older till the pitch is so high, nobody on Earth can hear you, and you slowly disappear!"

Their laughs abated, Saul wiped his eyes, and David came down to earth, unnerved by his mortality.

"It's like a Mayan calendar," the younger man said. "It's built right into the fucking piano! Right in front of me all the time! Jesus!"

"That's it, David. You were too busy to notice it all these years."

David noticed many things, but he missed their meanings just as often. For instance, New Yorkers don't look up. They don't realize that above the first couple of stories, most apartment buildings have different facades. David was just such a creature of habit. The same jazz licks on the piano, the same tired conversation with clients. When Saul put forth his theory, for David it was a revelation of truth that was always there but never before seen. Now he thought...twelve months in a year, twelve hours on the clock, twelve notes in an octave. How did this come to be? He knew that numbers had meaning, but he didn't really understand those meanings. He knew that mathematics must be significant, but he also knew that he was ignorant of the specifics of this significance. Sure, there was math in music, but he didn't think about it when he played. He was a product of the New York City school system, and he had hated math. He had spent years struggling in grade after grade trying to make sense of something that he could never seem to grasp. Now that he thought of it, music had all sorts of underlying mathematical and physical principles of which he had no understanding.

Still he knew how to manipulate music to effect changes in his listeners. He didn't really know why a dominant chord magnetically wants to return to it's tonic, yet he knew how to use this principle. He knew how to emotionally control his audience, yet had no clue as to why it worked. With the right rhythms he could take possession of their bodies and compel them to dance. He could make them laugh or cry or be wistful. But why did a certain melody, chord progression or use of phrasing have these effects?

Saul knew things that David didn't. They were eighteen years apart in age. Eighteen, which in Hebrew is *chai*, symbolizing life and good fortune. They would always have that magical temporal space separating and joining them together. Saul would always seem to have a wisdom that rang deeper than his own. As long as David felt younger than Saul, he would continue to feel ignorant. Always on the verge of thinking creatively, David was stuck. His career always simmering when it could have been boiling. Greatness eluded him by a moment. He could not step back and see himself in context. Mediocrity had him in a choke hold. If he could only stop and breathe, he might be able to become great.

Have you ever done something for years, over and over? You, an intelligent person? You do this thing forever, and you don't think about why. And then somewhere in your life you awaken and see the thing for what it really is, and it is an unimportant, meaningless thing? You think that you are different from all the others, but then you come to discover that you are as much a sheep as they are. The little endless maze that is your life is so frustrating. But then, something, someone, or a word from that someone, lights your mind on fire, or speaks directly to your soul, and then you are raised up, and you look down at that filthy maze with that sad little person trapped in it, who is you, and you laugh and realize that now that you've seen it from above, you never need to go back into it again?

Well, poor (in spirit) David Stein knew enough to know that somewhere in life one may rise to this realization, but he could not seem to extricate himself from his maze. He could not rise above his maze to be a-mazed. He saw himself as a rat in a tuxedo. All outer glow but putrid on the inside. He hoped that God loved the rat. And every other day, he almost believed it. Almost.

CHAPTER THREE

David Stein, forty-two, D above middle C, pianist or piano-player (depending on his self image of the day) sat at his Mason-Hamlin piano and played along with the music emanating from his stereo. Over the swinging groove of Paul Chamber's bass and Philly Jo Jones' drums came the sounds of a sure-footed elf. It was Red Garland's piano solo on "If I Were A Bell" with the Miles Davis Quintet of the 1950's. His use of space was impeccable. And it was not just the notes that mattered, but the way he touched the instrument that sounded like nobody else. And David knew that when Red Garland recorded this solo so many years before, the last thing on his mind would have been that some sad sonofabitch would be sitting in his living room decades later trying to imitate his sound. David could find the notes, but he couldn't sound like Red. He could not become this other man from another time. The turntable playing this old LP was indeed a time machine. It had brought Miles' band to his home. David was a phantom in their world, longing to materialize, but remaining discorporate.

Sometimes he thought that his own playing was remarkable. He would try to dissociate himself as he practiced and listen to his music as if it were coming from another. He would become an observer in order to give an impartial opinion of himself. This is not unlike the observer in Indian meditation who detaches itself from the meditator in order to focus on the breath. But David as the observer could not stop wondering who was playing the piano if it weren't himself. If he could observe himself play, then where were the notes coming from? Who was making the choices? Or was it just automatic pilot? Once, in college, he sat in a practice room working on a Beethoven Sonata. He didn't play it well, but, after a fashion, knew it by heart. He started to fall asleep at the piano, and actually let his head come lolling down towards the keyboard. In that moment, he realized that his hands kept playing the piece. His hands couldn't have cared less whether or not his head was upright with eyes open or not. And at that moment, the semi-comatose man saw that his head and hands were not in conscious accord.

He turned off the turntable. As was his habit, while the needle returned from the record to its holder, he switched to the tuner button to hear a moment of radio. Piano chords gripped his neck and shook through his spine. He gasped as if he had been electrocuted. Immediately a melody soared around the upper octaves that was like nothing he had ever heard. Agonizingly beautiful, pristine and moving from melancholy to inspiration, the music twisted through him. He sobbed loudly and fell to the floor. He lay on his back on the tattered green carpet crying and laughing hysterically as the music made his mind reel like a fallen-down drunk. Each note hurled him out of this world and into another where the rules did not exist.

He became more and more devoid of tension and slowly sat up to reach the tuner to turn up the volume. He reached for the button but inadvertently hit the tuning presets that were adjacent to the volume button. It had happened a hundred times before, but now his peace was smashed by the thump of techno-pop blasting through the speakers. It was as if a skydiver had reached for the rip cord and tore the parachute away instead. He squinted through his astigmatism and tried to get back. He hit the button. Rock'n'Roll. Again. Country. Again. Rap. He could not return to the station. He could not find the piano music. What station had he been tuned to? Was it the jazz station? Or that little hard-to-find station that had asked him for years to donate to keep them on the air? He tried the jazz station and heard the elevator music that passed for New Jazz. He tried the listener- sponsored station. He knew the frequency, but it seemed to be silent.

He called information and got the number of the station. He punched the numbers on his phone faster than most normal humans could. He heard the seven pitches over his receiver and then he waited. After six rings a recorded voice intoned "You have reached WBGI-FM listener-sponsored radio. At this time we are off the air due to court proceedings in relation to our lease. We hope to be back on the air as soon as our finances will permit us, so that we may serve you, the listening public. This machine does not take messages. Thank you."

He hung up. "Shit!"

Sitting down in the beat-up armchair, he shook his head back and forth. For a brief moment he had been exorcised and cleansed, and now he had been slammed to the earth. Both feelings coursed through him.

What had he heard? What pianist could move him so tumultuously, and in so short a time? He thought of Keith Jarret's crying passion, Art Tatum's roller-coaster balletic runs, Arthur Rubinstein's bell-like tones when he played Chopin. All of these were masters of their own styles. People whom he had tried to follow, with only minimal success. But this was something else, both foreign but familiar. The music had sounded like a name on the tip of his mind. Had he tried to embrace it, it would have vanished. And in his mind, he could feel it still, but he could not reproduce the notes. Like any great music, it went far beyond the notes.

CHAPTER FOUR

*A*bby Mitropoulos sat at the Steinway singing "The Girl From Ipanema" in a small, airy, jazzy voice. Hotel guests, mostly businessmen, sat around the piano on bar stools. The piano top was closed to be available as a table top for drinks. Abby tolerated this with a smile because she knew she had no choice and because it made it possible to have a tip jar on the piano. Every night she'd put a $5 bill in the jar to get things rolling. One night some wise guys from the mob kept stuffing it with $100 bills in return for repeated performances of "My Way." She sang it five times in a row and made every time sound like the first time. She knew how to please the customers.

The Sheraton Hotel stood at Fifty-first Street and Seventh Avenue. This was Abby's steady gig. It wasn't career-shaking but it afforded her a modicum of security in an insecure business. She played the part in a long black gown with a hint of cleavage. With her dark hair piled high and some well-placed cubic zirconium, she looked every inch the part. The businessmen loved her, and most of them were unaware or even interested that she was a good pianist. She had them hooked.

This evening, as David took the steps to the hotel at his usual two at a time, no heads flew off. As he strode into the main floor lounge, Abby spotted him. She knew by the short leather jacket and jeans that he wasn't working tonight, at least not on a gig that required a tux. He smiled at her, and in one brief instant when the businessmen weren't looking, shot him her goofiest cross-eyed smile. He sat down on one of the stools by the piano and listened for a bit. Then he made his request.

"Would you happen to know "Donna Lee?"

He'd hit her with a ninety-mile-a-minute bebop tune. Her lips pursed as if to say "you bastard!" but her eyes kept smiling. She immediately launched into it, but realizing that she'd probably have a musical car crash, decided to play it as a ballad. It almost sounded like Dvorak's *Humoresque* in this manner. David smiled at her resourcefulness and laughed. She knew that she had risen to the challenge without falling into his trap. This was the way of their relationship. The musical gauntlet always thrown, the sardonic remarks that marked their friendship. As she finished, he mouthed "Can you take a break?" She announced to the crowd that she'd return in a few minutes.

"Let's get a drink," he said as he motioned her to the bar.

Tonight he wasn't working, and she certainly wasn't as careful about liquor on the job as he was. They sat at the bar and he ordered two beers. Abby looked at him quizzically.

"How are you? You've got a different strange look in your eyes than your usual strange look."

He instantly became very serious, looking almost as if he were about to cry. He couldn't get words out.

"Did someone die? What is it?"

He looked down at the ground, took a deep breath and let it out slowly, trying to compose himself.

"Those are both good questions. I feel like I died today. I'm not quite sure who I am. I heard something on the radio today that was unlike anything I've ever heard before."

"What was it?"

"It was solo piano. I don't know who it was. It was music that was not of this Earth."

She looked disturbed. "David, you dick, have you been doing drugs?"

"No, no, no," he laughed. "I haven't done anything. I just heard this music and I was totally, totally overcome by it. I literally could not stand up. It was so powerful and so beautiful that I kind of...fell...on the floor. I started crying and laughing at the same time."

"My God, who was it already?"

"I told you, I don't know who it was!" he almost shouted. "I tried to turn it up and accidentally lost the station. I couldn't find it again."

"You asshole!" She realized that he was deeply upset and put her hand on his. "You poor asshole!"

"I thought that maybe you would have heard of anything new that this could have been. I have to find out who plays like that."

"How do you know that it's new? Maybe it was an old recording."

"It could be. The reception was so bad that with all the static I couldn't tell if it was an old or new recording."

"Do you know what station it was?"

"I thought that it was WBGI but I called them and they're temporarily off the air."

David felt panicky. This thing had happened and was sand-papering his nerves. God came out from behind the asteroid with a large cheese-grater and sliced him thin against it. Facing these feelings was a violent act. He could not escape the truth. Others could, but he didn't get it at all. How could people go through their lives as if they were in a parade of occupied beds rolling down the street? The concept "ignorance is bliss" made him drool. To not care! To not seek beyond the routine daily grind seemed a sedated luxury to him. If only he didn't think these crazy thoughts and feel the feelings, then he could get on the rush hour bus with the rest of them. Shit! But he was short-circuiting inside. Or perhaps he was being rewired by the master electrician.

"I'm gonna go fucking nuts over this, Abby!"

"Listen David, you know what? Leave yourself alone!" She stared at him wide-eyed.

"What do you mean?" But he instantly understood her as he asked for confirmation.

"I mean, stop analyzing yourself and everything around you. No wonder you're an insomniac! Stop picking at yourself. You're a nice guy with a gift. Enjoy it instead of tearing at the wrapping paper all the time."

He laughed nervously. "Jesus, that's funny. 'Enjoy it.' That's the problem. I never enjoy it. My gift is my curse."

"Why do you say that?" she worried.

"'Cause I can never leave it alone. It's supposed to go some-where. It's supposed to do something!"

"David, don't you ever play the piano just for fun? You know, stop and smell the ivory? Do you ever... *play* the piano instead of *work* the piano?"

"I can't. It's like I'm running out of time."

His voice grew into an intense whisper. "I want to make every note count, and it never works out that way. I play a gig and afterwards I've played nothing! Nothing!"

He was trying to let go, but he wasn't willing to let the other people at the bar hear him. And this is how he performed at the piano. *Please notice me, but don't make a big deal over me.*

This pattern went all the way back. When his mother had brought him late to nursery school one day and the little girls screamed excitedly "David's here!", he refused to go in. It didn't matter that he knew that they were glad to see him. The attention was too powerful. As a child he needed to be liked, but not be in the forefront. As an adult he started to observe this pattern (the word "trap" is hidden in the word "pattern") but couldn't seem to break out of it. In his twenties when he'd go to parties, if there was a piano there he'd be afraid that someone would ask him to play, but if they didn't ask he'd be disappointed. And there was no way that he could start to play on his own volition. And so you see that he was right. The gift was also the curse ("curse" contains "cure"). Because he used the piano as much to hide behind professionally as he did to express. The circuit of gigs that he played in was perfect for a man who didn't want to be noticed. How very safe! A life being given to deliberately be in the background. Musical wallpaper. An aural folded napkin for the rich to wipe their mouths with and then discard.

David and Abby went way back. But then, she went way back with a lot of musicians. That's why their relationship couldn't last. She was constantly playing a game of musical beds. He wanted a duet and she wanted the whole damn band, so to speak. Not that he was a saint. In fact, looking back on those days, he realized what a double standard he had played by. But it was her openness about wanting other men that he couldn't stand.

She was completely out front. Her hunger scared him. After it fell apart they remained musical compatriots. They'd sub for each other on gigs and compare notes on the music they'd heard around town. She was always a great source of gossip. Her tragic flaw in her own career was a tendency to complain out loud and a nagging case of self-doubt. She was much more talented than she knew.

She put down the beer, stood up and draped herself around him.

"We'll find out what you heard. Sometimes I hear a great player in the subway just as my train's leaving and I go nuts wondering who it is. It's a bitch pal, but that's how it goes."

David didn't answer. He kissed her on the cheek and finished his beer as she walked back towards the piano. Her natural step became slinkier as she became a performer again. The men around the piano sat up and smiled. David smiled too, watching the line between Abby his friend and Abby the Siren blur. He couldn't hear her talk, but her verbal repartee' with the customers took them in to her territory as surely as her music did.

She launched into "A Whole New World" from Disney's "Aladdin" but she played it in a slow soulful-funk groove. As David walked out, he heard her singing. It both soothed and aroused.

CHAPTER FIVE

*T*he elevator at 1036 Fifth Avenue opened on the 18th floor. There was only one apartment. David looked for a bell, but unable to find it, used the antique knocker. He waited. No answer. He tried it again. Still no answer. Finally, he turned the knob and entered. The neurotic yips of a Pekingese greeted him from the foyer. He attempted to ignore the dog and stepped through the marble foyer into the living room.

Tapestry from China, vases from India, a statuette from Africa which displayed its phallus. The windows looked out on Central Park. This he loved. The park made life in Manhattan worth living. The day had been cloudy and now at dusk a glance at the park did not reveal what century it was. Only the cars let on that it was now rather than then. He turned around in time to see one of the young men from the catering company set out a basket of cleverly cut crudite's on a table.

"Hi," David greeted him.

"Oh hello, the music has arrived!" he retorted.

"Yes, I guess he has."

"Greeat, play something from "Phantom.""

"You got it."

David always tried to ingratiate himself with the caterers, because that might determine whether he got fed or not. He was always afraid that the client might ask him to join the guests, and that made him feel overly conspicuous. He preferred to hang out in the always-spacious kitchens on his breaks and eat there. Worker solidarity, he thought. He was no snob. Of course, the head caterer could be snotty as hell. He would attempt to charm them, and so to feed.

By the time he had plugged in his amp, set up his mic and cleaned off the keys with wet paper towels from the kitchen, guests started to dribble in. He could smell their money. In their clothes, their hair, their tans, their high cheekbones. Old money passed down the line. They sipped their drinks and mingled. There were only fifteen invited. Dinner party.

Mrs. Catherine Ford, the hostess, finally made an appearance. Fifty-five-ish, one facelift so far, nice figure, nice dress. She carried the damn dog. She laughed with her guests.

She fed the dog carrots and broccoli from the crudite's as David looked on hungrily. She ignored Mr. David Stein, pianist apparently unextraordinaire. He thought it would be fun to yell "Hey! Hi! Fuu-uck youuu!", but he resisted this bit of would-be whimsy. Well, it's not nice to insult the client. David's agent Eddy Marsh had noticed this edge in David's voice lately. He could clearly see the disdain for the clients that David wore on his sleeve of late. It made him very nervous. So far, David had yet to ruin a job by exploding. But Eddy was watching him.

All through the cocktail hour, horrible things happened to the wealthiest-looking guests. The African fertility statue jumped up and slapped an old man in the face with its dick. An Indian vase landed on the head of a young lady, trapping her head inside it. She suffered and died. A thirty-fiveish Wall Street wonder-boy-type smoked a cigar at the window as David coughed dramatically loud. David pushed him out and he landed horribly on Fifth Avenue. And David played and sang throughout it all. A real trouper. Then the carpet growled at them and rolled them all up as they screamed. When their screams became muffled, the African statue started singing "I Feel Good" a la James Brown.

As this all happened in David's mind, he played the song at the piano, but softly and unobtrusively, so as not to bother the guests. No one noticed. No one cared. They were called into the dining room for dinner. They left him alone in the living room with no instructions. To play or not to play. Would they even hear him from the dining room? Did it matter? He stopped and listened. Mrs. Ford had apparently not thought him worth introducing herself to. No matter, he thought. Soon she'd get another facelift. Eventually she'd fit right in with all her artworks, accumulated from around the world on her many junkets. How could she travel around the world and still be such a vile human?

Alone in the silent room, abandoned by the elite, he started to play. He played Jerome Kern's "The Way You Look Tonight" in C major. This song always played itself. You'd have to be garbage yourself to ruin it. There was such yearning built structurally into the melody, the chord progression and the lyric that no idiot could stop it from expressing itself. Kern was a genius and had encoded his thirty-two bar pattern with musical DNA. Every time it was played somewhere in the world it became alive again. It was itself a genuine, passionate time machine. As David toyed with the melody, giving it frills and ribbons, he was pulled in and he pushed at the same timeless time. Every note became like a touch on an automatic supermarket door.

The sound whooshed around him and he became dizzy but kept going. His heartbeat raced and then disappeared altogether. He thought he would die but didn't mind. He felt the trees in the park down below. He felt the tapestry from across the room. Tears streamed down his face.

A man in a three-piece suit walked in to put his cigarette out in the ashtray. Instantly, David left his reverie and went on automatic pilot. All transcendent meaning was sucked out of his playing and he became David Stein again. The moment had passed and passed away. The man ignored him. He hadn't heard what had transpired. He hadn't even seen David's wet face, which David quickly lowered and wiped with his sleeve. The guest left the room, embarrassed to be near the pianist, who was not of his class. These people used this music for decoration and David played it that way. Suddenly he had played something else within it that had burst forth from the structure into other dimensions. And David Stein, professional hack, had been the vehicle to bring it forth.

He sat alone, shaken. He rested his head on an elbow, which wobbled shakily on the top of the piano. What the hell was happening to him? He realized that the music he'd heard on the radio had altered something in him. He had to find out what he'd heard. For the rest of the evening, he could not or would not let it happen again. He played safely till 11 p.m., as scheduled. He was not asked to play overtime. He was not tipped, but perfunctorily thanked by Mrs. Catherine Ford.

And then she added, "One of my guests said that you're quite a wonderful pianist. I'm so sorry that we couldn't hear better during dinner. I hope you don't mind."

"Oh, that's par for the course, Mrs. Ford. It's fine, really."

She handed him the check and he left. He walked out into the night, deeply confused.

CHAPTER SIX

L uis Silvera stood on a ladder among the ceiling high racks of LP records. One small section consisted of old 78's. Another held 45s. Another had CD's. A large area carried tape cassettes. Still, the bulk of the collection was 33 LP's. Luis dusted the LP shelves, both on the outer edge and in the space between the LPs and the next shelf up. To keep up his spirits he listened to "The Master Musicians of Joujouka" from Morocco. Luis wore a long sleeve shirt in bright Caribbean colors with the top three buttons open. He only stopped dusting when the intercom buzzed. He jumped down off the ladder, clapped his hands together to get the dust off and primped his goatee to remove any that had settled there. He pushed the talk button.

"Yeah?"

"Hi, WBGI?"

"The same."

"Can I come up? I'd like to talk to you about some music I heard the other day."

"You know we're closed, man. Shut down."

"I know. It's a shame."

"Yeah, well did you ever pledge any money?"

There was a pause.

"Well, no, I'm sorry to say I haven't."

Luis liked his honesty. "Ok, come on up. Second floor."

He buzzed David in.

David walked up to the second floor. The door was open. He entered. He looked up at the stacks. Luis was back on the ladder.

"Hi. Thanks for letting me in."

"S'alright. Wha'd you say your name was?"

"David Stein. And you're...?"

"Luis."

"Thanks Luis, I just needed some information."

"You didn't pledge any money. That's why we're shut down, my friend. So info gonna cost you."

And with that he pointed to a bucket of rags.

"You do the CD's and we'll talk,'kay?"

David, surprised at this, found himself even more surprised to be picking up the rag and starting to dust the CD shelf.

"Oh right," he said, "Dust destroys electronics."

"Yeah, and it makes your records sound like shit."

They spoke as they dusted.

"How come you're here if you're shut down?" David asked.

"'Cause I care, that's why. If nobody cleans, weeds grow through the cracks, you know."

"That's nice, man. I'd like to see the DJ's come in and do that!"

"You're seeing it now, man."

David stopped dusting. "You're a DJ here?"

Luis looked down from the ladder.

"Sorry pal, but I can only hear you when you move that rag over those CD's."

David laughed. "Got it." He resumed cleaning.

"Yeah, I'm a DJ. You don't know my show?"

"Luis what?"

"Luis Silvera. *Sounds from Uno Mundo.*"

"Is that the name of your show?"

"Yeah."

"You play Latin music?"

"Hey man," Luis' voice took on a hurried edge. "*Uno Mundo*, you know what that means?"

"One world."

"That's right. Wha'd you say your name was?"

"David."

"Well, David, maybe you figure I'm Latino, must be a Latin show, huh?"

"Sorry, *mea culpa.*"

"Hey, that's real Latin! My show is music from all over the world. You hear that?"

He pointed to the stereo speaker.

"Arab?"

"Morocco, baby. Joujouka. Transcendent music. That music will take you somewhere else."

David perked up at the word "transcendent."

"Luis, listen, that's why I'm here."

"Either you heard something extremely powerful, or you're sensitive to something in particular," was Luis' diagnosis after listening to David's story.

"Or maybe that's the same thing," David said.

Luis jumped down off the ladder and approached him. David stopped dusting, sensing that it was okay to do so.

"Listen, my friend. You know music is 'the language of God and the angels, now and forever'."

David was taken aback.

"Where'd you get that?"

"I read it and I believe it. Whatever happened to you went in your ears and wrapped itself 'round your soul!"

David laughed uneasily.

"What's funny?"

"I just...didn't think of it that way."

Talk like this made David squirm. He was wondering if he should leave.

"Well what did you think happened, man? This music bit you, knocked your ass down and left you like a pile of sand, didn't it?"

"I guess it did."

"You guess? That's what I got from your story. First-round knockout. David.... what's your name again?"

"Stein."

"David Stein, out cold from auditory KO punch!"

Luis brought his face up close to David's.

"Why do you really think you're here, my man?"

"You mean here at this station, or something more existential, like here on Earth?" David chuckled at his own remark.

"That's right. Same difference. Why do you think you're here?"

"I dunno, why am I here?" David retorted, waiting for the rhetoric to complete itself.

"I'll tell you why. You looking for something. You looking for the answer."

Luis was invading David's space, physically and psychically.

David pulled his head back. "What's the question?"

Luis let out a loud guffaw. A low-paced "hee-hee-hee-hee" that sounded to David like he was being mocked.

"You wanna know the question? It's differently expressed by different folks, but I would say basically the question is 'What the fuck are we doing here'? Now, the answer is also understood differently. Jews want to follow the Torah. Christians want to follow Jesus. Muslims want to submit their will to Allah. DJ's want to let you hear music to enrich your life. You're a musician. What are you trying to do?"

David was silent. He felt oppressed and cornered. He didn't like being on trial.

"I'm trying to find a recording I heard, and I thought maybe you could help me."

Luis looked at him and put his hands on his hips.

"Mm-hmm. I see. May I play you something?"

"Sure."

Luis walked over to a shelf of LP's and pulled out a record. He held it up for David to see.

"Do you know it?"

The title read *"Eric Dolphy. Last Date."*

"Dolphy. I know him, but not this record." David took the record jacket and looked it over.

"Lemme play you something," Luis said as he removed the record from its jacket and put it on the turntable.

A swirling, searching alto sax wailed over a rhythm section chugging along in 4/4. Dolphy's playing went in and out of tonality at will and into other ways. Always, his playing was in a swinging manner, but he added in honks and bweeps and sudden jumps in range that made it sound like he was another sax answering himself. After a brief piano solo, Dolphy reentered till the head of the tune came around again. Suddenly, without

37

warning, the piece ended on a staccato note. There was applause and then a drum roll fanfare.

At this point, Luis looked at David. Luis put his finger over his mouth and with the other hand pointed at the speaker. A high-pitched voice spoke softly but clearly. *"When you hear music, after it's over it's gone, in the air. You can never ...capture it again."*

The arm lifted off the record and returned to its handle. Luis looked at David.

"That was Eric Dolphy on June 2, 1964 playing in Europe. He died June 29th. This is what he left us."

David listened intently, with only a hint of a smile.

"You see, David, that man knew what he wanted to do. It's in his playing. But he was dead in his thirties. So were Gershwin and Mozart. Hendrix dead at 27, Lennon at 40. We don't know what they might have done. *It's gone, in the air.* Even worse. It was never born. How 'bout you, man? You think you need to find the recording you heard in order to be whole, don't you? Why don't you let it go and just play real shit from now on? Make every note count. You could die tomorrow. Play the piano that way."

David looked at him and then looked around furtively. "How do you know I don't?"

Luis just stared at him, his eyebrows slightly raised.

"Okay, so I don't," David said. "Nobody can do it all the time."

"Oh. I think there's cats who can. You give a performance or make a recording and you take it seriously. You focus on being right...there! It can be done. But your mind can't be somewhere else. That's what great players do."

"I'll give it a shot. Meanwhile, maybe you can help me find that recording."

"I'll see what I can do."

CHAPTER SEVEN

David stood in front of Manny's Music Store on 48th Street. He was window shopping. The window display included keyboards, P.A.'s, mixers, trumpets and guitars. You didn't have to buy to keep updated on what was on the market. The air was nippy and he kept his hands in his pockets.

Out of the corners of his eyes he could see the afternoon crowd milling about. He sensed something to his left and looked east to see a man towering above the crowd. The man was thirtyish, about 6'7" and built like a pro-football player. His eyes were glazed in a scowl. He was approaching fast, and the crowd seemed to fear him and sense his power. They parted for the Goliath. David assumed that the man was schizophrenic or on drugs, or both.

A very little old lady stood next to David eating candy from a white paper bag while she tried to find a taxi. The giant was upon them and David froze as this behemoth stared at the woman and her snack. David was sure that she was about to be attacked, when at the last possible second she reached out to him and silently offered the open bag of candy.

"WHAT IS THIS?" the giant roared.

"Jordan Almonds," came the gentle reply, muffled only by the candy in her own mouth.

His great hand reached into the bag, took one and popped it into his mouth. He started to chew, when suddenly his scowl broke into a boyish smile. His eyes lit up.

"Oh, wow! I had these in movie theaters when I was a kid!"

His voice had turned to music and laughter and had risen an octave in pitch.

"Have some more," she said good-naturedly.

"Thanks," came the now jolly giant's reply.

He took a few, put them in his pocket. And then, his eyes glazed over, his scowl reappeared, and the little boy inside him was once again gone. He stomped off, as the shoppers moved aside.

David, recovering from fear and shock, managed to blurt out to her, "How did you know to do that?"

She smiled, and held out the bag to him.

"Always offer food. Always offer food."

She shook the bag at him and raised her eyebrows. David took a Jordan Almond.

"Thanks."

CHAPTER EIGHT

David slept fitfully. Well, that's a meaningless phrase in David's life. A more realistic one would be "It was three a.m., and as usual, David spun in his bed, failing to lose consciousness." His father was an insomniac, and had passed the condition on down. David had "Restless Leg Syndrome", "Non-Specific Anxiety", and a host of other neuroses that all shall be revealed to you, dear reader.

In his moments of sleep in between this particular night's fits of agonizingly lonely wakefulness, he had a dream. He jumped out of a plane to skydive. He was in freefall and enjoying experimenting with hand gestures to direct the flow of air to simulate flying. Others from the plane floated down next to him. There was Paul McCartney! And now, Duke Ellington! And here's George Gershwin and Mozart!! They are all floating down alongside David Stein. David started to sing "Eine Kleine Nachtmusik" in tribute to Mozart. The great composer laughed wildly for joy and joined in, improvising a merry and clever counterpoint. Then McCartney sang a high harmony while

Gershwin and Ellington created fabulous rhythms by slapping each other's palms in a stratospheric jazz patty cake. David was ecstatic. He had never felt such musical fellowship before.

Then Mozart looked at David and pointed down at the onrushing ground, a few thousand feet below.

He yelled at David. "David, pull der ripcord! Pull der ripcord now! Mach schnell! Before it is too late!"

David waved and pulled the cord. It came off in his hand, unattached to the chute. His smile turned ashen.

McCartney floated over. "Bit of a drag, eh mate?" he said as he opened his chute. It disappeared above David's head.

Ellington came face to face with him. "Music is my mistress." Pop. Chute open. Gone.

Gershwin next made his way over, swimming through the air. "I believe that Jerome Kern's score for 'Showboat' is the finest example of a Broadway musical ever written." Pop. Gone.

Finally, Mozart, that little imp, approached.

"Help me, Maestro, I'm falling!" David yelled desperately.

Mozart put his finger under his chin and looked quizzical.

"Iss dat 'Help me Rhonda?' or iss it "Help me if you can I'm falling down'? I can't help you David, because you're such a putz!"

Mozart pulled his ripcord and a large eighth-note-shaped parachute popped open. Gone.

David screamed and fell. He hit the ground.

He woke up on the floor tangled in his blanket and sheets. "Jesus!"

He lay on the floor, bemoaning his lot in life. He wasn't an icon for the world. Didn't Arnold Schoenberg, the atonal composer, once say that all he really wanted was to have people walk down the street and whistle his music? David had no Elvishood.

Continents did not tremble to his every note. The tabloids did not blare headlines about the alien babies he had fathered (or mothered).

As he lay on that filthy, frayed green carpet, in a twilight, Twilight Zone, he saw the obese Elvis approach. Elvis was sweating through his sequined suit. He took his cape off, lay it on the carpet next to David and sat on it cross-legged, huffing and puffing all the while.

"Uh, say man," said the demigod. "Uh, whasamtta with you boy? Y'all lyin' on the floor like an old James Brown routine."

David sat up.

"Sorry Elvis, I had a bad dream and fell out of my bed."

"Man," Elvis chuckled, "You are a bad dream! You sure are one sorry sonofabitch. One sorry-assed old sonofabitch."

David pouted, while nodding in agreement. "Yeah, well it's easy for you to talk. Nobody's throwing ladies' underwear and hotel keys at me!"

Elvis squinted angrily and his bloodshot eyes flashed. "That's Tom Jones, asshole. He gets keys and underwear. I get the women who throw them."

"Right," David corrected himself. "Sorry."

"Um-hum..." Elvis managed to answer. "Now looky here, David Steinflubber, you a whining, low-down, pussy-wimp baby. You a mama's boy snot-faced brat who don't get his way and takes his toys and goes home. Is that how you want me to think of you? Is that the way your public should see your ugly face?"

"The public doesn't even know my face."

"Well hot damn, you poor little pecker. I was a truck driver with a face that only a rearview mirror knew before I hit big!"

"Sure, but you were a kid! Elvis, I'm forty-two. I'm not the next Beatles."

Elvis grabbed David by the neck and shook him as they sat.

"Don't ever use that word around me, boy! I don't wanna hear about those no-account long-haired no-talent English punks! They just got lucky is all."

"Sorry Elvis. I'm never gonna be big as you, is what I meant."

Elvis thought awhile. "Well, hey how 'bout Granma Jesus, the painter? She wasn't big 'til her 80's, right?"

"It's Grandma Moses, but you're correct."

"Course ah'm correct," nodded the big man. "You have to keep goin', no matter what."

He extended one arm and sang *"Dream awn, young man, and you'll... be a big... suc-cess!"*

And on that note, he faded away.

CHAPTER NINE

"**D**avid Stein?"

"Yeah."

"This is Luis Silvera from WBGI."

"Oh, hi, how's it goin'?"

"Listen, David, I tried to find out what you heard on the station that knocked you down, you know?"

"Yeah!"

"I asked around, you know?"

"Uh-huh! And?"

"And I think the tape you heard may have been thrown out."

"What? How could that be?" David's throat got tense and dry.

"Who throws out tapes after they play them on the radio? Who was the DJ?"

"Listen man, I'm trying to make you understand. So cool down and listen so I can get the information to you, okay?"

"Okay, okay. I just don't get it."

"That's right, you don't get it. Just listen. The day you were listening, the hour you tuned in, we let listeners who are members come in and play their personal tapes. You dig? Not necessarily music they created, but stuff from their collection by whoever they like"

"Wow."

"Now, the guy who came in that day, I got his name and number. You can call him and find out what the tape was."

"But why do you say it got thrown out?"

"'Cause this guy would tear up the cassette after each thing he played. It's like Eric Dolphy, man. *'You can never recapture it again'.*"

A chill went up David's spine. He couldn't speak.

"David? Listen, I got his name. It's Simon Purcell. P-u-r-c-e-l-l. His number is 313-4545. So good luck."

"Thanks, Luis."

"You're welcome."

"Hey Luis, did you speak to him?"

"Nah, this is your private mystery."

"Okay, thanks. Bye."

"Bye."

David ran his fingers over the phone. He hated calling somebody he'd never met. He dreaded having to explain to a stranger: "You don't know me, but, uh...." Finally, inhaling without exhaling, he punched the number. *"The number you have reached, 313-4545 in area code 212 has been disconnected."*

"Fuck!" David yelled to the ceiling.

"No further information is available."

David slammed the phone down.

Always on a rollercoaster, David was dizzily upset now. Feverishly he thought this out. How could he get to Simon Purcell? No working phone. He called WBGI. Luis answered.

"Luis, it's David Stein again. Purcell's number is disconnected. Do you have an address?"

"No go, David. This guy called up out of the blue and came down with his tapes. We never got his address. All that mattered was that he showed up. *Habeas Corpus* in the flesh."

Minutes later, David got out the Manhattan phone directory. There were three "S. Purcell's". His man was listed with the disconnected phone number at 318 West 14th St. David drummed his fingers on the directory. He hated doing what he was about to do on this evening.

West 14th Street was a strange and uncategorizable neighborhood. Once he got off the subway at 8th Avenue and 14th, his westward walk took him past the northern border of Greenwich Village, past a Latino funeral home, a lonely looking church, an Irish bar, an isolated upscale high rise, and then across the wide intersection at 9th Avenue. Here one entered the meat market, both literally and figuratively. Great 18-wheel trucks blocked the street, unloading meat to the meatpacking centers along the block from 9th to 10th Avenues. The Hudson river loomed not far beyond. The workers looked hardened and unapproachable. In the doorways not occupied by the workers stood the ladies who were also working. These workers wore hot pink miniskirts, high heels, mile-high wigs, and on rare occasion, vaginal condoms. Some of the ladies occasionally wore male condoms, as they were not really ladies at all, but remarkable external facsimiles. These workers awaited the New Jersey license plates that beckoned to them to get in the car for a very quick one. David stepped through these two concentric meat markets.

He walked past 316 West 14th St., a red door on a window-less brownstone. It read "Aikido." He assumed that it must be some sort of martial arts school. He thought to himself that one would want to be a skilled fighter just to hang out on this block at night. He came to 318, a wooden door reinforced with a number of powerful locks. There was no bell or name.

He knocked. He waited and knocked again. Frustrated, he took out his business card and wrote on the back: "Mr. Purcell, please get in touch with me regarding the tape you played on WBGI. Please. David Stein."

He tried to slide it under the door, but there was no space underneath. He didn't want to tape his business card to a door in a public place and besides, he had no tape. But knowing he had no other choices, he opted for taping. He looked down the block. The closest place to find a piece of scotch tape was the aikido school.

Surprised at his own nerve, he rang the buzzer. After a few seconds he got a response and entered. The stairwell was musty and the ceiling was in need of repair. He headed up the three flights to the school. At the top he came upon a heavy metal door that was slightly ajar. He slowly opened it.

Except for the area by the door, the entire floor was covered by white canvas. On the wall was a framed picture of an elderly bearded Japanese man wearing a traditional white martial arts *gi* and flowing black *hakama*. The *hakama*, which covered the body from the waist down to below the ankles was a garment of rank, but it also disguised the movements of the feet, thus leav-ing an opponent at a disadvantage as to which way the wearer was going to move.

At a desk facing the door sat a man who also wore a *gi* and *hakama*. He was white, about thirty-five, with a crew cut and mustache. He was reading. As David approached, the man's eyes looked up without his head shifting.

"Hi. Sorry to bother you, but I was trying to contact somebody in the next building."

David hoped that the man would keep the flow of conversation going by at least giving him a "Yes?", but he said nothing.

David continued, "He wasn't home so I wanted to leave him a note. I was just wondering if you might have a piece of scotch tape?"

The man gestured to the tape dispenser on his desk.

"Oh thanks! Just what I was looking for."

As he reached for the tape he noticed a pile of brochures about the school.

"May I take one?"

"Certainly." Now the man perked up a bit.

"Thank you."

David took pieces of tape and the brochure. As he walked toward the door glancing at the brochure, he turned toward the desk to repeat his thanks, but the desk was unoccupied. Over in the corner of the canvas mat, the man had silently walked over to a wall rack of wooden *bokken* practice swords. He began to practice fast powerful vertical strokes through the air with a *bokken* held by both hands. Each stroke commenced from above the head and terminated at abdomen level. David sensed power in the strokes and was impressed. He wanted to watch but felt that he was not welcome. He left and walked down the stairs quietly.

He went back to Purcell's building. Feeling conspicuous, he looked around and then reluctantly taped the business card to the door. Sensing that he was being watched, he glanced up and saw the aikidoist staring at him from the *dojo* window. He waved meekly to the man. The man did not return his acknowledgement.

On the uptown subway David read the brochure. It was a no-frills black and white folded sheet. At the top was a circle containing a Japanese character. The text read "Aikido - the way to harmony with the universe. Learn to develop power by using nature's most perfect form, the circle. Learn balance, strength, fitness and a sense of wellbeing. Learn to defend without attacking."

Crap, thought David. Mystical bullshit. Scam alert! Scam alert! But his mind went back to the powerful sword strokes that he had just seen, and he couldn't get those images to go away.

He had always been a non athlete. He'd been pushed around as an adolescent and he was still feeling pushed around by clients on the job. He wanted power. He wanted to feel in control, and not just at the piano. He wanted to have those steely eyes behind that desk and behind that wooden sword. But he knew that he'd have to suspend his instinctive skepticism that decades of reading the New York Times had instilled in him.

Two days later at just before 6 p.m., David Stein, surprised at himself, once again climbed the *dojo* steps. This time he was there to take class.

David paid his $15 to take a single class. He certainly wasn't about to commit until he saw more. He was at once apprehensive and fascinated about the idea of learning power from Steely Eyes. In the men's changing room, which was just a corner of the loft with a wooden wall and sheet posing as a curtain, he put on his clothes. Not having a *gi* he wore sweatpants and a yellow t-shirt with a picture of Charlie Parker playing sax. It said "Bird". Out of the sax, instead of notes, flew a white dove. The other men in the locker room all put on *gis* or *gis* and *hakamas*. Many were out on the mat stretching before David even entered the changing room. There were a number of men ranging in age from upper teens to their late 50's. Some looked bulked up, almost square, but a few seemed scrawny and passive in their demeanor.

David approached a bearded bespectacled man who resembled a college philosophy professor.

"Where do I put my wallet?"

"Just leave it in your bag."

"How do I know someone won't take it?"

The professor looked at him with a faint smile.

"How do I know you won't take mine? Just leave it in your bag. It'll be there when you're done."

This was how the cult takes control, David thought and shuddered. They smile and act nice, and then lift your wallet and you're a nonperson without a home. Then you're dependent on the cult. You're screwed. He rolled the pants up to hide the wallet and shoved it in the very bottom of his gym bag.

Onto the mat stepped a Japanese man about 60 years old. He had a grey ponytail and he stood only about 4'10". As he walked forward he did not bounce up and down in his stride but rather appeared to have ball bearings for feet. He seemed to roll vertically. His movements were immediately followed by all eyes, and all the students lined up quickly, sitting on both knees. The teacher, also kneeling, faced the picture of the elderly bearded man and bowed low with hands on the mat. The group, which was behind him, bowed with him. He turned around to face the class at great speed and bowed to them. They bowed. He clapped his hands and was on his feet before David could register that he stood up. The class moved quickly to one end of the room and proceeded to move in fast, small somersault-like rolls across the mat. David felt his heart pound with fear of attempting this. In front of him appeared Steely Eyes.

"Watch".

Steely Eyes got down on the mat and gestured for David to do the same.

"Keep your palm flat, think forward, your head tucked in. Now push off with your rear leg."

David started to push off.

"Your rear leg!" Steely eyes was holding David's T-shirt back to stop him. "Yes".

David pushed off. He forgot to tuck his head in and felt the pain of head rubbing on mat. He flipped over and slammed down on his back. Steely Eyes gazed off in the distance, ignoring David's ill attempt. The rest of the class was already at the end of the mat and rolling back toward them.

"I think I forgot to tuck".

"One more time," glared Steely Eyes.

David reset, tucked, and rolled sideways instead of forward, but this time he didn't hurt his head.

"We'll practice again at another time."

David was told to watch as the class practiced more elaborate warm ups. Various-sized rolls, backwards rolls, jumping rolls, breakfalls, slides and impossibly fast walking on the knees. David did try knee-walking and felt his groin muscles almost tear. The class now seemed to have ball bearing knees as they defied physics altogether. The teacher clapped twice and they returned to their kneeling lineup to await instructions.

The teacher pointed to a large barrel-chested man who looked like he might lead a biker gang. The man bowed to the mat and got up without using his hands.

In a high voice the teacher said, "*Mune-tsuki kokyu-nage.*"

The biker, who towered over the teacher, threw a mean straight punch to the teacher's midsection. When the punch reached the intended location in space, the teacher was gone. He had rotated his hips and moved ever so slightly out of the way, at the same time grabbing the biker's *gi* from under the elbow. The teacher made a curving motion with his arm and the biker was airborne. He ended up six feet away on his back.

David's brain stopped. The teacher clapped twice. Everyone chose a partner and bowed to each other. Steely Eyes bowed to David and David stiffly bowed back.

"Are we gonna do this?" he asked weakly.

"Punch," Steely Eyes responded, pointing to his own mid-section.

"I can't make a living without my arms," David retorted nervously, hoping Steely would ask him what profession he was in.

Steely pointed to his own abdomen. "Step with your left and punch."

"I'm afraid that I'll hurt you!"

Steely glared, leaned his shoulder forward as if to say "Come and get me!" and David found himself stepping and punching. An instant later he was whirling and riding a rollercoaster at the same time. He felt a wave of vertigo and landed on his back, but without a thump.

"Whoa," he mumbled and looked up at Steely. Steely had him repeat the technique many times and within five minutes David was winded. Steely had him kneel with his eyes closed and the weight of his rear resting on his heels.

"Exhale slowly through the mouth. Now wait a moment. Now inhale through the nose slowly."

David did as instructed for five minutes. He felt dizzy, but calmer as his breathing settled down. A warmth flowed through his body, but he was distracted by soreness in his legs from kneeling. Finally, Steely told him to slowly open his eyes. David noticed that colors seemed richer.

"Stand up."

David started to move out of his kneeling position. He couldn't.

"Ow! My legs!"

Steely walked away, back to the group. David knelt in pain, not sure how to get up. He decided to fall on his side. On his side his legs were still locked. He massaged them and slowly was able to stand. Rejoining the group, he made it through a half hour of the class. He then sat on the sideline morosely watching the rest of the class.

CHAPTER TEN

*H*e never liked to be on boats. He wasn't much of a swimmer, because he was always congested, which caused him to inhale through his mouth and swallow water. This caused him to keep his head high above the water, which in turn made his head heavier, which then caused him to sink. So he wasn't much of a swimmer. Boats made him nervous, anxious, panicky, nauseous.

David got a call to do a gig on a boat.

It was a cloudy afternoon when he got down to the pier on West 23rd St. There he was, rolling his keyboard, which was vertically strapped to its dolly. On his left shoulder was his amplifier hanging by its strap. On his right shoulder hung his bag of wires, microphones, music and a peanut butter sandwich. He wore his tux, and he was sweating profusely. The cologne was wearing off before he even got to the gig, and he was in no mood to be charming. It was early and the crew was preparing the gangplank for the coming party. The 75-foot yacht, "The Princess of Whales" was rocking in her berth, and the gangplank, which had no rails, rocked right along with her. David immediately felt tightness in his chest.

He yelled and asked if he could get some help getting his equipment across the gangplank safely. He was ignored. He was wearing his loafers, the ones that always caused him to slip. He lay down the keyboard and the amp. He gingerly stepped out onto the gangplank, carefully trying to balance himself with the heavy bag on his shoulder. The gangplank rose and fell. He made it across, and deposited the bag on the boat, then he returned and picked up the amplifier, which was even heavier. He knew that it would sink faster than a stone, and he also knew that if it fell and caught his foot, he'd become part of the bottom of the Hudson River till he rotted. Now he was mad because no one would help him, and he was scared to die. He carried the amp in front of his body like a bag of groceries. Step by step he made it across and lay down the amp next to the bag. He went back for the keyboard, which was still strapped to the dolly. At this point, he really could have used some help, but he was afraid that the crew might drop his keyboard into the water, so he decided to go it alone.

The gangplank rose and fell, rose and fell. He tried to breath and thought "If Roseanne Barr married Norman Fell from 'Three's Company' she'd be Roseanne Fell." The gangplank rose and fell and David, wheelbarrowing his keyboard on the dolly, stepped on. He instantly regretted it, as he felt the weight of the keyboard shift to first one side and then the other. He held onto his beloved equipment for dear life. He pushed directly forward and the dolly got stuck on the speed-bump-like safety board sticking up to help passenger's feet grip the plank. He lifted the dolly over the board using the toe of his loafer and resumed his forward motion. After doing this three excruciating times, he completed his crossing. His big ocean crossing.

David set up his equipment at the back of the party deck, which was below the top outside deck. As instructed by the crew, he set up by a spiral staircase that led up through an open hatch to the outside top deck. He started to attach his many wires. Wires for electricity, extension cords, a pedal for the keyboard, his microphone cord, cords to attach the amp and the keyboard to the power strip, and a cord from the keyboard to the amplifier. He set up his microphone stand, which was falling apart itself. The microphone would droop down like a dead flower while he was singing. The stand would swing all over like a windblown mast on a sailboat, causing him to stretch his neck along with the motion, following the stand wherever it went as he tried to sing.

Today, while he tried to arrange the stand, the guests arrived. It was a corporate party, a group of lawyers in New York for a conference, and now it was party time. And David Stein was going to sing and play for their enjoyment as the yacht circled Manhattan on a beautiful day. David checked the keyboard to make sure he had sound. He thought "Okay, it's going to be a good day after all." And then he looked for the adapter that made it possible to plug his microphone into the amplifier. It was just a little metal doohickey that just wasn't there.

David's heart froze at the realization that he could not plug in his microphone. The boat shoved off. The woman who had hired him, Ms. Margaret Olson, herself a rather high-powered lawyer, stepped over and introduced herself.

"Hi David! It's so nice to finally meet you in the flesh. We're really looking forward to hearing you sing!"

And then David heard a loud clap of thunder, and through the hatch above his head came the first drop of rain. It landed on his head.

"Hello Ms. Olson, how are you?"

"Oh call me Margaret, please!"

"Thank you Margaret." He inhaled and tried to calm himself as he spoke. "I seem to have a bit of a problem. I'm missing a microphone adapter."

The boat's engine growled as they picked up speed and pulled further away from the pier.

"Missing a what?" she yelled, turning her head to hear him better.

"Ahh, it's a little interface from my microphone to the amplifier, and it seems to be missing."

A shadow darkened her eyes. "What does this mean, David?"

"Well, it means that I don't think that I'll be able to sing and be heard."

"David, I've got a group of people who expect to hear singing today, and that's what I hired you to do."

Her tone was positively litigious by now, and he was on the witness stand being cross-examined. He cursed himself for having missed the adapter. He knew that he should keep a list of everything that he needed, but he'd put it off, and now he was just about literally up shit's creek without an adapter.

"I'm terribly, terribly sorry." (Two terriblys was like a dog lying on its back in submission to another). "I'll be happy to play all those songs, but there's nothing I can do. This has never happened to me before, I assure you." (Come on lady, work with me here!)

"That doesn't help me, David!"

She stormed away. A flash of lightning. A burst of thunder. He sat down to play. Rain started coming in onto his keyboard and amplifier. She started telling the lawyers what had happened, and they didn't look happy. And they were drinking. And the boat was rocking and the engine growled at him and the water came down soaking him and threatening to electrocute him. He was trapped on a deathship with a bunch of pissed-off, drunken pirates. He was Ahab strapped to the whale. The ship to hell headed out onto the Hudson River.

Four eternally long hours later a soaking wet, miserable-beyond-belief, unpopular David Stein brought his packed-up wet equipment back across the gangplank. The lawyers had already disembarked, and David, with his considerably lower-than-planned check from Ms. Olson, staggered from dejection once or twice, and he almost lost the keyboard to Davey Jones. The crew seemed to avert their eyes when he passed by. He felt that he was an object of derision and deep shame. To perform for an audience and to look at the floor at the same time is not a good thing. This is what he had done. He couldn't face their scorn. He had just played instrumentally for the duration of the cruise, all the while trying desperately to keep his feet out of the deadly puddles that sought out his wires. And now he was heading home.

He stood shivering from the wetness at the entrance to the Westside Highway, praying for a cab. The rain, which had let up, now returned. He and his equipment were drowning in water and self-pity. The cars whizzed by. His feet sloshed. The equipment fell over in a large puddle. He cursed at the top of his lungs, unheard by anyone but a couple of homeless men who were wandering through the storm. He knew he could never get a cab. After twenty minutes of self-loathing and accumulated moisture, he took out a twenty dollar bill and waved it in the air. A van from a small construction company hit its brakes, pulled up and offered him a ride for the twenty dollars. The elegant sponge boarded the unknown van and at last he was on his way home.

CHAPTER ELEVEN

*T*hat night in the dark, David saw the disembodied mime's head floating through his room. It floated at a slightly tilted angle. Luckily the mime had worn white makeup or he might never have spotted it. It glowed ever so slightly. At first David observed it with detachment, almost amused. Then it turned towards him and wailed in a low-pitched tremolo. David answered with a scream of adrenalized horror. The head fell and landed on the open piano keyboard. The loud dissonant chord ringing out in the blackness was rather unsettling. But it was only the introduction, for now the head bounced up and down on the keys facing David, who cowered under the covers, with just one eye watching the head. The head now bounced out a bass line, vamping a vaudeville-like introduction. It sang in a not-bad tenor, but with a lot of echo:

"Dancing with you is like going to heaven
You're such an angel in that lovely dress
Dancing with you is like going to heaven
I'm a very lucky little devil I guess"

It then flew over to David in the bed and pressed it's cold white dead cheek against his. He choked and ran out of the bed. It blocked his path, no matter which direction he moved. It coralled him to the piano. He sat down shivering in his pajamas at the keys and began to play the chords and jazz embellishments while the head bounced on the low keys, creating a duet from hell.

David, in shock, sang the song as the head bounced out the bass line in the dark. Halfway through he forgot the lyrics. He told the head. Large white words appeared in the dark and the head, acting as a bouncing ball in an oldtime movie singalong, bounced on each syllable to let him know what words to sing. When they had finished the song, David got up to pour himself some scotch. The head looked at him gravely 'til David offered him a glass. David held the scotch up to the head who greedily drank it. It poured into its mouth and out the exposed neck cavity onto the carpet (it had always been a frayed and filthy carpet). The head belched and flew out the window. David fainted to the floor. In the morning he awoke on the floor, next to a puddle of sticky scotch.

He got up and walked into the bathroom. On the mirror the head had apparently used it's tongue to write in soap. It simply read "Best wishes in all your endeavors."

He washed it off for a long time.

CHAPTER
TWELVE

*E*ntering the martial arts supply store on the third floor of a loft building on Twenty-sixth street, David was struck by the characters who were shopping. Mostly men, all different colors, but everybody had some sort of attitude. One short ponytailed man was built like a square. He stood impassively staring at a rack of *katanas*, Japanese *Samurai* swords. David guessed that he was Filipino, but he wasn't sure. A tall, thin Brazilian-looking fellow with dreadlocks carried a newly purchased pair of polished sticks about two feet long. Who was he going to do what to with those?

David saw a display case containing books and videos about martial arts. Karate, Jiu-Jitsu, Judo, Savate, Kung-Fu, Capoeira, Paqua, Kendo, Arnis De Mano. Bando, Tai-Chi, Aikido. Others that he couldn't even pronounce. There were photos framed long ago of great martial artists. He noticed a photo of the same elderly Japanese man that he'd seen on the wall of the Aikido *dojo*. Other frames contained equally mysterious-looking figures with piercing eyes. He wasn't sure who they were, but he knew that he wouldn't want to run into them late at night if they weren't in the best of moods. He thought of the powerful figures of his childhood fantasies. DC Comics' "Justice league of America" with Superman, Batman and the Flash among the heavyweights. He remembered Porky and Buckwheat on TV in "The Little Rascals" series arguing whether Flash Gordon was stronger than Tarzan. In high school he had read Homer's "Iliad" with its great array of warriors like Hector and Hercules. All were legends, but here were pictures of men who seemed to be genuinely great fighters and who had nearly magical powers.

An elderly Asian man stood impassively gazing from behind a small window opening in the wall. David approached him and attempted to bow as he'd seen in the *dojo*. The man took a drag on a filterless cigarette and looked back at him. The man blinked at him because of the smoke, and yet his manner remained as if he had never blinked at all.

"Hi, I need to buy an Aikido *gi*."

"Aikido *gi* same as Jiu-Jitsu *gi*. What size you want?"

"Well," said David, taken aback, and feeling out of his element, "they only told me to get an Aikido *gi*."

The man looked a little pissed off. David, feeling that he'd already insulted the man, corrected himself.

"Whatever you think is best is best, I'm sure. I'm a little new at this."

The man pointed at a sign by the sales window. "Tanaka Martial Arts supplies. Serving the public since 1966."

"Aikido *gi* same as Jiu-Jitsu *gi*. What size you want?"

He motioned for David to step back. David obliged and the man looked him up and down for one second.

"Four," he barked and disappeared.

David could see that the area behind the man was a storeroom containing his inventory of martial arts clothing. He could see a pretty young woman moving boxes. She suddenly looked up at him. He smiled and she smiled back and then resumed her work. He now assumed that the man was the owner and that she was his daughter or granddaughter. After a few moments the man returned. He put the folded *gi* on the counter.

"Size four, fit you perfectly. Padded shoulders for beginner."

The *gi* was white and felt like thick canvas. David also bought a white beginner's belt. On the shelf through the window he also saw black belts.

"I like those black belts!" he exclaimed to the man and the young woman.

The man snorted in disapproval and walked away. The young woman approached him. She was quite beautiful, and slight in build, but something in her manner made him believe that she herself was a skilled martial artist.

"These days," she began, "martial arts teachers purchase colored belts and present them to their students when the students have passed their tests and earned them. But that was not the old way."

"What was that?" asked David, feeling both flirtatious and curious, but not wanting her to know about the flirtatious part.

"It used to be that the student practiced for years until his white belt turned black."

"But don't you ever wash the *gi*?"

She laughed at his question. "Yes, of course you wash the *gi*, and you wash it before someone tells you that you need to wash it!" she said, holding her nose in mock disgust. They both laughed at this. "But you don't wash the belt. Let the belt age. Perhaps your belt will turn black one day from practicing. Or perhaps your teacher will buy you a colored belt. Either way, it is most important that you do not advance in color until you deserve it. Make sure that you do not study at a school that is really a factory, turning out black belts who have nothing to show for themselves except a shiny new belt!"

This last comment had just a touch of sarcasm in it. But he knew that she meant it. He thanked her and left.

When he got outside, he sensed that spring had come to the city, and he decided to walk for awhile, proudly carrying his *gi* in a bag. As was his sometime habit, he chose to walk on side streets that he didn't know well. Even after a lifetime in New York City, he still discovered areas of Manhattan that he'd missed.

He turned down a quiet street. In the middle of the block he passed a small neighborhood church. The doors were open, and as he passed them, he heard singing. The singing was in a language that he didn't know, but that he took for Chinese. He knew that New York had a number of Mandarin congregations. They were practicing, and it sounded like an English hymn. He recognized the harmonies and the style, even though he didn't know the specific song.

A really good musician can hear a song and guess how it will proceed harmonically and melodically. Even though he knew where it was going, he found himself surprised at the effect that it was having on him. Because the singing wasn't in English, he heard it all as sound and not as words that he could attribute images to. He felt a tingling in his ears and a chill up his spine. He involuntarily exhaled and found himself hyperventilating. Then he inhaled deeply and when his chest and abdomen were fully expanded his body froze. No exhalation came. The singing continued as he stood outside the church, motionless. Part of him wanted to panic because his body wasn't breathing. At the same time he felt as if the music were flowing into him like an injection. He was being held in place against his will. It was as if a dentist were pinning him while he pulled an infected tooth, except that there was no pain. The choir held a long note on a dominant chord and David's breath was held along with it. He could not exhale while the note was held. The world disappeared and as the note was released in a Mandarin "Amen" and the musical phrase completed itself by resolving through a suspended chord to a tonic chord, David exhaled with a loud cry. A woman walking her dog looked at him quizzically. His breathing immediately came back to normal. In fact, he was profoundly relaxed. Still, he sat down on the steps of the church. He knew that once again, something had happened to him that he couldn't explain. And he wondered whether he was going mad. And he wondered what going mad meant, because he had the barest of inklings that something good was happening. But he wasn't certain, and having no answer unnerved him.

David's world had always been a New York Times world. There were rational answers to irrational events. In that world, whenever there was a world crisis, the Times headlines would inflate to bold black letters. But inevitably the crisis would subside, and the New York Times' bold black headlines would always default back to their natural state of calm clear observation. Until recently, all that was mysterious in the world happened to others. He accepted bouncing heads and parachuting Mozarts as normal. For as long as he remembered he had had "visitation-like" dreams. But now, since the incident with the radio he felt different. Something new was in the mix and in his body. And it was music. Music was possessing him in a way that it never had. Yes, he had often felt thrilled, despairing, or captivated by music as a listener or in a band, or even alone at the piano at home. But something beyond his understanding was in command here. Something supernatural. And though he was not the sort of person to believe in such things, he knew that he was in deep.

CHAPTER THIRTEEN

*I*t had been a few days before he returned to the *dojo*. He
had washed the *gi* to shrink it as he had been instructed by
Aikido students in his class. He had neglected, however, to put
softener in the machine, and now he suffered the consequences.
The *gi*, already thick from the shoulder padding, was as stiff
as cardboard. He stood in front of his bedroom mirror. The
stiffness and the padding made him look impossibly buffed up.
A mini Arnold Schwarzenegger. The problem was that it wasn't
his body, just canvas. And he could barely move because the *gi*
was so stiff and also because his muscles ached all over from
his first class days ago. He knew that this was natural, but that
information didn't stop the pain.

He bounded up the *dojo* steps with his *gi* in an old gym bag.
He was excited, if still a bit apprehensive about class, but he
also felt that this was a place where he could change himself
into something new. Here he might put on the *gi*, break out of
his chrysalis and become the butterfly that he had always felt

was trapped within himself. If it wasn't going to happen in his musical career, then let it happen on the mat of an Aikido school.

As he reached the top of the steps he heard the thumping of a body being thrown hard to the mat. Entering the *dojo*, he immediately knew that something other than the usual class was in progress. Dozens of people in street clothes were crowded onto one side of the mat. Those in front were sitting, and those behind them stood. All were watching the action in the center of the mat.

On the mat, perhaps forty Aikido students sat. A few beginners sat cross-legged, but most were in *zazen*, the Zen meditative position. This is the kneeling posture that had caused David so much pain during his first class. It took westerners quite a while to adjust to. In the midst of all this knelt the *Sensei*. David joked to himself that because the teacher was so short, you couldn't tell whether he was standing or sitting. But his joking mood was stopped by the look he saw on the *Sensei*'s face. David now remembered that during his previous class, the *Sensei*'s face had had almost a sense of playfulness. It was gone now.

Five students in *gi*s and *hakama*s knelt facing their teacher in a straight line. One of them was Steely. Another student stood, awaiting orders from *Sensei*. The standing student was the professorial fellow David had met in the dressing room the first day. With his beard and ponytail and potbelly, he resembled a grizzly bear with glasses.

The teacher shouted out commands in Japanese. *"Shomen-Uchi Ikkyo!"* A young man charged at the professor and at the same time aimed a Karate chop at his head from above. The professor blocked it and simultaneously reversed the offending arm and with it, his attacker's body. He then pinned the attacker.

"Another," the *Sensei* called out.

Another student attacked in the same fashion. This time the professor rotated his hips to move slightly out of the way of the chop, which now reached only empty space. The professor, now positioned to the side of the attacker grabbed his wrist with one hand and with his other hand grabbed the *gi* below the triceps. David understood little else of what he saw at that moment, but saw the attacking student go flying far across the mat. Rather than land in a broken heap, the thrown student used the momentum of being tossed and dove into a flying somersault. He ended up standing and immediately ran across the mat back to his starting position to await further instructions. This throw brought gasps and cheers from a few of the visitors.

David realized that he'd walked in on a test. The energy in the room was electric. Feeling still that he was an outsider, he decided not to put on his *gi*, but rather to sit with the spectators, who he now realized were probably friends and family of the tested students.

After a few more attacks, a very winded Professor was told to sit down. David watched to see what would happen next. The *Sensei* studied notes on a clipboard that he was carrying.

Then he called out, "Simon Purcell!"

Steely Eyes jumped up and stood at the center of the mat. David jumped up. David's jaw dropped. For a moment he was totally disoriented. Finally he understood that the man he was looking for, the man who would have the answer to the crisis in his life, was standing right in front of him. Slowly, in a daze, David sat down. A couple of people who had stared at him for getting up so fast now returned their attention to the testing area.

Purcell bowed to *Sensei*, and then to the students who were to attack him. *Sensei* shouted attacks in Japanese. The students took turns attacking him, one by one. Charges, punching attacks, kicking attacks, grips, bear hugs, headlocks. Purcell threw each attacker hard and fast. He was in excellent shape and seemed unaffected by the attackers, who seemed nervous themselves. After dozens of throws, he was told to sit down. Then each testing student performed *katas*, choreographed routines with the wooden *bokken* swords and then other *katas* with *jo*, long wooden staffs. Purcell's *jo kata* was so fast that the *jo* was a blur, pinwheeling around his body, making it impossible for the invisible enemy to penetrate. After each testing student had finished his *katas*, *Sensei* had them kneel and wait his next instructions.

David felt as if he were caught between worlds of rational and irrational thought. Aikido looked too good to be true, too magical. Still, he'd been on the mat and felt the power of being thrown. It occurred to him that when he played jazz, some audience members would see the experience of watching improvisation as magical, and others wouldn't understand at all what a complex event was taking place. Only a fellow musician could really comprehend all the layers of thoughts and mechanical events that the improvising pianist was performing. And so with the Aikido test. It was too early for him to understand much about what he was seeing, but he knew that he wanted to uncover the process for himself.

The visiting audience sat quietly, whispering to each other, while the students who viewed the test stayed silent. Was it over? *Sensei* stood up, turned to his visitors, and smiled.

"Everyone work hard. Now final part of test. Test is to focus skill and power, stay calm when attack come. Student must perform *randori*, four-man free-style attack. One minute long. Today three students will each *randori*: Jenna Romano, Howard Masters, Simon Purcell."

He motioned for the three to kneel on one end of the mat. Then he chose four students to kneel at the other end. David knew that these four were advanced because they all wore the *hakama* over their *gis*. *Sensei* picked up a stopwatch.

"First Jenna. Close eyes."

Jenna and the four students who were to attack her closed their eyes and breathed deeply and slowly. David noticed how thin she was. After perhaps thirty seconds, *Sensei* clapped two wooden blocks together. They all opened their eyes and the four jumped up and charged her. Jenna was up in a flash and moving. The first attacker to reach her tried to bear hug her. She ducked and moved past him at the same time. Two more tried to grab her *gi* at the neck from the front. They only got each other. She was moving like a greased pig and they couldn't grab her. She kept spinning and running, like the offspring of a shortstop and a Whirling Dervish. Finally one attacker bear hugged her from behind, pinning her arms. She tried to bend and throw him forward, but she couldn't move him. Instead, she turned within the hug so that she was facing him directly. In the instant that his grip was loosened she expanded her arms and upper body, moving his arms up slightly. She then ducked and was gone. Finally, *Sensei* clapped the blocks and the action stopped.

For a moment there was only the sound of Jenna's lungs trying to get air. Then the crowd broke out in cheers and applause. She returned to her kneeling position.

"Howard Masters."

The Professor stepped up. He looked about fifty. He had a strong upper torso and a too-round abdomen. His glasses were held on by a frame band around his head. He looked nervous but determined.

"Close eyes."

During the breathing Masters kept one knee down and the other foot flat on the mat, ready to get up fast. The blocks clapped. The same four came after him. He wasn't fast enough and got cornered immediately. He shoved the first into the others and got out into the center. They surrounded him and he threw each of them one by one. David couldn't help but think that in a real street situation Masters would be in trouble. He broke out of the center and found himself in the far corner. He looked angry. His throws became ineffective. They piled up in front of him, grabbing him. It looked like a mugging. Two men had grabbed his hands on either side of him. He whirled around facing them, pinning the two against each other and threw them forward. They landed in a heap. Finally, *Sensei* clapped to signal the end.

Masters looked disheveled. His glasses were off his nose at an angle. His shoulders were heaving. He sat down. *Sensei* now ordered four new advanced students to step up for the final *randori*. David thought that if it weren't tough enough to do this, performing it at the end of a long test must have been excruciating, and nerve-wracking. He was glad to be anonymous amidst the crowd.

"Simon Purcell."

Steely bowed and got into his starting kneeling position.

"Close eyes." Clap.

Simon was up faster than David could understand. His eyes flashed as they charged. He ran directly into their charge. As they tried to grab him, his extended arms reached each one of them first and, grabbing their elbows, he simultaneously hopped past them and threw them. They went flying in all directions. One hit the wall in a standing position. Another had to dive into a somersault and landed so close to the crowd that the audience gasped. They could not touch him, and yet they fell. Purcell then remained untouchable and just out of their reach for the remaining time, like a basketball player running out the 24-second clock at the end of a game. The audience laughed and whooped in amazement. Clap.

They cheered, and when they stopped, they heard four sets of lungs trying to calm down. Purcell seemed unruffled and sat down. The audience buzzed. David saw one of the students who had attacked Purcell slap him on the back affectionately. Everyone sat and waited as *Sensei* wrote upon his clipboard. *Sensei* turned to address the crowd of visitors and the crowd of students.

"*Randori* is free-style. Purpose is to stay calm in action during attack by many people. Coordinating mind and body. No time to stop and pin attackers. Just best to keep moving. So today, everybody did good work. Promotion tests hard. Some people don't like taking tests. But it is important to show what you have learned. Results of tests are [he now read from the clipboard] Jose Manuel, Edgar Chen, Doris Keane, promoted to First *Kyu*."

The crowd applauded. David knew that this was the equivalent of high brown belt. Belts were not used in Aikido other than white and black, and often, you didn't know the rank of the person that you were working with in class, except of course, by their skill.

"Howard Masters, promoted to *Sho-dan*, first degree black belt."

They clapped for Howard. David felt that Masters' test was questionable, but guessed that he'd been a student a long time. Also, he wondered if it would have been a terrible loss of face to have *Sensei* fail him.

"Jenna Romano is promoted to *Ni-dan*, second degree black belt."

Applause and hollers. David clapped, and found himself fascinated by the pretty young woman who was clearly so powerful. She smiled as they applauded.

"Simon Purcell is promoted to *San-dan*, third degree black belt."

Louder cheers for Simon. David observed his reaction. At first he seemed stony-faced. Then a flicker of a smile passed his face. He bowed in *Sensei*'s direction from his kneeling position all the way down to the mat.

"Thank you for coming to see Aikido examination. For black belt students, is just the beginning of study. I study fifty years, and I am just beginner." The audience laughed. "Please stay for refreshments."

Sensei bowed and the audience applauded in appreciation. Everyone stood up and friends and family went over to congratulate the students. David was struck by the warmth of the moment, after such great tension during the test. He approached Purcell, but there was a crowd of visitors and fellow students around him. He waited till they had thinned out and gone on to the refreshments.

Purcell was sweaty and his face was flushed. He held a cup of soda brought to him by a friend.

As David put out his hand to introduce himself, Purcell said, "So, Mr. Stein, did you enjoy this performance?"

"You know who I am?" David stammered.

"You left your calling card on my door." Purcell was smiling.

"But you didn't tell me!"

"I knew you'd come to take class, David."

"But even I didn't know I'd take class, let alone come back again!"

"You knew it, David. You just didn't know that you knew."

David was taken aback by this comment. He was confused. His mind had already played tricks on him when he watched the test. Things happened that he couldn't quantify.

The world is full of things that we know for certain. We know them intimately and take them for granted, right up until the moment when we find out that they're not as we believed. People didn't *believe* that the earth was flat before Columbus. For them the world *was* flat. And perhaps for you, it's round. Or if you dabble in physics, perhaps it's a wave. Or if you're a Buddhist, perhaps it's all an illusion. It might sound ludicrous to say that the world is an aardvark. Maybe for you, this paragraph was acceptable until that last sentence. Well that's where your mind stopped. That's your unchangeable flat earth. Right before aardvark, it was okay to explore, but aardvark was too silly. Yet, tomorrow, you will find out that the earth is an aardvark. And after you go through the disbelief, the shock of the new, you'll believe it. At that moment, when you accept it, you'll look back upon the history of thought and see all the views of the world before as immature and ignorant. And then sometime after you learn that the world is an aardvark, and after it has been taught in the schools and become a basic tenet of understanding, you will be told that the earth is a pomegranate.

"Is there a time when we can talk about the tape you played at WBGI?" David asked.

"Yes, but not tonight. Can you come to class tomorrow night?"

"Yes."

"After class, we'll go out for a drink and talk about the tape that I played at WBGI."

Then Purcell walked away into the crowd of well-wishers.

CHAPTER
FOURTEEN

*T*he following evening, David took class. In his *gi*, which was still quite stiff, he felt like a toddler bundled up in a snowsuit. He did not feel like Bruce Lee. He worked with a number of different partners, taking turns as both *nage*, thrower, and *uke*, throwee. David was informed by Lionel, one of the students that *ukemi*, the art of falling, was the more difficult art. Every time he was thrown, he knew that it must be so. As he was tossed or pinned, he would tense up his body like a rock, and this would increase the pain of impact with the mat.

"You need to stay calm and relax when you're being thrown. When a drunk falls down and doesn't get injured, it's because his body is soft. He doesn't resist the fall."

Lionel continued to explain as he put his hand on the back of David's neck and spun him around. David was sent reeling face down towards the mat and then jerked back so he saw the ceiling and then ended up "whump!" flat on the mat face up. As David tried to stand up for more of this, Lionel went on.

"Aikido is about being calm in what otherwise might be a tense moment. Now me, I'm a subway conductor." He extended his wrist for David to grab. David obliged. "I work all night on the A train, uptown and downtown, uptown and downtown."

He suddenly stepped in next to David and in an instant, had disappeared behind him. There was a only a fraction of a second between the time that David felt Lionel's hands on his shoulders and the "whump!" of his own back hitting the mat hard. David just wanted to lie there and regain his wind, but Lionel offered him a hand to get up.

"Most of the time it's quiet, if you can call the subway a quiet environment, but occasionally, you have undesirable elements who are not acting in an appropriate fashion." Lionel faced him. "Those are the times when you want to have the ability to stay calm and not lose control of the situation. Your manner will deter a lot of these situations, and your choice of words will have an effect too, but..."

Lionel took a giant step forward into David's space and David stepped back, tripping and almost falling on his own.

"In the end, you want to have the physical skills to back it all up, just in case it gets nasty. You will find many people in Aikido who have also studied other arts."

"You mean like Karate?" David asked.

"Exactly. You learn what you need to learn in life wherever you find the information. And now it's your turn to throw me."

Brendan's was a little bar on Ninth Avenue off Fourteenth Street, just a block and a half from the *dojo*. The decor was dark wood booths and the crowd was a combination of blue collar workers from the meat markets and yuppies who were gentrifying the neighborhood.

David sat opposite Simon Purcell in a booth. They ordered beer and David nervously tried to chitchat about class until the bottles arrived at the table. Then Simon spoke.

"You heard the tapes I played on WBGI."

"I heard a few seconds of one tape. It was solo piano music, and I need to know what I heard. Would you tell me?"

David tried not to sound desperate, but he felt very awkward, because Simon had all the power here.

"I didn't announce what I played when I played that tape."

Simon looked down at his beer pensively. This man seemed wise, insane, centered and dangerous all wrapped up into one enigma.

"I thought that if I announced who it was, things might get out of hand."

"What do you mean, out of hand?" David asked, even though he had a feeling that he understood.

"Why do you want to know who you heard? If you knew who you heard, what would you do with that?"

David gulped and sat back. He didn't want to play chess. He just wanted to know who the hell could play music that could plumb the soul that he hadn't known he possessed.

"Whatever I heard did things to me that I can't explain. It was frightening and fantastic at the same time. I'm a pianist and I feel as if I must understand how someone could make that come out of a piano! Please! Who was it? Why did you destroy it? Where can I find a copy?"

Simon Purcell took a swig of beer and put down his bottle.

"Listen to me. You heard a bit of this music and it has affected you in a very powerful way. If you heard enough of it often enough, it would affect you in other ways."

"What do you mean?" David's voice was getting a bit shrill now. "Why are you doing this? All I want to know is who it was! Come on, I just want to know! What's the big secret?"

"You heard it," Simon replied. "The secret is out. You felt it."

David stood up. "You're not going to tell me? I can't believe this. I don't know what to say."

Simon stood up and looked down at David. "Sit down!" he hissed softly. David sat down. "I will tell you what I can."

"Last summer *Sensei* told me that the State University at Stony Brook on Long Island had contacted him to informally teach Aikido there for the summer. It wasn't a credited class, but rather, a club that had formed and needed a teacher. *Sensei* suggested that I teach the classes. When *Sensei* suggests you go, you go. In fact, I was happy that he asked me."

"The classes were held in a building that normally served as a cafeteria."

David decided that by not interrupting, he'd get information quicker. He sat forward with his hands on the table and listened intently.

"I taught class three evenings per week. On the final night of summer classes, I was invited by a couple of the students to a party in one of the dorms. At that party, I hung out, listened to jazz and talked Aikido with my students. I deliberately did not drink because I knew that I'd have to drive back to the city. At one point a very wild-eyed young man approached me. He told me that he had been listening to me discuss Aikido and spirituality. He handed me a cassette and told me that he thought that I'd benefit from it. I asked him what it was and he said only that it was not to be described in words. I said 'Let's put it on now!' but he stopped me and said 'It's not for this place. It's not for driving home either. Please.' (and he emphasized that word) 'Please wait till you're home.' I agreed, because there was something serious and imploring in his eyes. The tape had only the stick-on label that comes with a blank cassette when you buy it. It was marked only with the number "7" on it. The recording tabs were knocked out to prevent someone from accidentally recording over it."

David's curiosity got the better of him. "Did you wait until you got home?" he asked, and immediately regretted it. Simon gave him a withering stare and David sat back. Then the stare dissolved into a relaxed and almost mischievous smile.

"I made it halfway home without playing the tape. After driving for awhile it started to seem ludicrous, and so I played the tape."

"What happened?"

Simon looked up at the ceiling and his eyes reddened with tears. His armor dissolved.

"What happened is... that I heard the music. I heard this.... light. I was electrocuted... and hugged... and I disintegrated... and I lost control and went off the road."

"Jesus."

"I was very lucky. I hadn't reached the expressway yet and I was in the right lane, taking my time. Otherwise I'd have been doing seventy and we wouldn't be having this conversation."

"Were you badly hurt?"

"No. I ran off the side of the road and hit the brakes. I ran up onto the grass and stopped. I sat there a long, long time. I got out and looked at the stars, as much as you can see stars on Long Island."

A waitress passed by. David waved her over. "Two more beers". He returned his attention to Simon. "Go on, please."

"I sat on the grass and did some deep breathing. I still felt bodiless, but at least I was calm. I drove on the service road in the right lane, as slowly as I could get away with. I was determined to get home alive. That night I had wild dreams that I can't describe. I remember them, and how they felt, but I have no words."

"Did you listen to it again?"

Simon looked uneasy. "When?"

"When you got home. Did you listen to it that night? Or ever again, for that matter?"

Simon looked down, and David realized that this man, who seemed so fearless, was afraid to meet his gaze.

"I didn't listen to it again that night. Days later, I heard it one more time."

"And what was that like?"

Simon took a long swallow of beer and then put the bottle down on the table. He leaned in very close to David's face.

"One listening is the right amount."

David blinked. "What do you mean, the right amount? What does that mean?"

"One listening is the right amount. You're not to listen to it more than that."

David was confused. "I don't get it, where did this rule come from?"

"That's just the way it is. Nobody had to tell me. I just know it, in the way you know your own name. It's meant to be heard once, and then not again." Simon slumped back in his seat, looking exhausted.

"But what happens if you hear it more than once? What happened when you heard it again?"

Simon shook his head 'no'. Then he got up and walked out.

CHAPTER
FIFTEEN

A few days later, David walked into Penn Station to take the Long Island Railroad out to Stony Brook. The trip was just over an hour and a half. On the way, he stared out the window. Long Island had changed deeply from his childhood visits to family friends. There was much less green, and much more development. Places that had been fields when he was a kid were squashed suburbs. Quaint little old train stations now looked like corporate complexes. It seemed as if the island that one once could escape to, was now an island to escape. He remembered visiting Great Neck during holidays as a child. His family didn't have a car, and they'd take the double decker trains. It was a mysterious adventure to climb into the monstrously large train and decide whether to sit on the upper or lower level. For a city kid, it was a thrill.

Now as he got closer to his destination, the land opened up a bit. There were more trees, and some of them were close enough to almost smack the side of the train. But a lot of the farms were gone. The houses looked more "old money" out here. The conductor called out "Stony Brook" and the train squealed to a halt. David stepped down off the train. His adrenaline shot up, knowing that he was a step closer to finding out about the tape.

The University stretched out before him. It was massive. He saw buildings across an extremely large athletic field. He decided to walk across. Students were jogging or practicing team sports. Others had stepped off the train and were returning to their dorms from ventures into the city. When he reached the other side, he saw a young man and woman that he took for students. He took out a piece of paper from his pocket and read it. He asked them where Roth Quad was. They pointed.

"It's about a fifteen minute walk," one said. Walking across the campus, he was amazed by its size and by its bustle.

Stony Brook, the largest of the State University system, had gone by many nicknames. He remembered many years ago that friends who had gone there had called it "Rockefeller's Pet" and "The Berkeley of the East." It had always been under construction, but seemed on the verge of finally being finished, in the sense that it had expanded as far as it could. It was renowned as a science school. The undergraduates were primarily from Long Island and New York City, but there was also a smattering of international students, many of whom had come to study the sciences. He also remembered from his college days that it had a reputation as a party school.

The architecture reminded him of the movie "The Time Machine" with Rod Taylor. In the film, in the far off future, a terrifying looking building sounded a siren and swallowed up the unsuspecting Eloi people, after which they became food for the evil Morlocks, who lived underground. Every building here looked like that to him. Cold, cement, faceless, few windows, tomblike. In fact, to David, it seemed as if for the last thirty years or so, every institutional building in the world had been built by the same architect. And he didn't like this architect. He longed for something old fashioned that was long gone.

He reached Roth Quad, a group of three and four-story buildings, all grey, built around an artificial pond. The pond water was covered in algae. The buildings looked as if Hobbits must live in them. He located Cardozo College, one of the Roth Quad dorms.

"Hi, I'm looking for Karen Lister."

The student who answered the door looked to be about nineteen. She wore a sweatshirt and blue jeans, and could have been a college student in any number of eras.

"Kaaarennn!" she yelled, still looking at David. David shrank in embarrassment when she yelled. "Visitor!"

David looked down at the ground. Karen Lister came over to the door. She had long brown hair and an old soul in a young face.

"Hi?" she ventured.

"Hi Karen, we haven't met. I study Aikido alongside Simon Purcell in the city. Can we talk?"

She gestured for him to come in. They sat in the living room of the dorm suite, which also served as a kitchen and dining room.

"You study with *Sensei* Simon?" she asked.

"Yes, at the main *dojo* on 14th Street." David was surprised to hear Simon referred to as *Sensei*.

"He's a great teacher," Karen offered.

"Yes, he is. Karen, you invited *Sensei* Simon to a party on the campus last summer. Do you remember this? It was on the last night of classes."

"Yes, we went to a party at my friend Stefan's dorm."

"Can you tell me where that dorm is?" She pointed out the window to a building in the same Quad, just a couple of hundred feet away. "It's called Mount College. You want to talk to Stefan? What's this all about?"

David lied, "Simon has asked me to speak to Stefan."

She called his number. When she hung up, she told him, "His roommate says that he's at the library. I can take you there if you want."

The Stony Brook University library was a marvel of very strange construction. There had been an older library on the campus. In the early seventies it was decided that the library was too small for a fast growing university community. But just as you can't shut down the New York subways to upgrade them, you can't shut down a university library to rebuild it. So the new library exterior was built around the old building, completely encasing it. Then, the old shell was taken down from the inside. A bit like a snake shedding its skin, filmed backwards.

They wandered through the reading rooms, looking for Stefan. Finally, Karen spotted him. He sat alone. He had long unkempt hair. He had bad acne and an overly serious built-in scowl. He sat reading a book entitled "Plato's Republic: An Analysis." They approached him.

"Hey, Stefan." she said.

Stefan finished reading his sentence and then looked up. "Oh, hi, Karen!"

He instantly knew that whoever David was, obviously he had come to speak with him. He stood up and extended his hand.

"I see that you're reading Plato," said David.

"Well, sort of. Actually a critique of Plato by an idiot, but what do they say, 'opinions are like assholes, everyone's got one.'"

"Whoever they are," David retorted.

"Huh?" Stefan looked quizzical.

"You know, the 'they' that say things about opinions."

"Ah." Stefan shrugged. They were sizing each other up.

"Mr. Stein studies Aikido with *Sensei* Simon, the man I studied with last summer," Karen said.

"Please, it's David."

"David wanted to ask you about the party you had in your suite last summer."

"Do a lot of students stay on campus during the summer?" asked David.

Stefan just blinked back at him.

Karen felt the tension. "Okay, you guys talk. I've got a class soon."

David thanked her and she left.

"Look Stefan, I'll get right to the point if I may."

They sat down at the table. They spoke in hushed library tones.

"Somebody at your party, a young man, gave a cassette tape to my friend, Simon. That tape had a profound effect upon both of us. I'm trying to find out more about it. I'd like to know who the musician on that tape was, and where your friend got it. This is very important to me or I wouldn't have bothered to come out here. Perhaps you can help me."

Darkness passed across Stefan's eyes. He looked at David, and then he looked down at the book that he had been reading.

"Who's your favorite philosopher, David?"

"I'd have to think about it."

"Mine's Plato. He had a very clear world view. You might even say that he created our world view."

David listened.

"The great philosophers constructed a reality that we still subscribe to. Whether or not it's so, we've bought into it. Do you understand me?"

"I think so."

"But maybe, just maybe, things are not how they told us. Maybe reality is completely different from whatever we thought it was. Perhaps we've even constructed a society based on the realities that the philosophers told us about. We've made the society function, more or less, even though it's a complete illusion, a false premise."

At this point, David would have thought that he was talking to a drugged-out idiot, but too much had happened to him lately to do so.

Stefan grinned at him and held it long. And then he said, "Alex Hirsch."

"Excuse me?"

"Alex Hirsch would have been the person who gave your friend the tape."

"Thank you, Stefan! Is he your roommate?"

"Was. Well, my suite mate. We lived in the same suite. He was in the room next to mine."

"Is he on campus today?" asked David in a hurried manner.

Stefan shook his head "no".

"He's not here. He's not even all here." Stefan pointed to his head.

"What happened to him?"

"Some say drugs, some say a psychotic breakdown. But I'll tell you, I don't think that's the whole story. I think that he heard the tape too many times."

David sat back. The wind had been knocked out of him. How could he get so near to this...thing...and yet not dare to experience it?

"Do you know where I can locate him?"

"He's in a place for people that don't fit in."

"You mean an asylum?"

"That's right. You want to see him?"

"Very much."

"You want to see him now?"

"Is that possible? Where is he?"

"Not far from here. About ten miles. I can take you if you want to go see Alex. I can help translate for you."

"Doesn't Alex speak English?"

"He speaks his own way. He's like Quasimodo pretending to be deaf. He can speak, but he may not choose to do so in a way that you can understand too easily."

"Do you have a car?" said the non-driver.

"Can do." said Stefan.

CHAPTER SIXTEEN

*T*he clinic was in Northport. David didn't like these places, because he felt that he might end up in one someday. It wasn't a new feeling. He had always been a bit different, and though he didn't dwell on it, he knew it to be so. He also knew that he had experienced many strange states of being long before he heard the tape. Perhaps he was due for madness. There had been enough crazies in his family to fill the place. The ones in the arts got away with it, because a little madness goes so well with being an artist. But he wasn't comfortable here. What was madness, anyway? Was it quantifiable? Or was it a whole palette of different ways of being? Different ways that neither the society nor the victim could handle? The more he thought about it, the more he was confused.

He looked at the patients. Some pretty far gone-looking, and others who looked as centered as anyone he'd ever met. They lined the antiseptic hallway in chairs. Some stayed in their rooms, but others took part in organized activities in a large day-room. Same sonofabitch architect. He ran the world now.

They came to Alex's room. As they entered, David noticed the personal trappings and paraphernalia without seeing the body lying face up on the bed. Alex had been invisible to David for a moment. Stefan walked around the bed to him.

"Hey, you, wake up! Lou Gehrig broke a finger nail, and I'm putting you in the lineup!"

Without moving, Alex answered, "Lou Gehrig is dead, Stefan, and so am I. Today, I consider myself the luckiest man alive."

David recognized the last sentence as the opening of Gehrig's speech at Yankee Stadium on the day he retired with the killing disease that would come to be known by his own name.

"Sit up and meet somebody, Alex," said Stefan, reaching for Alex's hand. Stefan pulled him up.

Alex looked at Stefan, but commented on David. "He looks funny but sad. Has he come to worship my unruly ass?"

"No, oh Machiavellian wannabe, he has come to glean info from you."

"What sort of info, and what am I in fo'?"

"You're in fo' some conversation, s'what you're in fo'."

Alex, sitting on the bed, swiveled his head towards David. He stared at David. Alex Hirsch had closely-cropped red hair and his face was covered with freckles. It was easy to picture how he had looked as a child. David couldn't tell if Alex was smiling or sneering.

Alex raised his hand and pointed at David. "Are you Billy Joel, or are you George Gershwin?" Then he laughed.

David felt a chill go through his body. "Either one would be a good gig," he answered.

"Well, if you were Gershwin, you'd be dead like me. And if you were Billy Joel, then Long Island is the right place to be." Alex stared deeper. "What have they got that you haven't got?"

His tone seemed sarcastic and mocking. David was trying to stay calm in this place, but the inmate had become the inquisitor, and he knew too much that he couldn't have possibly known.

"Actually, I am a pianist."

"Yes, you're a pianist, friend of Jonathan the warrior, who died in battle."

"I don't understand."

"Because you're not him."

"Not who?"

"The king whose friend was Jonathan."

David looked at Stefan for an answer.

"Alex, are you referring to King David from the Bible?" asked Stefan.

"They were very, very close," answered Alex. "Jonathan's death was a great loss to the King."

David shook his head in confusion.

"Am I supposed to believe that he knew my name?"

"I have no idea," said Stefan. "Alex, how did you know the man's name?"

"Did you call ahead?" David interrupted. "Did Karen call here? What the fuck is this?!"

"Don't curse in my room, mother*fucker*!" growled Alex.

David was steaming, but held his tongue.

Wisely, he said only, "Sorry."

"Sari? *Dashiki, kimono, gi, hakama. Hakama* you come to see me, Aikido man?"

David had sat down in a chair but stood up again. He was very frightened.

"How do you know so much about me?"

"*Hakama* you don't know so much about you? You want to know about the fucking tape."

Alex's head was nodding long slow negative drunken nods. He looked like a blind man who had suddenly regained his sight.

"Yes that's correct. Please tell me about the tape."

Alex closed his eyes. "You wouldn't believe what it's like in here."

"Maybe I would."

"David, you would hate it in here. You'd be really unhappy. And you can't get away."

"Did the music make you feel this way?"

"Music made me feel...made me feel like...he cared about me."

"Who? Who cared about you?"

Alex pointed straight up. "Him."

"Do you mean God?"

Alex nodded.

"How many times did you hear the tape?"

Alex held up his hand and wiggled his fingers very fast. "How many fingers am I holding up?"

There was a long silence. "Alex," David said, "Would you please tell me who is playing the piano on the tape?"

"He doesn't know that," Stefan said.

Alex looked blank.

"Well can you tell me where you got the tape? Who gave it to you?"

"Alex, tell him where you got it, man."

Alex smiled ear to ear. His smile was held so tensely that it looked as if he might explode into tears. He spoke slowly through clenched teeth.

"I received.... the tape... from Thossian."

"Who is Thossian?" asked David.

"Thossian," said Alex, relaxing now, "is our friend."

David looked at Stefan. "You know this Thossian?"

"Not exactly," replied Stefan. "Alex has told me many things. That the tape came from the universe, that it came from hell, heaven, any number of sources. He has mentioned Thossian, but I've never been clear about who or what Thossian was."

"All of the above," said Alex.

"Alex," said Stefan, "is Thossian a person, place or thing?"

Alex looked at Stefan coyly. "Are you a person, place or thing? What are we? Animal, vegetable, mineral, legume, jellyfish, gods or roaches?"

"How 'bout Thossian, Alex? Is he a person?" said Stefan.

Alex nodded very slightly.

"He's a person?"

Alex nodded again.

"So he is a person!"

"YESSS! PERSON!"

Alex lay back down and stared at the ceiling. "He's our friend," he muttered.

"He's your friend." said David. "Stefan, Alex says he's a friend to both of you." Stefan shrugged.

"*Our* friend, piano man," said Alex, still staring at the ceiling.

"You mean that Thossian is your friend and my friend?" asked David. Alex nodded.

"Why is Thossian my friend, too?"

Alex said nothing.

"Alex, tell me why Thossian is my friend too."

"Thossian is your friend, too, because he gives you the advantage. He gives you the advantage, and the disadvantage. He gives you the game of love. He jumps over the net with you.

He puts you in the court and on the court, and he takes away the boundary lines."

"It sounds like a game of tennis."

"It is a game of tennis. But there are no spectators in this game. And the serve is hit hard at you, and you'd better not miss. And the fault you make is bigger than the San Andreas fault. And the shorts you wear will short circuit you.... like they did me." Alex turned away from them and started to sob. "Go away! Get the fuck out of my world!"

"I'm sorry, Alex."

"Get... the fuck... out!"

CHAPTER
SEVENTEEN

*H*aving cajoled Alex Hirsch's mother on the phone, David found that the tape had come from one Thossian Lewis, in Florida. Alex had met Thossian when he worked down there at an EZ Time Inn over a winter break from school.

And so David Stein, who did not like to fly, found himself on a flight down to Fort Lauderdale. He was at best an uncomfortable passenger, and more often, a white-knuckle flyer. During the flight, fighter jets zoomed past and shot his plane down repeatedly. Fires broke out, crazy violent people took over, noxious fumes overcame the passengers, and gremlins chewed off the wings. Other than that, it was an uneventful flight.

David hit on the blonde flight attendant. She had heard it all before, but smiled at his jokes. Telling jokes eased his terror of flying. As long as he was laughing, he wasn't gripping the armrests quite as hard. As the plane came in for a landing, he tightened his seat belt and slouched down low to avoid injury in the crash he imagined coming. It didn't help when the mime's head came sailing past and smashed itself like a tomato at the front of the cabin. Nobody but he seemed to notice. When the plane landed, he clapped out loud for the pilot.

He stared out the window at the runway and the palm trees and the glaring afternoon Florida sunlight. He had never been to Florida. He was a provincial New Yorker. He was as culturally trapped in New York as anyone who grew up in an isolated small town anywhere in the world. Coming to Florida was not a simple choice for him. It took him way out of his comfort zone. But then, the tape had taken him way out of his comfort zone, and so it followed in a peculiar new logic that he should take the initiative in this adventure.

At the baggage claim, he was amazed to see the clothing people wore. Bright Hawaiian-looking shirts, polyester suits in outlandish colors, shorts, tank tops, sandals. When the baggage came, he noted three or four sets of golf clubs.

Why did people play golf, anyway? What did they get out of it? Didn't playing golf mean hurrying up and waiting? Standing on line for a turn? He remembered that from playing miniature golf as a child. Wasn't it the same with gigantic golf? He couldn't conceive of spending hours out in the sun, waiting for one second of movement. It seemed to him like some sort of ultra-slowed-down baseball game. To a basketball or soccer fan, baseball seemed like a slow game. You wait your turn and then take your chance in the batter's box. You're usually not moving. To David though, baseball had a dramatic plot. A rhythmic arc like a great symphony. Tension built and subsided and built up again. But golf? Wasn't that where people go to die? He didn't get it. He did, however, admire the paucity of clothing on the women at the baggage claim. He had always liked warm weather for that reason. The legs came out, the shoulders, the cleavage. And here in Florida, he figured, it's always warm and it's always half naked. This was good.

The cab driver took him to the EZ Time Inn. Being a non driver, he knew that it would be tricky to get around. Everybody else in the world drove. He had never learned. Such a city slicker. He was the world's number one passenger. On the plane everyone was like him. A passenger. Nobody expected them to fly the plane, did they? Yet everyone in the world was supposed to know how to drive. But not David.

The humidity was overwhelming. Oppressive, if you were used to it. Being fair-skinned, he was miserable without sunglasses and squinted the way he had squinted since he was a kid. He wanted to look cool in sunglasses but it was so hard for him to find a pair that looked right. And they'd just get broken like the watch straps. He had a pile of old sunglasses in his dresser drawer. He was a middling pack rat. He needed to be *Feng Shui*-ed. He needed his possessions to be exorcised. He really owned very little of worth besides his grandmother's piano.

The hotel was in a large parking lot. It was nowhere. Across an open plaza he could see a Jukefood fast food joint. He was in the desert without a camel.

He went up to the check-in desk at the EZ Time Inn. He felt stupidly out of place in his long sleeved shirt. He knew he appeared as foreign as exotic foreign visitors appeared to him in New York. He liked to laugh at them, and now he felt as if the Floridians must be secretly laughing at him.

He handed over his credit card to the young man behind the desk, the young collegiate-looking fellow with the EZ Time Inn uniform on.

"Can I get an ocean view?" asked David, with a smirk.

"The ocean's just fifteen minutes away sir."

"No ocean view from here, huh?"

"That's correct, sir. Not from the hotel. But we do have a view out to the highway if you'd like."

"Is that better than the other side?"

"Well sir, the other side looks out on the parking lot. I'd suggest the highway view."

"Does it cost more?"

"It's twenty dollars more per night."

"I'll take the cheapo view."

"Okay sir. You're in room 219. Here's your key. You can also use the gym."

"How 'bout the pool?"

"Well actually, the pool is in the process of being built. This is a brand new EZ Time Inn. We just opened three months ago."

"How come you opened before the pool was built?"

"That's just what happened, sir. I don't really know more than that."

"Shouldn't there be a discount for a new hotel that has a pool that the guests can't use?"

Collegiate boy shrugged. It wasn't his job.

David brought his luggage up to room 219. The hall smelled of disinfectant. He walked in and immediately walked over to the window to look out. The window was sealed with central air conditioning. Claustrophobic no-no number one.

The view indeed looked out on a grey formless parking lot with nothing of color or humanity to break its spell. This was no-no number two. He switched on the TV to calm himself down, but it was a hotel promo channel with muzak. The oasis in the desert was a plastic palm tree.

He checked the toilet to make sure it worked. He checked the shower to make sure it worked. Soap, shampoo, little shower cap, all there. He felt an overriding urge to be with people. Without unpacking, he left the room, closing the door and then opening and shutting it again to make sure the lock worked. He walked down to the lobby and out the front towards the Jukefood.

The sun blazed down on him, and he was sure that he'd get skin cancer and heat stroke before he reached the restaurant. As he walked he rolled up his sleeves, wishing that he had changed into short sleeves. He was the only human in the state of Florida wearing black jeans today. Maybe they'd think that he was a rock star.

Upon reaching the Jukefood, he could no longer bear his outsider appearance. He turned around to cross the asphalt desert one more time. He was getting pissed off and tense. Here was this city boy who should have been overjoyed to be in the Florida sunshine, and he was getting pissed off instead.

Sweating and angry, he went back to his room and changed into his Charlie Parker t-shirt with the bird flying out of the saxophone, and a pair of grey shorts with an elastic band that made him look supremely stupid. He had on tennis sneakers with black socks.

Back out again and across the desert to the oasis. His eyes were tearing up from the sun. He reached the Jukefood entrance, and by now had worked up a great thirst. The air-conditioning hit him all over and in two seconds he went from relief to feeling too cold. He had no jacket! He'd freeze! He only liked the world from 68F to 72F. Everything else was too cold or too hot. But he knew he was right to feel the way he did. He had once read that the best temperature for mental work was 68F and that that was why England had done so well, historically, as a thinking society. 72F was the best temperature for physical labor, and that's why the U.S. had been able to build itself up into a gigantic industrial society. So wasn't his body thermometer perfect? So he didn't like extremes (below 68 or above 72). Big deal!

He sat in a freezing booth by the window, staring out at Florida. Everyone else seemed to be comfortable. Didn't they know how cold it was? No, they didn't know because they were so fat! Everyone looked fat to him. Not fat, obese. A lot of customers at this Jukefood on this day looked disastrously fat in a dangerous heart attacking way. He saw a couple who waddled. The only skinny folks he noticed were the retirees. They were too skinny, and should have felt as cold as he did. So how could these old geezers in shorts sip iced tea in this air-conditioning? He crossed his legs to keep warm. He remembered that if you fall into the ocean, you should cross your legs and keep your arms closed so that heat doesn't escape your groin and your armpits. He did this. At a window booth on a 90 degree day in Fort Lauderdale. In a Jukefood. To keep from freezing to death.

Melba brought the menu (it said Melba on her name tag).

"How you doin' today?"

"Oh, I'm okay, just a little cold."

"You mean you have a cold?"

"Umm, no, just cold in here."

"Oh, is it cold in here? I just keep movin' so much that I don't even notice."

He hoped she'd follow up by offering to have the AC turned down.

"Can I bring you some coffee to warm you up?"

There was no way that Melba was going to turn down the AC. To her, this was alien stuff. Where was he from?

"I'll have tea, actually."

"Okay, tea coming up."

As she left he picked up the menu. Even though it was afternoon he went for the breakfast menu. He loved ordering breakfast, anywhere, anytime. Being able to get scrambled eggs gave him the illusion that he was getting home cooked food and that somebody loved him.

"The Original Rock'n'Roll" listed "Rockin' eggs, Rollin' pancakes, Boppin' bacon, Swingin' sausage, Rock'n'Roll!" And all for a few bucks. How could you beat that? When Melba returned he ordered "The Original Rock'n'Roll". It sounded so cool, so American, like it had been around as long as Rock'n'Roll. He felt that he was part of a great tradition, ordering "The Original Rock'n'Roll". He was smart enough to not sound like an outsider and say "I'll have the Original Rock'n'Roll Breakfast." Instead he said, "I'll have the Original Rock'n'Roll. And grits on the side." What were grits, anyway? He'd heard about them in Country Western songs, but he had no idea what they were. So he was going to try grits today.

He looked at the mini-jukebox on the table with its selection of songs. Mostly country, some Elvis. He looked for Frank Sinatra. No, not "My Way", he thought. Swinging Frank. He found it. "Live At The Sands" in the '60's with the Basie Band. Nothing was playing. He put in his coins. "I've Got You Under My Skin" or as David liked to introduce it on gigs, "A song about crab lice."

Those horns started chugging and David relaxed. He felt safe and he felt like singing. He snapped his fingers under the table.

Melba came with "The Original Rock'n'Roll". It was really big. And she brought him a side of grits.

"Melba, whaddya put on grits?"

"Try butter, honey. Lots of it."

He slathered the butter on and looked at the Rock'n'Roll. What a name. How could anyone shake their butt with that in their stomach? He stared at the grits and brought the spoon slowly to his mouth. Then he looked at the spoon again and smelled it. Finally he tried it. New world. Grits world. Great new world of grits. How had he come this far without grits in his life? Well, that had to stop. From now on he would be hooked. And it didn't hurt that Sinatra was singing the crab lice song to imprint the joy of discovery. Music could always imprint an experience into your DNA. You hear an old song and "poof!", you remember your childhood, or someone you loved. The music was the time machine to take you back instantaneously.

"What the hell is that crap you're eatin', pal?"

It was Frank. In a tux. Here at Jukefood. David jumped up and spilled buttered grits all over himself.

"Omigosh!" he said.

"Cheesh, what is this, piano player's nursery school? Here, clean that crap up, kid."

Frank handed him a white silk handkerchief with F.A.S. emblazened on it.

"Oh, I couldn't", said the grits-laden David.

"Go ahead pally, I got a trunk full."

"Thanks." David wiped himself off as Frank sat down facing him in the booth.

"You gigging down here, sonny?"

"Well, actually, I'm searching."

"Have you tried pool side? That's always a good place to look. The broads are out in force today at the Sands, where I'm working."

"I'm really searching for something else than broads."

"Well don't look at me! I'm no pansy ass."

David laughed. "No no, I meant that I'm searching for something. Some music that I heard, but I don't know who was playing. It really shook me up."

"Um hum. Was it that god damned Rock'n'Roll? I hate that shit. Noise. Noise from longhaired pansies from England. Makes me never wanna go back to London. Makes me never wanna sing 'A Nightingale Sang In Berkeley Square' again. And after we saved their asses in the war, they send us that crap. Was it Rock'n'Roll?"

"No, it was something that didn't fit into a category. It was played on the piano, and it turned me inside out. I'm down here from New York to talk to a guy about it."

"Oh, you're from New York," said Frank, lighting a cigarette. You know, I'm from New Jersey, myself."

"I know. Everybody knows that."

"Good boy," said Frank. "When you find out whose music this is, be sure to give credit to the composer. That's one thing I always do on stage. I always credit the songwriter and the arranger."

"I know," said David.

Frank blew a great cloud of cigarette smoke, filling the restaurant 'til David could no longer see him.

When the smoke cleared, David was alone at the table. His grits were still in their bowl. He finished the grits, and stuffed himself with "The Original Rock'n'Roll". Feeling greatly rocked, rolled, and very original, he headed back across the asphalt to the hotel.

Not due to meet Thossian till tonight, he decided to see the ocean. He hadn't seen a lot of ocean since he was a kid. Back then, his parents would borrow a car from a friend and drive out to Jones Beach on Long Island. Jones Beach, though mobbed in summers with New Yorkers, was actually a world-class beach, and was unfairly maligned. You go to the French Riviera, as famous it is, and the beach itself is no great shakes. Yes, to the topless women, but no to the pebbles. But Jones Beach was very deep and covered with fine white powdery sand. It was a great beach. And though people from the west coast laughed at the Atlantic, it was a perfectly nice ocean. The surf wasn't Hawaii, but it was all he had known, and he respected that ocean. There were parts of the Long Island shore where a riptide might pull a powerful swimmer out to death. He had heard that you were supposed to go with the pull and not fight it if it took you out, but he knew that if he got pulled out, weak swimmer that he was, he'd fight it. And lose.

He remembered the stickiness of the floor in the Jones Beach refreshments building. The tough guys from Brooklyn and their bikini-clad babes. The Rock'n'Roll blasting on the transistor radios. The coolers with the cold chicken and the hardboiled eggs. Somehow, no matter how careful you were, you'd be ingesting some sand with your hardboiled eggs. He could still smell the suntan lotion. He could feel the pain of his feet running through the hot sand, and stepping on sharp shells that had somehow worked their way inland. And he'd always get sunburned. When he was a kid his hair was platinum blond. He was a burner.

Awash in memory, he called a taxi from Seagull taxi. He packed a backpack, put on his horrendous old baggy tangerine swirled bathing suit, which was professionally crumpled, and waited downstairs for the cab. He wore an old light blue NY Mets cap and cheap sunglasses with brown plastic frames and dark blue lenses. In his mind, he was the picture of cool. As he rode beachward, he found himself still amazed that the palm trees weren't just props. When he reached the beach, he involuntarily took in a deep breath at the sight of the ocean. Still there. Following him through life the way the moon used to follow him when he was a boy as he walked down the street.

It was a weekday, mid-afternoon, and the beach was almost empty. A couple of joggers, an old man lying in a chaise lounge. With an unnatural tan. Skin like leather, wrinkled up. A full head of grey hair. A wealthy man of leisure. David took off his sneakers and walked through the hot sand as he had remembered doing, so long ago. His heart and breathing slowed. He reached the water and sat down cross legged. He took another deep breath. The sun was hot. He took off his cap and wiped his head and then fanned his head with the cap. Then he put it back on. He closed his eyes and just listened and felt.

He couldn't hear fire engines or police sirens or subways or breaking glass or shouting. Just wind and surf and the occasional cry of the seagulls. Even though he was the only person on earth to take a cab to the beach in Florida, he felt at home. He stopped bitching for a moment. After awhile he got up and walked along the edge of the water down the beach. He was so stuffed from "The Original Rock'n'Roll" that he knew he'd either not last long walking, or that he had to walk forever to compensate for what he'd eaten. He walked silently. He was rarely silent. He was always yapping or singing or whistling. He was afraid of silence. Who knew what he might hear if he stopped making noise? What strange voices within him might make themselves known? Noise made things normal. Silence was a dangerous void. And yet, here he felt the urge to keep quiet.

And now he sat on the beach and closed his eyes. Music swirled through him, like so many radio channels competing for his attention. Songs stuck in his head, repeating in loops. He tried to direct his attention away and to the sound of the surf. The gentle but demanding swooshing of the waves slowed his heart. He was trying to let the city go. The heat burned through his clothing. Still he sat listening. He wondered if God were there. At that moment three gulls flew along the beach over-head. As they cried out he heard a cry in his head, "Beware of Mahozada!" And then they were gone.

David thought that he must have had too much sun today. The sky looked grey. The waves were a bit too loud. His skin was starting to hurt. He stood up and walked away from the ocean. He called a cab from a pay phone. In the cab he sat sing-ing softly, "Mahozada little star, how I wonder what you are."

CHAPTER EIGHTEEN

*T*hat evening, a red skinned David cabbed it to La Luna, a jazz club on the water. Dr. Armando, the legendary turbaned wizard of the Hammond B3 organ, was in residence with his band. The crowd was loud and beer-driven. The band was playing gut-bucket funk with Dr. Armando's organ lines swirling above and through the sound. David was immediately captivated and intimidated by his technique. And between the beer he was drinking, the babes at the bar and the music, he was buzzed.

A young black man with white slacks and a button-down short sleeved shirt tapped him on the shoulder.

"You're David!" he yelled above the din.

"Thossian?"

"That's me."

"How'd you know me?"

"I knew you." They sat at the bar.

"What can I get you?" asked David.

"Same as you."

David ordered another bottle of beer for Thossian.

"You like the Doctor?" said Thossian, pointing to the organist.

"He's a great player!" David answered.

"He makes things happen," said Thossian, smiling down at his beer.

David accepted the remark without delving into any subsurface meaning.

"Thossian, I came down here to Florida to meet you, because ever since I heard the tape that your friend Alex heard, I feel as if meeting people and talking to them makes more sense than telephone calls."

"Uh-huh. I understand."

David shifted uncomfortably on his barstool. His skin was burned and the air conditioning and cigarette smoke was not helping matters.

"So," David went on, "I'm here to find out from you what I can about the tape."

Thossian took a sip on his beer and said nothing. David waited. Their silence was filled by Dr. Armando's angular lyricism and the driving rhythm section.

Finally Thossian looked him in the eye.

"My grandfather gave me the tape. He told me that I should listen to it twice and then give it to someone else with the same instructions."

"Listen to it twice?"

"Just twice."

"And did you?"

"I did."

"How did he know you would do that? Just listen twice?"

Thossian grinned. "He knew, like I knew who you were tonight."

David felt a chill go through him.

"Besides," laughed Thossian, "in my family, you don't cross the paternal figures. "Grandpa said twice, twice is it."

"Thossian, my friend told me that once is all you should do. What do you think about that?"

"Once will take you somewhere. Twice will take you somewhere else. Depends how you're wired. Twice was right for me. Once was right for your friend. Some folks shouldn't hear it."

"I only heard part of it," said David "and yet it's affected me in many ways."

Thossian nodded in understanding.

"What about your friend Alex Hirsch?" David asked. "What happened to him?"

"Alex was like one of those rats in those psychological experiments. Every time the rat pushes a lever with his paw he gets a little dose of cocaine. Then they keep pawing that lever over and over till it kills them. That's Alex. But he only wishes he were dead."

David took a swig of beer. The band finished their number to tumultuous applause from the crowd. Dr. Armando took the microphone.

"It's always a good night to jam at La Luna. Anyone wants to sit in with us, they're most welcome. Just come on up and talk to me."

David's heart beat fast. He wanted to play, but Armando's playing was so stellar that he didn't know if he could cut it. He saw an electric piano on stage.

"Excuse me Thossian. Please don't leave."

David walked over to the organ. "How ya doin?" he said to Armando.

Armando smiled broadly beneath his goatee. "I'm doing just wonderful! What do you play?"

"Piano."

"What would you like to play?" David was about to answer something safe. A jazzy blues like "Route 66" or "Blue Monk" perhaps. As he opened his mouth, a gruff voice next to him said "Stella",

David turned to find a crew cut leather-clad sax player. He was big, and he was mean-looking. David knew what "Stella" meant. It was short for "Stella by Starlight." A basic stand-ard that every jazzer knew. It also just happened to be one of those rare ones that David didn't know well. He knew that he should speak up quickly before he agreed to play "Stella By Starlight" with no music in front of him with a strange band, in front of a live audience. He should have spoken up.

"Sounds good!" said Armando. "Come on up, guys."

David rolled his eyes as he mounted the bandstand. He stood over the old Fender Rhodes electric piano, a dinosaur from bygone days. Armando asked them their names. Then he went on mic.

"Hey folks, we've got some special guests in the house tonight! Two gentlemen who I haven't had the pleasure of meeting before. On tenor sax, a big man, Eddie Clovis!" Mild applause. "And all the way from New York City, a piano player... and they're all good up in NYC, aren't they? David Steinberg!" David winced. Mild applause. "Are we ready boys? A one, a two, y'all know what to do!"

And they barreled into "Stella." Not only did David not really know the chord changes, but it was at a faster clip than he felt comfortable with.

Clearly, these guys were great players, and they were on their turf. David immediately sensed that they were taking this tired old warhorse of a tune and giving it meaning. He played sparsely, because he wasn't really sure of the chords. In jazz, there's an expression "When in doubt, lay out", meaning that if you're not sure of the notes at any point, it's better to stop playing than to play the wrong notes. David was timidly comping (playing rhythmic chord accompaniment). Clovis' tenor sax wailed out the melody. He had a big growling sound that sounded the way he looked. There was nothing David hated more than competition on stage. The old jazz "Cutting contest" where players try to outplay each other in a musical one-upmanship. He just wanted to enjoy playing, but at the end of thirty-bars, Clovis launched into something else.

It was jazz but it wasn't. His tone seemed to get even fatter and his notes sounded like Coltrane mixed with Hendrix and a dash of broken glass. The solo was distinctly unnerving, and David noticed that Armando was staring at Clovis with a rather incredulous look. Clovis stood on the front of the stage and the crowd was listening intently. After three choruses, Clovis stepped back. Some in the crowd cheered, others seemed disoriented.

Armando looked at David. "Do it, man!" he shouted.

David took off on his solo. Except, he didn't know quite where he was going. He remembered the piano recital at thirteen years of age. He was to play Chopin's "Minute Waltz." He knew it inside out, but as soon as he had started to play he went blank. It was a horrible moment. And so, he kept playing a waltz pattern in his left hand while he improvised on the spot in his right. It wasn't Chopin, but it was something. Something Chopinesque. To his teacher he had screwed up, but he knew that he'd created something new rather than lay down and die onstage.

And now, here at La Luna, he tore into a quasi-Stella solo. In a quasi-Stella mode. A Quasimodo. And he soared above the chords in his Quasimodo solo, trying not to let his nerves stop his technique. He could feel the rush of the bass and drums percolating away under him. He was one step from disaster, skateboarding down a handrail. Armando smiled but Clovis looked at the ground as if David didn't exist. His solo was clearly not kosher, but neither was the sax solo. David made it swing, wrong chords be damned! And when he stopped, he received mild applause.

Armando launched into a swirling hot solo on the organ. He was in total command. He was no slave to anyone else's style. He was his own man on the keys, and the audience loved it. After short solos by the bassist and the drummer, Clovis replayed the head of the tune and the band took it out. David shook Armando's hand and walked over to Clovis. Clovis turned away.

David went back to Thossian at the bar.

"That was cool," he said to David.

"What's up with that sax player?" said David. "He must have a rod up his ass or something."

"He's a Mahozadian," Thossian offered.

"A whosy whatsy?"

"A Mahozadian. He studied with Bob Mahozada."

"Never heard of him," said David, as his insides shook with remembrance of gulls gone by. "Sax player?"

"Yes. A sax player. And his students are very clannish and clandestine. And they all seem to have an attitude problem."

"How d'ya know he studied with that guy?"

"I know. That's the sound. Or a pale imitation of it."

"If that's a pale imitation of Mahozada's sound, I don't think I'd wanna hear the real thing," David said.

"It'd be hard to hear the real thing."

"How so?"

"'Cause Mahozada has no recordings out."

"So how do people hear him?"

"He performs live."

"Have you actually heard him play?"

"No, I haven't. I've heard his student offspring, so I've only heard him second generation."

"You know Thossian, I have recordings from 1905 of Chopin's student's, students playing Chopin. And I wonder if they sound anything like Chopin did."

"Good point. Think of all the Bird and Coltrane wannabes who don't get close to the sound."

"So I wonder what this guy sounds like, and what he's got going."

"Well," said Thossian thoughtfully, "it seems to me that if Eddie Clovis is a hint, then Mahozada's channeling some kind of energy through himself into the sax. Some kind of energy that isn't putting the world at peace."

David thought about what he had heard in the dressing room at the Aikido *dojo*. The Samurai would extend their power, their very soul, into the tip of the *katana* sword. All power went through them and from them into the sword. Was Clovis some sort of aspiring musical Samurai warrior? How different Clovis' playing had made him feel from the music on the tape. Both had startled him, but whereas the tape had made him want to follow it, the Mahozada technique had left with him a feeling of dread. He ordered another beer.

Late at night, after finding out as much as he could from Thossian Lewis, David headed back to the EZ Time Inn. Between performing, the beer, and a terrible emerging sunburn, he was extremely nervous. When he lay down shirtless to try and get some sleep, he found that he was in pain from the sunburn no matter what position he tried. He lay in the dark, sweating and agonizing. He hated hotels. To him, they were only a half step from prison. He half expected to see the ghost of Jacob Marley walking through his door. He closed his eyes reluctantly. He did not trust either himself or the room in which he lay. Eventually he nodded off.

One hour later, at three a.m., the witching hour for insomni-acs, David bolted up with his heart beating like an express train. He couldn't see where he was in the darkness and he fumbled for the lamp switch. He knocked over the lamp. The crash was very loud. He felt his way slowly to the door to find the overhead light switch. He found it. The room looked alien to him. It was not his home. He was suddenly horribly lonely. His chest was tight and he couldn't get a deep breath. The panic fed on itself. He went to the window for air. The windows were sealed. He pulled apart the shades to see the outside world, knowing that that might calm him. There sat the parking lot with only a dim lamppost casting a ghostly silence over the parked cars. He was nowhere at no time. He went to the bathroom and filled the plastic cup with water. It tasted like disinfectant. He gagged and spat it out. He turned on the TV and found only infomercials and programming guides. He sat on the floor and tried to do the stretches that he'd learned at Aikido class. He tried to calm his body, but his head was pounding. He couldn't stand it any longer. He had to get out of there. He threw on his clothes and left the room.

The hall was silent except for the hum of the fluorescent lights, and at the end of the hall, the ice machine whirred. There was no human to talk to here. He took the elevator down to the lobby. There was no one there. He was alone on alien earth. The lobby was plastic and fabric and bad art and an artificial environment with none of the healing power of nature in it. He saw nobody at the front desk. He walked out of the front door into the night.

Ahead lay the asphalt desert towards Jukefood. He looked up. If he could at least see the stars he would know that God loved him. There were no stars. Light pollution had taken care of that. He was afraid to step across the desert. He was afraid to go upstairs. He was afraid to stand still. He wanted to scream but he was afraid to attract attention. And even if someone came to his aid, how would he explain? The sunburn was making him sick. Suddenly he bent over and threw up on the cement. He almost fainted from the effort. He staggered back up and leaned against a car. He leaned carefully, because he didn't want to set off the car alarm. He looked at his vomit. He started to laugh at what he had done. All the tension had vomited out of him and he finally felt better. He laughed and cried, softly but almost uncontrollably.

When it ended he walked back to the hotel door. It was locked. He banged on the door. Nothing. He rang the bell and waited. After a few minutes an old man came to the door.

"I'm sorry, I'm a guest and I got locked out."

The man let him into the lobby. He said nothing to David. David thanked him. He saw that there was to be no conversation with this fellow. He headed back to his room to try once more for blessed sleep.

CHAPTER
NINETEEN

"**S**o now what happens?" asked Abby, sipping Chardonnay at the Sheraton Hotel bar.

"So now I guess I go out and meet his grandfather."

"Why don't you just call him?"

"I can't just call him. I have to physically be in the presence of people who've heard the tape. That's how it is."

"So if he lived on a mountain top in Tibet, you gonna go there to talk?"

David didn't smile. "I have to be in his presence. I just know, that's all."

David knew now that something happened when humans were in physical proximity. Though the music could be recorded and be effectively played anywhere, people a few feet apart had powerful effects on each other. Sexual attraction, hostility, love, telepathy, all increased geometrically in strength when people were near each other. He needed to meet Thossian's grandfather.

"You gonna ask me to lend you plane fare to Indiana?"

"No. I have gigs coming up this week, and then I'll go out there."

"'Cause I'll lend it to you."

He finally smiled at her. "Thanks. But no thanks."

Her dark eyes widened. "You wanna play for me?"

"What, now?"

"Now."

"Sure. What are we doing?"

"A ballad."

"Name it."

They walked back to the piano. A few people were sitting at nearby tables. He sat down on the bench and she reached for the mic. It was a kick for her to be able to stand up and sing and not have to play. She looked at him. " 'I Lie Awake and Dream", in C." He smiled and nodded.

David loved to accompany female singers. Especially beautiful and musically coherent female singers. And he knew that she liked his phrasing and he liked hers. He set a luxuriously slow tempo to indulge her sense of time and her lyrical *savoir faire*. From the moment his intro started, it was as if he was slowly pulling back the sheets on the bed. She was his from the first bar. When she opened her mouth to sing, the combination of her voice and his rich chords altered the energy in that room. Almost immediately, a couple of people came over and sat on the stools surrounding the piano. She started the line at the bottom of her range on a low 'G'.

"There's no way I can keep you off my mind"

And as it climbed up to high 'D', Abby charmed her way through her mix into her head voice. She was so good at this when she played, and now she was free. Look Ma, no hands.

"And I can't see straight, because love is blind
No, late at night I won't be sleeping"

She lowered herself slowly back down over his accompaniment.

"I Lie awake and dream of you"

She turned to him and stared at him as he pressed the keys so softly but firmly. He tickled the keys and ran his fingers up and down them between verses.

"Each day I wake up from the thoughts I've felt"

Now she toyed with the melody, teasing the crowd by back-phrasing and causing them to lean in with anticipation.

"And I'm not quite here, cause I'm somewhere else"

She let them all know that she knew what she was singing about.

"I'm in a world where I can touch you"

And as pianist and singer smiled at each other, the crowd realized that they were sharing intimacy with two people who had shared it with each other.

"I stay awake and dream"

The verse ended and the mood changed as David modulated to E minor.

"I'm shy but I want to reach out for your hand"

And now, in the melancholy romance of the bridge, he followed her phrases with musical caresses.

"I'm aching to be wrapped in embrace by your arms"

And he let her know.

"And when our eyes meet, my heart skips a beat
And I'm overcome by your charms"

He gently brought her back to the final verse.

"How can the passion in my dreams come true
Though the night is cold still I burn for you"

She sang "passion" in such a truthful, bluesy way that the crowd could barely hold onto themselves.

"No there's no chance that I'll be sleeping"

The people at the tables and on the stool were smiling as they watched Abby and David serenade each other.

"I lie awake and dream"

Now David took his solo on the verses as Abby introduced him to the crowd, who applauded noisily. David could hear female voices whooping for him and it just made his playing get sexier. The alcohol was just enough to get him to loosen up without his time sense falling apart. With the crowd attentive and Abby listening to every note, he knew he couldn't throw this solo away. He made it count and created long lines that swam through the tune. On the second eight bars of his solo his left hand started to walk and as he swung more and more the crowd got into it. When he finished they erupted in applause and joyous shouting. David smiled and nodded at the crowd in thanks as Abby retook the bridge, rephrasing the melody with wonderful little twists and turns and surprises. David laughed at her inventiveness as she had during his solo. She sang her final verse and then...

"No there's no chance that I'll be sleeping
I lie awake"

And they both knew to repeat it as a tag.

"I lie awake"

He changed chords on each repeat to color the meaning differently.

"I lie awake"

She stopped and David played a beautiful swinging cadenza and slowed it down till they met at...

"and dream"

As the audience gave of themselves, David stood up and Abby came over and hugged him. She kissed him on the cheek, but it meant more than a kiss on the cheek. It meant that no matter how different they were when it came to relationships, no matter how crazy they might make each other, right now they realized a closeness that others could neither understand nor share. And he knew that tonight they would be together.

CHAPTER TWENTY

David and Luis sat on the floor of the WBGI studio listening. They listened to late Coltrane. They listened to John Mclaughlin playing acoustic guitar. They listened to Keith Jarrett's piano improvisations, and Miles, and Rubinstein playing Chopin, Monk playing Monk, Glenn Gould playing Bach's Preludes and Fugues in "The Well Tempered Clavier". Music from Pakistan, India, Japan, Turkey. Ravi Shankar's lightning fast sitar explorations. Louis Armstrong's incredible take on "Stardust". Live Grateful Dead followed by Debussy's "Sunken Cathedral."

It was three in the morning. They weren't smoking or drinking. Just donuts and Pepsi. But they were very, very high. Bing Crosby from the thirties, Sinatra Live in Vegas in the sixties with the Basie band. They ended with the original 1924 recording of "Rhapsody in Blue" with the Paul Whiteman orchestra and Gershwin himself at the piano.

David slowly shook his head as it ended.

"Jesus."

"What?" said Luis.

"It's Black and Jewish and Latin and jazz and European all in a stew! All my life I heard orchestral versions of it and I never really got it. But this... this is amazing. From the first clarinet gliss it's klezmer music! Why didn't anybody tell me?"

Luis smiled. "They made it safe for democracy. They watered it down so it wouldn't speak straight to the heart. That would be too powerful."

"And it's funny," David laughed. "It's got haha-funny built right in! Why do they always have to take the fun out of everything and make it so fucking serious? Fucking serious music. What's that about?!"

"Listen man, governments, religious fanatics, people who want to control you either water down the music or take away the music altogether. You're not supposed to have any tools that'll let you find out who you really are. You're supposed to be a busy bee clone."

"And beehive ourself," said David.

Luis laughed. "That's right, beehive yourself and don't think and don't feel and don't get into trouble and don't ask questions. But you, my friend, have had the doors of perception ripped open."

"Um-hum, that I have. I don't know if I'm hearing these records differently now because of the tape, or if I'm just listening differently because we're bothering to listen to them."

"Does the sugar taste sweet because I told you it's sweet or because it's sugar?" said Luis.

David nodded. "Are you sorry that you didn't hear the tape, Luis?"

"Yes and no. I always like to hear music that's gonna move me. At the same time, I been listening to great music all my life.

And because of my job, I been listening wholeheartedly to great music. All kinds of music. So, who knows, maybe I heard it already...so to speak."

"And sometimes good music is mystical in its effect."

"Right," said Luis. "The mystic power of music is always there. You have to be receptive to it. Maybe somebody who doesn't respond to music hears the tape and nothing happens. Jesus said he could heal because the 'healee' had faith. If he didn't have faith, he wouldn't get healed."

"So, a deaf person or a tone deaf person doesn't respond to music's healing powers."

"Exactly. And yet, there seem to be natural laws about music that you would think effect everyone, like gravity affects everyone."

"Natural laws?"

"Like the law of the octaves."

David shook his head. He'd never heard of this.

"Don't ask me, man," Luis went on. "I'm not an expert, but I think it has to do with understanding the universe as you would a scale. The whole universe is vibration. We're vibration and we respond to vibration. Coarser vibrations are more earthbound and physical-oriented. Finer vibrations take us toward heaven. You know Miles' tune 'Seven Steps To Heaven'?"

David indeed knew Miles Davis' composition, and he could sing along with every solo on it.

"So, seven steps like a major scale. Each vibration finer and faster and a higher note and reaching towards heaven."

"But high notes can't be the way to get to heaven," said David, "or the dogs would get to go and all the tuba players would end up in hell!"

They both started laughing.

"I think they're there already!" laughed Luis, and this brought them into gales of laughter.

Calming himself down, David said, "Who came up with this idea?"

"It's in a lot of mystical traditions. It's everywhere. You know, you hear about the 'Word' of God creating. Chants in other cultures. Primordial sounds. See, you're already part of a mystical tradition, but no one ever told you that you were in the club. You play and people feel. People feel and they are transported from their earthly cares to a better place. The whole idea that 'entertainment' is not important is a dumb fucking idea. Life needs work and life needs play. Play has value that they didn't tell you 'bout when you were a kid. You worked in class, and when it was time to play, they sent you out of the school to the yard for recess. They left you on your own. Your play time was not considered meaningful as compared to your work time. But play is when you create. Creation is God's function. Entertainment is you taking the audience on a journey, or better yet, helping them to permit themselves to take a journey."

David listened intently.

"And when you improvise, you're the ship's captain on that journey. If you play what they expect all the time, they get bored and leave. If you only play the unexpected, most of them get lost and they leave. But, if you give them some of what they expect to hear, and then you twist it and turn it with unexpected permutations, they will follow you on that trip. So you gotta be a good captain. You gotta be worthy. You can't play bullshit if you wanna be a leader. You have to respect your audience and the job that you've been given. Now all this shit's goin' on, and it looks like some dude's at the piano playing 'Night And

Day', see? But beneath the layers of the onion, something else important is happening. Something holy should be happening. Something that swings like crazy but it's holy, see?"

These words reverberated through David: Something that swings like crazy but it's holy.

So many critics down through the decades had maligned jazz as unholy and dirty. It certainly could be dirty. It had developed right there in the brothels. But it wasn't stuck in the brothels anymore. How does something secular become something spiritual? Is it a change in the content, or a change in the intent? If the attitude of the creator changes, doesn't the creation change too? David was jogging on that tightrope between heaven and earth. Between heaven and hell.

CHAPTER
TWENTY-ONE

*T*wo nights later David came home at night from playing a wedding at Tavern On The Green. He played back the message that had come in on his answering machine: "Hello David, it's Thossian Lewis. I'm calling you because I know that you had expressed an interest in visiting my grandfather in Indiana. That, unfortunately, is no longer possible. My grandfather has died. I'm going out there for the funeral. I'm sorry that you didn't get a chance to meet him. He was a unique individual and you would have liked him."

David called Thossian.

CHAPTER
TWENTY-TWO

*T*his time passenger Stein was out of his league. It's one thing to get around Fort Lauderdale without a car. It's another to get to Angola, Indiana.

It was hard enough to get a flight to Fort Wayne, but this time the trip included a sixty mile bus ride to Angola. City boy was way out in the boonies now. Rolling down the highway with never ending cornfields on either side, David half expected to meet Judy Garland in pigtails skipping along with the scarecrow. He hadn't realized that corn came from cornfields and not from Fairway's supermarket on Broadway. He was the only person on the bus with a leather jacket. Perhaps, he thought, he was the only person in the state of Indiana with a leather jacket. Really, he was very smug.

Heading North on Highway 69, the bus turned east onto Route 20 and into Angola. Just a little circle of low-rise, very early twentieth-century commercial architecture. A movie theater and a few stores and a statue in the middle. For David it was like an old "Twilight Zone". He'd been transported back to another time.

He carried his one bag off the bus and looked around. Lost, he walked into a sporting goods store for directions. An elderly red-haired freckled-face man stood behind the counter.

"Afternoon," said the man. "Been traveling?"

"Yeah, I just got off the bus from Fort Wayne."

"Fort Wayne? Um hum. I got a cousin there."

"Actually, I'm from New York."

"New York? Whoa! You're a long way from home!"

"Well, I guess I am."

"What line of work you in?"

"I'm a musician."

"Is that so? That's what you do?"

"Yep," said David.

"For work or for pleasure?"

"Both, when I'm lucky."

"Um hum." Awkward pause.

"I'm supposed to meet a friend in front of the Best Western. Could you tell me where that is?"

"Come on outside and I'll show you."

They walked outside the store and the man pointed.

"One block down that way, make a left, and you'll see it. You can't miss it. Says 'Angola Best Western.' Good hotel. Great food. You'll like it."

"Thanks. Actually I'm just getting picked up there. I'm staying at a lake."

"Oh, 'Laker', huh?"

David detected a bit of coldness in his tone. "I'm just visiting the lake. Lake Jeremiah."

"Bye now, good luck to you," said the man and walked back into the store.

"Thanks for your help," said David to empty air. When he reached the Best Western, Thossian was waiting for him in a beat-up pickup truck. David was glad to see a familiar face. He climbed into the truck.

"Hey Thossian, thanks for letting me do this. And thanks for picking me up."

"That's alright. It seems like you couldn't stop yourself from coming out here."

"You're right. I could not stop myself. I had to stay on the trail and follow the tape upstream to wherever it came from."

"I dunno if you're gonna find out where it came from. Your source is no longer with us."

They talked as they drove out of the town and past miles of strip malls.

"This place is a little different for me," David offered.

"And I'm a little different for this place," responded Thossian.

"How so?"

"Not a lot of black folks around here. More than there used to be, but we're still a novelty. A few years ago the Klan had a rally right in town."

David felt a chill.

"The good news is that the anti-Klan demonstrators vastly outnumbered the Klan, but still, it was a little weird."

"Did you grow up here?"

"Nah, Army brat. Grew up all over. But I spent some summers here at the lake. It's a great lake."

"I didn't know there was even water in Indiana."

"Yeah, they got electricity and everything now."

David laughed. Just after reaching the end of the last strip of stores, they turned left and were soon into a wooded area on a smaller back road. Thossian pointed to the sky and they stopped the truck. A hawk was circling overhead. David stared in awe. A real bird. Not a filthy pigeon in Central Park. Not a "flying rat" at all. They rolled on slowly past horses grazing in small shaded pastures. They rolled down the windows and the sound of the truck kicking up gravel passed through him as faint memories were also kicked up. But rather than images, they were feelings. The air was becoming so pure that his lungs didn't know how to process it.

After a couple of miles they headed slightly downhill until David saw the bluest blue water that he could remember. As they emerged from the woods Lake Jeremiah grew and grew before him. Hidden away in Indiana was an incredibly beautiful lake that went on for miles.

"Take off your watch," said Thossian.

"What?"

"Take off your watch and put it away, man."

"But how will I know what time it is?"

"You won't *care* what time it is."

He took off his watch and looked at it for one last time. He put it in his pocket. He felt naked, but he felt stupid for feeling that way. And so what? He was a total alien here and he had better figure out how the natives lived.

Thossian drove along the circumference of the lake until he had actually left the main body of the lake and reached a small inlet which became a series of marsh canals. They drove on a road directly behind the lakefront homes. The homes on the other side of the road looked less expensive. Those were the homes, he figured, of people who were almost at the lake, but who would never quite get there.

They pulled in behind a modest brown house on the canal side. They got out. The sound of his own truck door closing was pleasant. After that, was silence. Then, gradually, other sounds came into play. Wind, birds, children laughing. Space.

Thossian led him around the house to the front lawn. The canals came into view. Weeping willows swept the lawn. The weather was hot. Thossian's relatives sat at a table drinking lemonade and Mint Juleps. David was the only white person on that lawn, but he felt that he had come home. A feeling that he didn't understand. But he liked it.

David was introduced to the family. They greeted him warmly. Thossian's father, Cameron Lewis, was a big square-jawed man with a crew cut, who David knew to be an army colonel. His grip was like an iron clamp. Thossian's mother was petite. She held his hand for a long time and stared into his eyes.

"Welcome to The Lake, David. This place will work its magic on you."

She had no idea how much magic had already been worked on him. Amazingly, nobody asked him to explain what he was doing there. Thossian brought him, and so he was accepted by them immediately.

Thossian handed him a drink and took him down to the water. They sat on a bench at the water's edge. It was late afternoon and the sun was beginning to hang low in the sky. The reflected light on the water moved in the breeze and hypnotized. If death was like walking out of a stuffy room into fresh air, then this must be what death is. David involuntarily became calm.

"What's in this drink?" he said.

"Sugar and lemons. It's not the drink, it's the lake."

"You're a lucky man, Thossian, to have a place like this to come to."

Thossian nodded. "My great grandfather came here in 1925. The legend is that he walked the whole circumference of the lake to find a perfect spot on which to build. This place has been in the family since then. He wanted to be on the lake, but sheltered, so he chose the canal. When his son, my grandpa, grew old, he decided to retire here. He loved it here, as do we all."

"I'm sorry that I didn't get to meet him."

"His death was sudden and unexpected, and....there's something that I haven't told you."

David looked at him expectantly. Thossian looked not at David, but out at the water.

"My grandpa, who was a peaceful man, did not die as he should have. He did not die in a peaceful way."

"What happened?"

"He was found by a neighbor, who walked into the house to check on him when she hadn't heard from him or seen him in a couple of days. She found him on the living room floor, face up. He had blood coming from both ears and she also said that he had a look of terrible pain on his face."

"Jesus!" said David. "What did he die of?"

"They wanted to do an autopsy, but the family didn't want that indignity foisted on him. The police medical examiner told us that his best guess was either head trauma or a tumor in the middle ear canal." Thossian paused and looked at David. "But they found no trauma to the skull other than the fall to the floor. And without an autopsy, they couldn't find evidence of a tumor."

"So what is it that you think happened?"

"I'm not exactly sure, but I have feelings."

"Feelings?"

"You know that people who've heard the tape develop skills and feelings. Those come in images and knowledge. And I have those feelings, but in this case there's a wall in the way of those images and that knowledge. All I can tell you, is that I believe that someone killed my grandpa."

"That's a pretty intense thing to say. You're scaring me."

"It's scary stuff. Somebody wanted him dead. Nothing was missing, so I don't think that robbery was a motive."

"What else?"

"I'm not sure. As I said, something is blocking the knowledge."

"Ordinarily I'd say you were crazy, but 'ordinarily' seems to have slipped away from my life lately."

"I'd say it's gonna get weirder."

CHAPTER
TWENTY-THREE

*T*hat evening after dinner, David washed the dishes. This both gave him visible credit with the family and aided in bonding time. Everyone sat around the table after dinner talking. Some of the older ladies played cards. There was no television by choice. They actually communicated with each other. Relatives had come in from all over the Midwest for the funeral, and they had a lot to catch up on. When he had finished with the dishes, David sat down at the large round table with the others. Thossian's mother smiled at him.

"I hear that you're a jazz singer and pianist, David."

"Something like that," said David, feeling a bit shy.

"Will you sing us something?"

David's heart beat fast. Behind the piano he was totally at ease singing, but here he was on someone else's turf, freeloading and crashing a family gathering. And there was no piano and no microphone. His voice was not that big, and while it worked great on a sound system with him playing for himself, he didn't have one of those voices that make you sit up straight. It was a voice that just worked fine for what he did.

"Ahh, I'm really more of a pianist, Mrs. Lewis."

The Colonel, whose biceps were bulging and who had a bottle of beer in his hand looked at him.

"Come on man, let's hear you sing something! We won't bite you...maybe."

This may have been meant as a joke, but it made David a little paranoid. He knew he was either going to have to sing or turn them down and offend everyone.

> *"I ain't foolin' around, no foolin'" he started.*
> *"I ain't foolin' around*
> *Though I'm a fool for you and your tender kisses*
> *I ain't foolin' around"*

He swung it at a nice slow tempo. A few words in he became confident and started to have fun with it. And then... Thossian Lewis' family, his parents and his cousins and aunts started to add harmonies and sing jazz bass lines. In that house by that canal, that family backed him up and made him sound like the God of Singing. He started to laugh and then tried to keep the song going. He could not believe how good they sounded and how much fun they were all having. Everybody had ears! Everybody sang harmony! When he finished the thirty-two bar song he started at the top again, improvising around the melody and scatting as they bounced notes off him and he off them.

Finally he came to the end with

> *"I'll stay cool and I know that you know,*
> *that I ain't foolin' around"*

They all whistled and applauded, and so did he. Somebody brought him a beer. Then The Colonel looked hard at David with a furrowed brow and stood up. He leaned across the table with his palms flat and got his face uncomfortably close to David. Then he opened up his mouth and sang "I've Got You Under My Skin." And he had a rich baritone and he made it swing. And David laughed again and started singing with him. And the beers flowed and the voices flowed and they were at that table for hours 'til the beer made them get up to go pee and then come back to the table for more music and more beer. There were no instruments but the human voice and there was no sound of machines to be found. Just people communing in the ancient mode of singing.

His gigs had made him almost forget what music could be about. All the peripheral crap. The *schlepping* of equipment, the thoughtless clients, the resentment he had towards them. Suddenly here he was in the purest of musical environments. Human voices making a joyful noise. Just for the love of it. The magic of organized sound as a tool of transformation.

Late at night when the party had finally ended and he had been hugged by many former strangers, he walked down to the canal and over to the boat dock. He had to maneuver very slowly in the darkness, and was torn between his feelings of joy at being with a great bunch of people in a beautiful setting, and his fear of the dark and of the woods and too many bad horror movies he'd seen. When he reached the dock, a small light on a post helped him find his way forward safely. He walked out as far as he could 'til he knew he was near the edge. Then he looked up.

The night sky was overwhelming. He gasped audibly at the sight of the stars. Not only had city life taken away his memory of the plethora of celestial ornaments, but it had also denied him the full scope of viewing. He hadn't realized nor remembered that the sky would appear shaped like an inverted bowl.

For a brief moment he remembered being a nine-year-old boy at New York's Hayden Planetarium on Central Park West at Eighty-first Street. The sky show was as close as he often got to the real thing. He had sat in the darkness, mystified as the great robot projector sent images of comets and meteors over his head while the live narrator told of big bangs and the end of time.

And now here he was completely alone before that sky in Indiana on Lake Jeremiah. Everything that had ever bothered him seemed stupid and petty and unimportant at this moment. He lay down on the dock on his back, gazing upward. A shooting star flew overhead and by the time he realized what had happened, it was long gone. He had a rumbling of vertigo as if his body were being lifted up. He was afraid that he'd splash down in the darkness of the canal. He was afraid that the bogeyman would come out of the woods onto the dock and kill him with a knife, and that little evil girl demons would come up out of the water and touch him with their horrible little demon hands and get seaweed all over him and sing in little horrible high voices, horrible demon songs. *Aieeeeee!!! Aieeeeee!!! Ayaaaah yah-yah yoo*!! *Hoofamoofa hoofamoofa shom shom shom*! Luckily this night they did not.

He felt like crying when he looked up. He just wished that God would cradle him and lift him high enough so that he could look down on the insanity of humankind. All of this welled up in him and poured forth. The good, the bad and the cathartic. He wanted to close his eyes, but he didn't want to miss an instant of this astronomical panorama. Little laughs began to surface from his chest to his lips. He could not stop them. They turned to little sobs. Back and forth for a few minutes, laughter and sobbing. They were the same. They needed to come out into the clean night air.

Finally, they subsided and he lay totally relaxed. He contemplated sleeping on the dock, but could not quite commit himself to it. He stood up, took one more look up at the sky. He knew one constellation from his planetarium days. The Big Dipper. He located it. It was still there after all these years. A blink for God and a lifetime for him. He walked off the dock and toward the house.

CHAPTER
TWENTY-FOUR

*I*n the morning David put on a jacket and tie for the funeral. The family had prepared enormous platters of bacon and eggs for breakfast. They looked different in their Sunday best. For a moment he was afraid that their formal dress meant the end of the familial feeling he had had with them last night. Then Thossian's mother came over and hugged him good morning. They were quieter this morning. Today they would bury Thossian's father's father.

At 10:00 a.m., they all left the house together on foot. The church was only half a mile away on a hill in the woods. They walked down the road past other homes. When they came to a small road entering the woods, they headed up the path. Ten minutes later they reached the church. The church stood in an area thick with pine trees. It was a beautiful day and seating for the service was outside the church on benches. The ground was covered with red pine needles. The breeze blew softly as relatives and friends gathered and greeted each other. The preacher shook hands and hugged many in the group. Clearly, he was an old friend.

They took their seats. The casket was open. Mervyn Lewis lay there peacefully. There was no blood coming from his ears. His face had been manipulated into a calm facade. Harold P. Owsley, the preacher, stood in the dappled sunlight at the lectern and spoke into his microphone. He wore a black robe with a white collar and to David he looked like an African prince at his princely inauguration.

"Yes, yes, take seats now please. How wonderful to see all these friends and family members who loved our Mervyn. Isabelle, there's a seat right over there. Um hum. Um hum. What a beautiful and glorious day God has given us today! What a wonderful day for us to celebrate Mervyn's reunion with his heavenly Father and with his earthly parents."

Scattered "Yes's" from the crowd.

"Even as I speak these words he is hugging his parents and they are loving him right back!"

"That's right," from the crowd.

David was enjoying himself, as were most of the folks there. He shot a glance at Thossian a few seats away. Thossian was not smiling. Something was bothering him. He looked extremely anxious.

"What can we say about Mervyn Augustus Lewis? That he was a loving son to his parents? A wonderful husband for fifty-two years to his beloved Esther, may she rest in peace? Can we say that Merv was a daddy who would do anything for his children?"

"Anything!" from The Colonel, who sat with his arm around his wife.

"Yes we can!" said Harold P. "Can we all agree..."

"Yes we can!" from the crowd.

"Can we all agree... that this man, who worked so tirelessly for the good of his family, for the welfare of his friends, and for the betterment of the community, was a great man?"

Applause from the crowd. Hollers and cheers.

"Of course we can agree. Of course we know this to be the truth." His voice then shot up an octave. "Well what is greatness? Just what do we mean when we say that a man was great? Do I mean accumulation of worldly goods?"

"That's not it" said a man.

"Of course not!" His voice came back down and he leaned forward at the lectern and spoke deeply and somberly. "My friends, my beloved friends. I think that you all know that God can raise your pay....but God can take it away!"

High-pitched lady laughs from the crowd.

"Yes, you know that already...I'm sure. They say that 'All your wealth won't buy you health'. And that is so true. So true. The Bible tells us that a camel can get through the eye of a needle quicker than a rich man get into the Kingdom of Heaven."

Applause.

"So, greatness is not about money. No, greatness is not about money. And Merv was not a rich man in economic terms. He was Merv Lewis, not Merv Griffin."

Laughter from the older folks.

"But let me tell you something that I know, as surely as I know that the IRS wants to hear from me on April 15th every year."

"Tell us!"

"Merv Lewis had a greatness about him and a great greatness inside him, that suffused him! Merv Lewis had an innate greatness that you could feel when you were in his presence!"

David was very moved and found himself clapping and cheering along with the congregation. He looked at Thossian, assuming that the speech would lift Thossian's spirits. Thossian looked as if he knew a terrible secret. David didn't know if he should enjoy himself or be alarmed by Thossian's expression.

"At this time, we're going to sing. Mervyn's daughter Leticia has told me that this song was a favorite of his. If you will notice, a lyric sheet has been provided for you."

Everyone picked up their lyric sheets. The organist was inside the church but as his cue was given, the music was piped out on speakers to the crowd outside. It was strange and almost humorous to hear a blues shuffle coming from a church organ. Those who knew it sang it.

> *"I'm gonna take a little trip*
> *Got my suitcase in my hand*
> *I'm gonna take a little trip*
> *Got my suitcase in my hand*
> *I wanna see blue water*
> *Put my feet down in the sand*

The people began to sway and clap, and those who didn't know it learned it a minute.

> *"Tell the boss I'm busy*
> *And I just can't take his call*
> *Tell the boss I'm busy*
> *And I just can't take his call*
> *Cause I'm down on the beach*
> *Drinkin' beer and playin' volleyball*

By now everybody was standing up. The organ wailed on.

There's a time to work and
There's a time that we should play
There's a time to work and
There's a time that should play
And I know one thing for sure
I ain't gonna work today!"

"One more time"! yelled Harold P.

Now they sang it again even louder. The joy was palpable. David let himself go, even as he watched Thossian. Thossian looked even more frightened and frightening. What was going on with him?

They reached the final verse.

"I'm gonna take a little trip
Got my suitcase in my hand
I'm gonna take a little trip
Got my suitcase in my hand
Well I ain't comin' back
Hope the boss will understand!"

"Last line two more times!" Harold P. shouted.

Well I ain't comin' back
Hope the boss will understand!"
"Here we go!"
Well I ain't comin' back
Hope the boss will understand"

The organist inside the church played a big bluesy ending. He held the chord. He couldn't hear the crowd outside finish their note so he held it a little longer. One gravelly wailing voice was heard holding the last note of the song over the organ after everyone else had stopped. Everyone laughed and looked around to see where it was coming from. Thossian slammed his hands over his ears and put his head down facing the ground. David looked over at him and then looked around for the singer of the long note. When he saw the terrified look on Harold P. Owsley's face, he knew where the voice was coming from. It was coming from the coffin.

CHAPTER TWENTY-FIVE

*I*n the days following the funeral, many of the mourners refused to talk about what had happened. Better to remember Mervyn the way they had always known and loved him. The way that the preacher had spoken about him. Not this way. Not in this macabre, unspeakably gruesome way. Lying in that open coffin with blood coming out of his ears and his face contorted into a hideous look. Like a demon. And those who did speak of it argued with each other and with each other only, as to whether or not Mervyn's body had actually let forth with that banshee scream to finish off the blues.

Well, Mervyn had always liked the blues. He could sing, just like everyone in the Lewis clan. They were the envy of their friends because music bonded them together in such a warm manner. It rubbed off on everybody outside the family. You always felt at home went you visited Lake Jeremiah, and wasn't Mervyn Lewis a big part of that? Wasn't he the patriarch both spiritually and musically? Well then, to have this... thing, happen was just not decent. That poor family did not deserve this travesty, this blasphemy. And The Colonel, well, he was a strong and hard man when he needed to be. He had been a young man fighting in the jungles of Vietnam and then later a leader of young men, fighting in the Gulf War. He was not easily shaken. But this was too much. For the next couple of days while the family was still at the lake, Colonel Lewis just moped. It would be too obvious to say that he had a haunted look. He did, but even more so, he looked disappointed and angry. Like a coach whose team has lost the big game. Like the father of teenagers who roll their eyes when asked to behave. He kept to himself and did not sing at all. Even when the family held hands and sang a prayer before dinner, Colonel Lewis didn't join in. His wife tried to prod him into being sociable, but he would have none of it. He had been shaken to the core and didn't like that feeling. So, he masked it in a cold, downcast frown. People stepped aside when he passed through the house.

Grampa was buried that day in the little cemetery on the hill just behind the church. But, it just wasn't the way it should have been. The women up front were biting their nails, and some of the biggest, strongest men were cowering in the back. Folks were half expecting Mervyn to throw off the closed lid and wave. Fortunately, he did not.

David saw Thossian sitting by the canal later that day. He sat down on the bench next to him.

"You knew, didn't you?"

"What?"

"You knew that what happened at the funeral was going to happen...didn't you?"

Thossian didn't answer. He stared at the water. At that moment the largest bird that David had ever seen flew by, only inches above the water. Between the marshy vegetation and the bird's long legs and incredibly wide wingspan, it seemed to David as if he were witnessing a prehistoric event. The bird flew slowly enough that it looked impossible for it to stay aloft.

Both men watched attentively.

"What is it?" cried David in amazement.

"Great Blue Heron."

"Unbelievable! He's so big!"

"He is beautiful. But not to the frogs on the lily pads. They'd like to steer clear of him."

They were silent for a bit. Then David said, "I'm really confused now."

"How so?"

"Because I had thought that I'd come out here and meet your grandfather. I was sure that he'd link me to the source. Now that's not going to happen."

"At least not the way you thought."

"Not at all."

Thossian looked thoughtful. "You can't really know that."

"Your grandpa's gone, man."

Thossian shook his head as if he were trying to puzzle something out.

"Folks leave part of themselves after they go, and maybe we'll discover a part of him that we didn't know he'd left. A part that we didn't even know existed."

David listened.

"Grandpa left us memories and impressions. He may also have left writings or recordings or who knows what?"

"Good point, and I guess that when someone dies, maybe later on we find out new things about them. Things that maybe weren't really new, but are news to us."

"And then we get a new concept about who that person was", said Thossian. "You'll never really know everything about them, but as new information comes in, history gets rewritten in your mind and in your memory. You will now remember that person in a different way. So let's say you remember, say, your mom as a loving and sweet woman. Then decades later you find out that your mom was a serial killer. What happened to the memories of the sweet woman you thought raised you? Was that real, or is your new understanding the 'correct' one?"

"You're making me think more than I want to in this place."

"That's The Lake."

CHAPTER
TWENTY-SIX

*T*hat night, a group of them went out onto the lake in a
motorized pontoon boat. The cloth-canopied craft looked
a bit like a floating picnic table. They brought lots of beer. The
stars came out and they moved along very slowly in the dark.

The Colonel did not come. Nor did his wife. David and
Thossian did, along with a number of cousins of varying ages.
Riding in boats in the dark was beyond David's frame of reference. The only light was a small red light up near the canopy
to warn other boats of their presence. It was still spring and the
summer crowds had not yet arrived.

The air grew cool. Thossian's cousin Marshall turned off the
motor. Between the stars, the water, the darkness and the silence,
David felt pleasantly disembodied. A guitar was produced and
somebody started to sing Beatle songs. Harmonies were improvised by others on the boat. Disembodied voices sang. The
sounds had a different quality floating around the water than on
land. There were ten people on the pontoon boat facing each
other in a square, but you could only guess the number by what

159

you could hear. Those who weren't singing were only secretly present. This time instead of singing, David felt like listening. For a musician, he wasn't usually able to listen in conversation without interrupting. Tonight he listened. The sounds of voice and guitar seemed to become the lake around him. Later on, less people sang, until he heard only cousin Sam who played the guitar and sang, and cousin Martha, who sang along with him. Finally, there was silence. No wind, no music. Almost no reference point to the world. He could have been in a dark closet or floating in space. Then he heard a splash.

"That's Reginald," said a voice.

"Who's Reginald?" asked David to no visible person.

"The biggest fish in the lake. The king. Nobody's ever caught him," said another voice.

David could imagine Reginald down there in his dark domain. If it was spooky on the water, what was it like down there in the depths?

"How deep is the lake?" he asked.

"I once measured the depth with a rock tied to a rope," said a voice. "It was over a hundred feet deep."

"Really!?" said David.

Deeper than a ten-story building. It made him queasy. This dark airless void under him.

He remembered summer camp in Maine. He was thirteen years old. Most of the kids were from places like Scarsdale and New Rochelle, and they all knew how to play tennis and baseball. They'd all been swimming forever. He was a skinny runt of a brick in the water. He was always cold in the water and could only swim a few strokes. After a month of feeling less than human at the camp waterfront, he found that he could swim on his back by doing a frog kick and keeping his hands in the water, pulling them from shoulder to hip. He couldn't see where he was going, but he could stay afloat.

The waterfront counselors convinced him against his own good judgement to take his lake swimming test, which meant swimming a distance of a half mile across the lake with a rowboat at his side to monitor him. They started on a sunny morning. As soon as they got out past the enclosed swimming area he had felt panicky. He was not comfortable and didn't trust his own body. The water was now deeper than any he'd ever been in, and he could hear the sounds of campers at play growing fainter as he swam out. All the while he lay on his back looking up at the sky. Water and sky, sky and water. The two counselors talked loudly to him as they rowed alongside.

"You're doing great, David."

"How you feeling, David?"

"I'd like to stop now, o-okay?"

"Nah, you don't wanna stop now, you're just getting started!"

"Just starting? Aren't I most of the way there yet?" said David, feeling more alarmed.

"It's a big lake, David. Just relax. Take your time. Don't be in such a rush."

David tried to figure out if they could actually convince him to relax while he, basically a non-swimmer, swam half a mile with death all around him. Not to mention that he was getting cold.

He decided that they couldn't convince him unless he wanted to be convinced. He wasn't even sure that he wanted to be. He'd heard too many haunted campfire stories about dead people and he didn't want to become next year's story. All he needed was some kid roasting marshmallows in a fire as the counselors told of the horrible drowning of David Stein. The body found weeks later, half eaten by water snakes. No eyes left. Just a torso wearing a bathing suit with a label in it from his mom that said "David Stein, Bunk 13."

He swam on, trying to believe that their voices could calm him. He hummed "Help" by the Beatles. Everybody sang that song that summer. But now he really meant it. This almost calmed his thirteen-year-old nerves. Almost.

And then, with his ears below the surface, he heard it. He heard the sound. It was coming from beneath him! It was the sound of a great whirring machine. A flying saucer on the bottom of the lake. A great big whirring flying saucer that at any moment would suck him down to the bottom of the lake. He involuntarily threw his head out of the water and turned over into a prone position. His nose was full of water and he started to choke.

"Whatsamatter Davey?"

Didn't they hear it? How could they not know?

"I heard something!" he yelled, spitting water and floundering.

"Whadja hear?"

"I don't know! Something. Some machinery! In the lake!" He was treading water badly, and losing his composure. "I'm stopping!"

"Don't stop, Davey. You're getting there. You don't wanna quit now, you're too far along."

"I DO wanna quit!" He started to swim towards the boat as best he could.

They rowed away. Just a few feet, but they rowed away.

"No! Don't!"

"CALM DOWN!" yelled one of them.

He was going to die. Horribly, painfully and all alone. They'd never even recover his eyeless torso, because the aliens on the bottom of the lake would keep his body for study.

"Stop!" he screamed and started to cry hysterically.

The rowboat stopped.

"Get back on your back, Davey."

He did.

"That's better. Now move slowly and don't lift your head up so high. That's what's making you sink. He listened, crying and trying to calm himself.

"Just don't DO that again!" he shrieked at them.

"Okay, sorry, buddy. Keep swimming. We'll stay right alongside you."

Now that he knew that they wouldn't row away and let him drown, he had nothing to worry about, except for his inability to make it to the other side of the lake and the Martians underneath him and their stinking machine.

David noticed that whenever speedboats pulling water skiers passed by, the Martian people-sucking generator got louder, and whenever the speedboats pulled away, the Martians got softer. He hoped that the Martian sound was just the sound of the speedboat engines. But what if he were wrong? What if the stinking lousy rubber-faced devil-ish aliens used the sound of the boats to cover their engine noise? What if they had a dimmer light switch like on the lamp at home where they could just turn their engine noise up and down as boats passed by? He was the only person on the lake who knew what was going on here! If he drowned now, the world would never know. He couldn't afford to abandon mankind.

He decided to make it to the other side of the fucking lake! He saw his picture in the paper: Hero Kid Saves Earth and Passes Swim Test All In One Unforgettable Day!

He frog kicked onward. He had lost all sense of direction and the sun was now in his eyes. He no longer felt as if he were moving. He knew that the rowboat was alongside him. He could hear the oars in the water and he heard the two counselors discussing breasts. He was quieter inside now and closed his eyes, knowing that they would correct his direction if he headed the wrong way.

AAAH! His foot touched something! Something slimy was trying to grab him! AAAH! Martians!

"AAAAHHH! They're trying to grab my foot!"

"What?" said the counselor. "Turn over, Davey."

David turned over onto his stomach. More slimy things trying to grab him. He punched and kicked the water desperately.

"Davey, relax. Stand up."

"What?" yelled David the thrasher.

"Stand up."

David stood up. He was standing in the weeds on the far side of the lake. The water was only up to his waist.

"Holy shit!" said the boy.

"Holy shit is right, Davey. You swam across the lake. You just swam half a mile. Congratulations."

"I swam across the lake!" he screamed. "I swam across this fucking lake!"

"Alright, watch your mouth."

"Yeeahh!" he beat on his chest like Tarzan. "Swam over this lake! Whoooo!"

They helped him climb into the boat.

"I beat this fucking lake!"

"Say that again and you're swimming back."

"I swam across the lake."

It was a good day.

Adult David's summer camp reverie, which had brought a great smile to him in the darkness, was bumped out of existence, by a bump beneath the pontoon boat, which almost lifted his side of the boat out of the water.

"What the hell was that?" he said. None of Thossian's family answered.

"Hello, what's going on?" he said as he gripped the wooden bench with two hands.

Nobody answered. Again the boat was bumped.

Bum, ba DOP, baDUHbubb, ba DOP! Bum, ba DOP, baDUHbubb, ba DOP!

Whoever or whatever was smashing the bottom of the boat understood funk. He was a great drummer and probably a Great White shark. Wasn't anybody else still on the boat? David gritted his teeth and bent down to untie his shoes in case he had to swim for it. Then he realized he only had flip flops on, but still he took those off. Off to the side of the boat he both heard and felt a gigantic presence. An entity rising up on its great tail. It was about eighteen feet high, give or take a millimeter. It was a giant fish who stood up on that tail with its fins crossed like arms, staring at David, who now seemed to be alone on the boat. David cowered in fear as he tried to make out the fish in the dark. It was Reginald.

"Are, are y-you Reginald?"

"Wittle biped," said the fish in a loud wet lisp. "Why ith a fith like a piano?"

"Why is a what?"

"Why ith a fith like a piano?" roared Reg.

"I d-dunno. Why?"

"Because they both have thcales. Har har har!" The great fish reared back its fish head and guffawed amphibiously.

David knew he should shut up, but he was never capable of shutting up when he should.

"Yes," said David, "and you can t-tune a p-piano, but you can't tuna fish."

There was silence. The fish then took a great bite out of the boat and it started to sink. David held on for dear life.

At that exact moment in the space-time continuum, thirteen-year-old David, who was rowing back with the counselors to the camp side of the lake, saw in his mind a giant fish biting a boat while a man held on in terror. Both David's saw each other, though one had just left the water in Maine and one was entering the water in Indiana.

Big David fell into the dark lake. It was surprisingly warm. The fish swallowed him whole. It really wasn't any darker inside the fish than out, but it was still disconcerting. It smelled terrible though. David looked for an escape tool. His eyes started to adjust to the darkness. He noticed the fish's great uvula hanging at the back of his throat. Mounds of old weed were wrapped about it.

"It will be my pweasure to digest you, you sowwy, helpwess wittle man."

David heard the fish's words reverberate through the cavity of his great fishy body.

"If I can help you, will you wet, I mean, will you let me go, oh great Reginald?"

"Har har har! I waugh merciwesswy at your wudicwous attempt to mowify my gweat anger! How many humans have been swawowed and excweted by my gweat bowels? None have exited by the same door they entered! Why on Earf would the wikes of me help the wikes of you, siwwy wittle sad excuse for a wiving being?"

"Because I can help your speech impediment."

Silence.

"What thpeech impediment are you thpeeking of?" said Reginald with a dark tone in his voice.

"Your lisp."

"If you mock me, it won't help you, biped."

"No, really, I know what's causing your lisp and I really can help you. I really will help you if you promise to release me."

"What is the cause of my, ahem, 'winguistic eccentwicity' ?"

"Your uvula is totally covered with lake weed. That's why you talk the way you do. You're a legend in this lake, and you need to be able to command the respect that you so richly deserve."

"I'm wistening."

"So, I can undo this knotted mess of weed. I'm sure that you'll have instant vocal relief."

"Pwoceed."

"Nah, [bluffed David from no position of power] I don't 'pwoceed' till I get some sort of guarantee that you'll let me go."

Reginald let out a great scream of anger.

"How dare you chawwenge my integwity! No one has ever spoken to me with thuch insowence! I should thpit you out now, just so I can chew you up."

David was so scared that he didn't know if he could sound convincing in his bluff.

"Swear to me on your mother's gills that.."

"Don't talk to me about my mother, biped."

"Swear to me..."

"She abandoned me at birf," said Reginald in a low and mournful voice. "And when I'd thwim by her, she'd act as if we were total thwangerth."

They were both silent for a moment.

"Reginald?"

"Why do you torment me, wittle worm of a man?"

"That must have been vewy, uh, very painful for you."

"Vewy."

"How did that impact your life?"

"How did it impact my wife? I'll tell you how it impacted my wife. I became hungwy for wuv. Vewy hungwy for wuv. And tho I ate, and I ate, and I ate to fill the void in my heart. I became extremewy warge, ath no doubt you have notithed, and then I thtarted to eat my fewwow cweatureth. Fish wike mythelf."

"What kind of fish are you, by the way?"

"Bwuegill."

"Aha."

"So, I ventured on, eating my fewwow bwuegill. It's been a thavage existence, cannibawizing my own fish. I became the biggest, baddest fish in the wake. No hook could catch me, no wine could hold me."

"No what?"

"No wine! No wine! Fishing wine, like on a fishing wod! Wod and weel? Kapeesh?" Reginald was getting perturbed again.

"Oh. Sorry."

"So that's how my mother's abandonment impacted my wife. I'm a vagabond monster... with a speech impediment."

Reginald now began to sob great heaving sobs, though no tears flowed from his lidless eyes. The sobs shook the great fish's insides and David almost fell over.

"Reginald," said David, trying to find a space to speak between fish sobs. "I'd like to help you. Will you let me go if I help you?"

"I will wet you go uneaten, unharmed and undwowned."

"Very well. You sound like a fish of your word. Give me a moment to see if I can undo the weed around your uvula."

David started trying to untie the great clump of weed around the fish's uvula. His uvula was so big that it looked like a hanging punching bag in a boxing gym. He pulled on the weed.

"Ha ha ha ha!" laughed Reginald. "That tickleth! Oh, ha ha ha!"

"Sorry. Try to stay calm. Your laughing is gonna knock me down! Think of mathematics or something."

This time Reginald stayed quiet and calm. David was having a devil of a time with the weed, and he knew that his life was in the balance. Finally, realizing that he had no other tools, he began to chew through the foul old lake weed, desperate to free the uvula and thus himself. He was forceful yet careful, knowing that if he bit the uvula he'd be in deep, so to speak.

After what seemed an interminable amount of time (that was really only ninety-three seconds), the weed fell off in great clumps. There swung Reginald's uvula, free at last!

"Alright Reginald, I'm done. I sincerely hope that this works. Please remember that I really tried my best."

"I'm sure you tried."

"I really did... Wait a minute! Say that again!"

"Say what again?"

"What you just said."

169

"I said 'I'm sure you tried'."

"My God, I think it worked! Keep talking! Try the 'typing sentence'."

"What typing sentence?"

"You know, the sentence everybody learns when they learn to type. The one that uses every letter of the alphabet."

"Ah, I know the sentence of which you speak. 'The quick brown fox jumps over the lazy white dog'."

"That's great!"

"Was it good? Was it really?"

"Yes!" screamed the now elated David. "You sound so, so eloquent!"

"Thank you," beamed the fish. "Twenty Twickenham twits at twilight twirled in their tweed."

"Magnifique, Reginald! Formidable!"

Well now, they were both so happy that they sang all of "The Rain in Spain" out in that lake in the darkness. They sang with great glee. And when the song was over, Reginald opened his great mouth and spat David out.

"Hop on my back, biped. I'll not break my promise to you."

David climbed onto Reginald's back and held onto his fin. Reginald swam towards the shore. When he reached the entrance to the canal he stopped.

"Shallow water here, biped. This is as far as I can go."

David climbed off and stood next to him in the water. It was up to his neck.

"Thank you, Reginald."

"It is I who should thank you. You've given me back my pride. Perhaps I can be of service to other creatures in the lake now. Creatures who are less fortunate than me."

"Than 'I'," David corrected him.

Reginald bit David in half.

Just kidding!

Reginald actually said, "Perhaps I can be of service to other creatures in the lake now. Creatures who are less fortunate than I."

"Good luck," said David.

"And the same to you, biped."

Reginald swam away in the dark. David started to dogpaddle towards Thossian's family dock.

He climbed up a set of wooden steps coming out of the water onto the dock. At the same time he found himself stepping off the pontoon boat onto the dock. As Thossian's family disembarked from the pontoon boat, David helped to tie the boat to the dock. They silently passed him on the dock, and he thought to himself *Where have I been*?

He went to bed.

CHAPTER TWENTY-SEVEN

*I*n the middle of the night David was awakened by a howling wind and a hard rain. His bed was one of many in a communal open loft balcony situated above the dining area. In his NY Mets shorts and his t-shirt, he found his trusty mini-flashlight and walked down the stairs to the dining room. The wooden steps were cold under his feet. The wind was talking to him. Nobody else seemed to be awake.

He walked down the long hall of family bedrooms until he entered the large living room with its bay windows overlooking the canal. Not far away he could see flashes of lightning over the main body of the lake. Then he saw immense jagged bolts. The drummer in the sky bashed away at him with thunder. This storm was onstage and in control of the crowd. In the wind he could hear musical intervals of perfect fifths becoming diminished fifths. Diminished fifths, the "Devil's interval", banned to church composers in the Middle Ages, lest they be burned at the stake. It was such an important part of jazz and blues, blended in to the harmony, but tonight it blew at him like Satan's horn section. It was nature's soundtrack to a horror film. He should have loved the storm, but not at night in a place where there was no light and no one to talk to.

Out of discomfort with the darkness he switched on the light in the living room. The view outside became invisible. He looked around the room for something to keep him from feeling alone. On a bookshelf he saw a group of tattered, leather-bound photo albums. He reached for one. He opened it to the middle and saw a number of photos of groups of men posing together. Most of them were black, a few were white.

David understood immediately that they were groups of musicians. Some pictures were taken outside nightclubs. A couple were inside clubs, posed on the bandstand. One picture showed a group of about fifteen men standing out-side a beat-up old bus. Many of the pictures were captioned: "Toledo w/Sky Martin", "Denver, Moe Cantrell", "Biloxi, Red Phillips".

And in almost every picture, was a younger Mervyn Lewis. Thossian had told David that Grandpa played the bass, but David hadn't grasped that he had been a touring jazz musician.

David scanned across the shelf and picked up another album that looked newer. The lake house with family members on the lawn. The Colonel as a boy, then as a young man in his army uniform. Pictures in the church. People clapping along as a band played. Mervyn on bass. And in every photo of the band playing, the light of the camera flash bouncing off Mervyn's bass. The people clapping along with ecstasy on their faces. Mervyn's face was serene as he played.

Who would kill such a man? What had happened at the funeral? David knew that whatever had happened was perceived by most of the people there. It wasn't just in his mind. What had Thossian known?

Mervyn had given Thossian the tape and Thossian had heard it twice. Thossian gave it to Alex and Alex had played it too many times. Alex gave it to Simon who heard it twice. Simon had played it on the radio and then destroyed it. The tape was gone and the man on the high end of the chain was dead. David's trail seemed to stop here in Indiana. Still, he sensed that there was more he could learn from the life of Mervyn Lewis.

He picked up a third album that had been closer to the first one. More pictures of musicians. A band in a nightclub. There was Mervyn on the bandstand. A picture taken at night in a smoky club. Once again the light bouncing off the bass. Something odd, though. The two men on trumpet and sax standing next to him. Their instruments were close to the bass, yet no light seemed to be bouncing off their horns. Why not? Was it the angle of the flash? David took out the newer album again. He flipped through until he found the pictures of Mervyn playing in the church again. Drums, organ, bass, guitar. The flash only showed on the bass, though. Perhaps the photographer had only aimed at the Mervyn and his bass? But wouldn't other objects in the room reflect the flash too? The lightning flashed again and again. The wind blew. Thossian's mom came in.

"Oh, hi," said David.

"I came in to close the windows to keep the rain out," she said.

"Oh! Let me help."

"Thank you."

They shut all the windows in the room. The carpet had indeed become wet and David felt stupid that he hadn't gone ahead and closed them upon entering the room in the first place. He sat down.

"Looking at pictures?"

"Yes, I'm interested in Mr. Lewis' life."

"Well, he was quite a man."

"Yes, I get that. I hadn't realized what an accomplished musician he was."

"Oh yes, he traveled for many years on and off with all the big bands."

"Yeah, so I see. Might I ask you a question?"

She stood still and smiled, waiting for him to speak.

"I noticed something in the photos that was, well, different."

"Hmm?"

"Have you ever seen all these performance pictures?"

"I believe I have."

"What I noticed was that in all the performance pictures, the flash from the camera seems to always bounce off his instrument and back at the viewer."

She was grinning.

"I'm sorry," he said, "am I missing something obvious?"

She sat down next to him.

"You're not missing anything, you're noticing something. Come with me."

She led him down a flight of stairs. They walked quietly in the dark as the storm raged on. He shined his light in front of her protectively. She led him into one of the downstairs bedrooms. It was the only room with no guests this week. She stepped in, and he followed. Then she closed the door and flipped on the light.

"This was my father-in-law's room."

David looked around. It was a small room. There was a single bed. On the walls were more framed pictures of musicians. He recognized Miles Davis, Thelonious Monk, and Dizzy Gillespie. In the corner stood the bass, zipped up in a cloth case.

"Take out the bass," she said, matter-of-factly.

David raised his eyebrows and shook his head.

"Me? I couldn't. I'd feel out of line. I'm just a visitor here. I'm not even in the family."

"Take out the bass," she said again, in an authoritative manner.

"Okay, if you say so."

"I say so."

He still felt like a grave robber opening the instrument case of a dead musician so soon after his death. He unsnapped the snaps and unzipped the zipper and carefully removed the bass. It was the middle of the night and though thunder boomed, he didn't want people to hear him knocking over their beloved lost Mervyn's bass fiddle. The bass was covered with a layer of dust, even beneath the cloth. It had obviously not been recently taken care of or played.

"Mervyn's arthritis stopped him from playing in the last few years."

"It's a beautiful instrument." David wanted to pluck the strings, but the late hour stopped him.

"Go into the bathroom next door. There's a cabinet in there with towels. Go get a couple of towels." She was clearly giving orders, yet her voice was not harsh but soothing. He obeyed without a word. When he returned he reached out to hand her the towels. She pointed to the bass.

"Wipe."

He wiped. The dust came off. It was moist enough in that house that the dust came off on the towel rather than flew around. David's eyes widened. Beneath the layer of dust, the bass was glowing. It glowed just as surely as if it had internal lighting.

"What am I seeing?" he said, slightly raising his voice.

"You're seeing what you saw in the photo albums."

"I can't believe this! This is amazing! What is it?" he whispered excitedly.

"What do you think it is?"

David hated it when people said that. He always misread that comment. Did that mean that he should know what it is? Or that he should think for himself? Or that she had no idea? He knew that whatever he said would be wrong or taken badly.

"Something beautiful," he ventured.

"Yes, it's something beautiful. It is the light of God that Mervyn instilled in the instrument. It his spirit shining outward."

David sat down on the bed. He felt faint and put his head down between his legs.

"This light," she said, "shines on even though Mervyn has passed."

David slowly reached up and tentatively touched the bass, half expecting an electric shock.

"How was he able to do this?" he whispered.

"I can't tell you exactly. Cameron and I know that he studied with certain people, but we don't know who those certain people are."

"What did he study?"

"Well now, we don't exactly know that either. We just know that over the years there were places he went and people he knew whose identities were not revealed to us. But as the Bible says, 'By their fruits ye shall know them.' In this case, whatever

Mervyn studied, goodness came from it. The light in that instrument is just a symptom, an outward manifestation of the spirit within the man."

"Ms. Lewis."

"Amanda."

"Amanda, what do you think happened to your father-in-law?"

"God took him back."

"You don't feel that anything unusual took place?"

"I know that Thossian thinks that. I also know that he is sensitive to certain energies. He is so much like Mervyn in that regard. And so, I'm in a quandary about that."

"What about what happened at the funeral? Forgive me for asking."

The wind blew against the sealed bedroom windows. The rain beat down and lightning flashed.

"There is more to this world than we see, David. More than most people see. I choose to focus on his life, David, and not on his death. Look at his work, David. Look at the bass."

David stared at the incredible sight of rays of light streaming from the wood.

"You must remember your loved ones for who they were in life, not for who they appeared to be in death. Mervyn is no longer in his body. He has returned to the state of being with God that he carried with him in life. What happened at the funeral means nothing to me." She put her head down for a moment and sighed. "All mysteries will one day be unlocked. Until that day, I will continue to live each day with gratefulness to be alive. Good night."

She stood up.

"Will you please put the bass away before you go to sleep?"

"Of course."

She left the room. David stroked the bass. He picked up the towel and cleaned the rest of it off and watched it for awhile as if were a Christmas tree on Christmas Eve. Then he returned it to its case. As he left the room he put out the light and closed the door.

CHAPTER
TWENTY-EIGHT

*A*fter flying from Fort Wayne to Chicago's O'Hare, David boarded a late evening flight to New York. In his zealousness to savor every moment of being at the lake he had fallen behind on sleep. He had used up his anxiety about flying during the first flight and now found himself more relaxed. He slept for awhile.

He dreamed that he was floating above an immense Indiana cornfield. He felt fine about this until he saw a clearing in the cornfield hundreds of feet long. It was shaped exactly like a giant saxophone. As David floated, birds flew by him. He thought that they were a reference to Charlie Parker, Bebop god of the sax, whose nickname was "Bird." He smiled at the birds. They turned and faced him.

A little bird (who looked like a baby eagle from an old Bugs Bunny cartoon) cried out "Ma!" David thought that it must want its mother. "Ma!" it cried again. David felt bad for the little bird flying over the giant saxophone in the corn field. Then all the birds looked at him and cried "Ma! Ma! Mahozada! Ma! Ma! Mahozada!"

David was taken aback. Then the earth split open where the giant sax lay. Horrible noise and smoke came out from the field and the birds scattered. The smoke threatened to overcome him. He flapped his arms trying to get away. The airplane was shaking. He woke up.

He was on the plane to New York. The warning bell sounded and the co-pilot came on the intercom.

"Folks, we're over Pennsylvania and I'm afraid it's going to get bumpy." David's newfound calmness evaporated. "There's quite a stretch of storms up ahead and we will do whatever we can to avoid some of them, but the whole northeast is covered with T-storms. Please return to your seats and put up your trays and fasten your seatbelts."

David hated turbulence. He hated it even more in the dark. At least in the light you could get some reference point, but who wanted to ride a rollercoaster in the dark? He over tightened his seatbelt and slunk down as low as he could in his seat. He was crammed into the middle seat between the aisle and the window.

Hefty sleeping men hemmed him in. Maybe if they crashed he'd land on them and survive? Hefty Man on his left still had his tray open. Bump! He gripped the armrests tightly. Bump! The window shade was open and the dark rain smashed into the window. Bump bump! The peanuts on Hefty's tray started screaming and ran back into the peanut wrapper. The cabin lights blinked. David prayed. He didn't even work up to it. BUMP! Lateral shaking.

If it had been a subway he would have been standing, reading a newspaper and not even aware of it. But here? Here at thirty-thousand feet? Who would miss him if he died horribly?

Who would come to his funeral? Would all his old girlfriends show up? Would they cry because he was the best thing they had ever had so why did they dump him? Would the coffin be open and would he sing a Blues shuffle like Mervyn, or would he be so blown up by the crash that they couldn't display him? BUMPABUMPBUMP!! How come he never BUMP! got married anyway? How come he didn't B-B-B-BUMP! have kids? Was he going to puke all over the jet? How come nobody else seemed to notice what was happening? Didn't they care? Weren't they scared shitless like he was? RATTLELATERALSHAKEBUMP-UMP! Hefty Man Two on his right woke up. He waved down the flight attendant, Neal.

"Yes sir?" said Neal to Hefty Two.

"Can ah git a scotch on the rocks?"

"Sure," said Neal. "Anything for you sir?" he said to David.

BUMP! UMP! UMP! UMP! and the plane went down and David's guts went up. He could barely get the words out.

"Ginger ale. Just half a glass."

He didn't want to fill up now on liquid and then have to pee and be trapped in his seat in the storm, and he sure wasn't about to walk to the bathroom while the plane was being buffeted around in the dark. He might hit the ceiling. Now the plane seemed to be aimed down at a steep angle and the pressure changes made him more nauseous.

Hefty Two looked at David and said, "Storm like this pulled down a plane like this last month over Iowa."

"It did?" croaked David, as faintness surrounded him.

"Shore did. That plane saw a McDonald's in Peoria from two miles up and just landed right down on the roof for a cheeseburger."

They stared at each other blankly.

Finally David said, "What?"

Hefty Two elbowed him and guffawed.

"Har har! Ah'm jes' kiddin' you. We ain't goin' down. Not unless we find us a couple of fine lookin' women who'll oblige us! HarHARHAR!"

David tried to smile through his pale face.

"My friend," said Hefty Two, "looks like you need somethin' a little stronger than ginger ale to put the color back in your cheeks."

BADUMP! David's eyes widened at the sound. Were they breaking apart? How could the wings possibly stay on in this? Didn't they know about that old Jimmy Stewart movie where the plane develops metal fatigue and disintegrates up in the air?

Neal returned with their drinks. The trays stayed shut and they held their glasses as Neal handed Hefty Two his little bottle of scotch and a glass of ice. He poured David a full glass of ginger ale.

Now I'm stuck, thought David. I don't want to drink all of this and there's no place to put it down and BUMP BUMP BUMP!...BUMP! it's gonna spill all over the fucking place.

He took a small sip. He couldn't put the drink down and he needed both hands to grip the seat. He was miserable.

He put on his headphones. The audio quality was pretty bad and the storm and plane noises didn't help. He jacked up the volume. He flipped through the channels. Talk, Country, Muzak, Classical. He stopped when he heard the violins, thinking that it would calm his nerves. It was the thunderstorm from the second movement of Beethoven's "Pastoral" symphony. He kept flipping. It was Bill Evans. Bill Evans was one of his early pianistic influences. BUMP! He knew the recording. It was Bill playing an extended solo piano version of "On A Clear

Day". He had heard it a million times, but he always discovered something new in it. BUMP. This guy swung so effortlessly. And his harmonies! He was like Debussy playing jazz.

Bump. Bimp. Bimp. His chest muscles loosened and he closed his eyes. Not to go to sleep, but to go Bill-land. Bill-land was a very intimate, private place. He had once gone to see Bill Evans play at the Village Vanguard, New York's original smoky basement jazz club, where you could hear the subway rattle on the other side of the wall. Evans had been so impossibly hunched low over the keys that David had felt that he was intruding by being there. After the first set he left because of that feeling.

It was the opposite of whatever "performing" meant. But every note counted for Evans. Nothing seemed wasted. Every note seemed simultaneously composed and improvised. Like Bach. As he listened on the plane he tried to hear things that he hadn't heard before. The plane leveled off as the storm moved away. They swung on into the night.

CHAPTER TWENTY-NINE

*I*t was June in New York. Eddy Marsh booked David a few wedding gigs. On a Saturday evening he took a car service over the Verrazano Bridge to Staten Island. As he traversed the bridge he remembered all the great cheap dates he'd had on the Staten Island Ferry, riding across the harbor from Manhattan. And when he was a little kid his grandfather used to take him and they'd ride back and forth, back and forth, a nickel a ride. The ferry would pass Ellis Island and the Statue of Liberty. It was like riding the back of an old whale. The boat would huff and puff across the water until it docked, grinding into a wall of timber that acted as a buffer. The creaking, scraping sound of the boat hitting the timber sounded like the whale had been harpooned.

Now he glided over that harbor, high up on the bridge in a Lincoln Town car. He opened the windows into the hot June night to let the harbor air into the car. Haitian pop music played on the radio.

Twenty minutes later he arrived at the wedding site. He paid the driver, who helped him unload his equipment from the trunk. With his tux on, he was sweltering almost immediately. Outside the house in the backyard was a tent large enough to hold a couple of hundred wedding goers.

He scanned the area to see where the band was setting up. It was a pickup band and there was a reasonable chance that nobody in the band was anybody that he knew. The sax player looked liked he'd once been a very cool looking ladies' man. Once. Now it appeared that he'd fallen on sloppy times. His skin looked ragged and a pot belly greeted anybody who got close enough to shake his hand. The deeply etched lines on his face seemed to reflect the physical and emotional wear and tear of a life that consisted of playing too many of these. The drummer was a young hotshot who still had the fire and the desire to play. To him each gig still mattered. The female singer was still in fine form and had on a blue gown cut low in front and in back. David decided that he'd enjoy watching her from behind all night. The bass player was about six feet five. His name was Sal. He had a beard and a somewhat rumpled tux with a string tie instead of the standard bowtie. David introduced himself and noticed that Sal had a relaxed, lighthearted manner.

Tonight David knew he'd have to play a lot of music that he really did not want to deal with. Disco hits, The Electric Slide and The Macarena topped the list. If it had just been jazz he'd have been happy, but that was not going to be the case with this crowd. It was a wedding. People wanted to dance and art was the last thing on their minds. It was possible to have a good time on a job like this. The factors affecting this included getting fed or not (and not at the end of the night, thank you), who was in the band, how the client regarded musicians (as humans or not quite), weather, the crowd, etc. It was your basic New York June wedding in a tent with a band.

Large electric fans had been set up along the periphery of the tent to keep the humidity blowing in everybody's faces. Ellen, the singer, counted off and the band swung into "In The Mood."

The dance floor immediately swelled with couples. All ages. The sax player played the melody while Ellen snapped her fingers and smiled at the crowd. Staying with Glen Miller's hits, they moved into "Chattanooga Choo Choo" with Ellen singing. As they would approach the end of a song, Ellen would flash them finger signs to let them know what key to modulate to for the next song. David didn't know what song was next, but he knew what key to move to. Two fingers up for B flat, three for E flat, and so on. Fingers down for sharp keys. The audience would never know that this wasn't a regular working band that had been together for years. Everyone spoke the same musical language and they pulled it off well, as so many bands have done at so many weddings. After about forty minutes of this, Ellen motioned David to take a break.

"Come back in ten," she said as he walked off in search of food and drink. He looked back to see that she had sat down at his keyboard and was singing "The Rose."

He ambled through the crowd. They were loud and uninhibited. He wanted to stare at every woman there, but he also didn't want to get beat up or fired for doing it, so he put on his professional non-predatory face so as not to piss off any jealous boyfriends. He hoped that the women would notice him and that their dates would not.

As clusters of people gathered around waiters who carried trays of hors d'oeuvres, he tried to get close. Every time he took

an hors d'oeuvre off a tray, he felt the waiter's eyes were bor-
ing into him as if to say "Not quite human." He smiled at each
waiter, took an hors d'oeuvre and skulked away angrily and then
proceeded to the next waiter, whereupon he would smile again.
Feeling the heat, he ordered a ginger ale from the bartender,
gulped it down and then asked for another. He didn't want to
die from heatstroke in the middle of playing "Louie Louie." If
only he could have taken off the damn jacket!

Plenty of guys were dancing with no jackets on. But they
were guests. He was supposed to keep it looking formal. Even
if he fainted and ended up in the hospital it'd be less than a foot-
note in the guests' minds.

With one minute to go on his break he was on his way back
to the bandstand when he heard a different kind of loudness from
someone in the crowd. Two big men in their forties were insult-
ing each other and people around them were nervously laughing
as if that might resolve the argument. One guy called the other a
Fucking Crook and the other called the first a Cocksucker.

Whether or not these bold accusations actually had any truth
behind then didn't seem to be the real issue. The real issue
seemed to be about who had ingested more booze and who possessed more testosterone. The accused Fucking Crook had a
trace of humor in his inebriation, but the accused Cocksucker
looked like a mean drunk. His eyes were dark pools that spoke of
ruthlessness. The Cocksucker returned to eating as his wife put
her arm through his. Fucking Crook kept staring at Cocksucker.
David took one last look and relieved Ellen at the keys.

"Rock'n'roll time, boys," she said, strapping on an electric guitar. She flashed them two fingers. "'Jonny B. Goode'.
One. Two. A-one-two-three!" And she tore into the Chuck
berry lick.

Dah dah dah

DUH duh duh duh duh duh duh duh

DUH duh duh duh duh duh duh duh

DUH duh duh duh

DUH duh duh duh

DUH duh duh duh DUHHHH!!!

A million bands from The Rolling Stones to The Grateful Dead had beaten out that riff a million times. There she was in her low-cut full-length blue gown, ripping out a guitar solo you could chew on. The crowd loved it. When she got to the chorus the sax player joined her on the mic and sang harmony with her.

The crowd was singing it, too, and the dancing got wilder. David pounded out the classic kind of Boogie Woogie licks that Johnny Johnson had played on the original record. Ellen played a soulful roots rock solo and then the sax player blew blues licks like it was 1955.

Then Ellen motioned to David to take a turn. With the back of his hand he glissandoed up and down the keyboard, almost knocking it over in his excitement. He jumped up and down at the keys and felt all sense of control disappearing into ecstasy. Life was good.

And then out of the corner of his eye he saw something. A wave of people parting like a well-dressed Red Sea. In an instant Cocksucker had crossed the dance floor to Fucking Crook and was on him in a flash. He pounded Fucking Crook in the teeth. David expected Crook to fall backwards, but instead he doubled over forward as if he was checking his mouth and Cock smashed him over the exposed back of his neck with two hands entwined. Ellen turned to the band in complete shock. Her eyes reflected horror and confusion.

Sal looked at her and yelled, "Keep playing."

Crook slowly tried to stand but Cock brought his knee up into his already broken mouth and Crook came up and went down flat on his back. The screams of the people who could see the fight mixed with the cheering of the Chuck Berry fans.

The band kept playing. Ellen sang the last verse but the right lyrics escaped her.

"One morning in the moonlight you became a man
Your father and your mother had a baby band
Tired old keeper had a daughter, Jim
She was not a her and she was not a him
Her mama had a baby and she knocked on wood,
saying
Sonny be good, tonight"

As people gathered over the downed man, the beater went back to his table. The song ended.

Ellen flashed a letter "C" with her hand and called out "You Belong To Me", the old fifties slow dance. She told the sax player to play the melody. She was trying to cool off the crowd. Someone was screaming. A woman.

"I can't find his pulse! I can't find his pulse!"

The bride, still in her wedding dress, came up to Ellen.

"I'm not letting that bastard ruin my wedding! Just keep going! GodDAMMit!" She stormed away.

The musicians stared at each other, incredulous. Then the bride's mother came up on the stage. She grabbed Ellen's microphone and waved the band to stop.

"Excuse me", Ellen said, "Your daughter just came up here and told us to keep playing!"

"She doesn't know what the fuck she's talking about! We're paying for this wedding, so stop playing now, okay?!"

Ellen stopped the music. The bride came back and yelled from the front of the crowd.

"What are you doing? I told you to play, for Chrissakes!"

"Your Mom just told me..."

"Angela," said the bride's mother, "shut up for a moment!"

She addressed the crowd. The mic switch was off and she couldn't be heard.

"How do you work this thing? Come on!"

Ellen ran over and switched on the mic.

"It's on now," she said.

The bride's mom started again.

"Everybody listen!" she yelled. Crowd noise. Not everybody listening. "Will you please all shut up for a second?!" She got their attention. "Some people do not know how to fucking behave at a wedding! This is our daughter's wedding, and anybody who'd stoop to wailing on a guy like Joe at our daughter's wedding can stop calling himself family. This isn't the fucking street! If you don't know the fucking difference between a wedding and the street, then get the fuck out of here!"

Cocksucker got up from the table and screamed something unintelligible but threatening at the bride's mother. She was a little afraid, but shot right back at him.

"You talk that way to me at my daughter's wedding? You're an animal!"

Now Cocksucker started to come forward. A group of men blocked his path. It looked like more blood might be shed. Suddenly police sirens were heard. In came the cops and the paramedics. They hunched over Crook and took his vital signs. Then they put him on a stretcher and got him into the ambulance.

The cops encircled Cocksucker to talk to him. He sucker-punched a cop who went flying. The others tackled him, punched him, kneeled on him and cuffed him. He looked like an angry trussed up oversized rodeo calf wearing a nice suit. He screamed obscenities and oozed blood from his mouth as he lay face down on the ground. A cop still sat on his back for good measure. Then they lifted him by the arms and led him to the police car.

Ellen sighed and told the band to play "That's Amore."

Sal laughed.

CHAPTER THIRTY

*I*t had been a few weeks since David had been to the Aikido *dojo*. He saw some of the same people, but some new faces also. The *dojo* was not air-conditioned and the temperature had climbed to a hundred and one degrees. The windows were open and a single fan blew, but it was beyond stifling. Wearing a padded *gi* and spinning and falling and being thrown for an hour wouldn't help.

David changed in the locker room. A student visiting from an out-of-town *dojo* came into the room, having just bought a book about Aikido from Sensei. He was counting his money.

"Whoops, Sensei gave me back three dollars too much."

"Who's gonna know?" said David.

The visitor stared at David.

"I'll know."

As the visitor walked off to return the three dollars, David immediately felt stupid and ashamed. How did he get to a point where he could so easily rip off someone who was teaching him something valuable? Was he so desperate for money that any sense of decency went right out the door? Morosely, he finished putting on his *gi* and stepped out on the mat to stretch before the class started.

Simon was there, off in the corner with the wooden *bokken*, slicing through the air at an imaginary opponent. He looked all business and David didn't feel good about making conversation.

Instead he got down on the mat to stretch. Yogic stretching was not about reaching hard into the stretch, but rather about releasing. It was a new concept for David. Releasing. The music business had always been one of struggle for him, and his physical reflexes operated the same way. Everything he did involved tensing up. When he played the piano his shoulders tightened. Anytime he'd ever gotten a shoulder massage, the first thing he heard was "Your shoulders are very tight."

So here he was on the mat, trying to not try. Just sitting on the floor was new to him. His life had been spent sitting at the piano, usually a bench with no back, and his back often hurt during the later hours of a gig. Being vain, he didn't want to slouch, but holding a straight posture wasn't easy for four hours at a time. Now his legs were stretched straight out in front of him and he was trying to touch his toes. He had quite a distance to go and was about to give up when he felt hands on his back. A woman's voice.

"Take a gentle deep breath through your nose."

He did.

"Let it come through your nose and downward till it reaches your lower back."

He didn't turn around, but did as instructed. He imagined the air coursing through his body, beyond his lungs until it rested in the base of his spine.

"Hold it gently for a moment. Good. Now, exhale, making a 'ha' sound, slowly, without forcing it."

He exhaled on a long 'ha' and as he did, he felt her hands pressing with surprising strength on his back. His torso moved forward, to his utter surprise.

"Omigosh," he said.

"Shh. Don't talk, just breath. Again."

He repeated the process. This time on the exhale, she pressed and his torso went further forward then he could ever remember.

"Stop trying. Just let it happen. Just let it happen."

On the third breath, his hands reached his toes. She gently but firmly kept the pressure on his back. And there he was, sitting on the mat with his torso almost completely bent over to his outstretched legs, his face only inches from the mat.

"Good," she said and walked away.

David turned his head slightly to see who his benefactress was. He recognized her as Jenna Romano, whose second-degree black belt test he had witnessed. He had always liked to look at women from the rear and he recognized her shape and her hair. He stood up and he felt weightless. It was a bit disorienting, but he liked it.

Sensei stepped onto the mat and all the students who had been warming up immediately lined up in rows on their knees. Sensei bowed his head almost to the mat from his kneeling position and they bowed back. Immediately he went into action and motioned to a student to attack him. David thought to himself that no matter how powerful this man was, he was still a seventy-year-old person working out hard in unbearable heat conditions. Would it kill him? Five minutes later, David was huffing and puffing and Sensei still seemed calm. His skin glowed a bit, but he didn't look bothered by the heat.

Every time Sensei taught a new technique, the class would pair up with new partners to practice. Fifteen minutes into class, David had to excuse himself and walk off the mat to get a drink of water. He felt embarrassed to do this but knew that if he didn't both drink and catch his breath, he'd never make it through the class. As he started to step back on the mat, a student told him that he should bow before re-entering the practice area. He bowed standing, and then stepped back onto the mat. His *gi* was soaked from sweat but at least now his heart wasn't racing quite so hard. The phrase "Whatever doesn't kill you will make you stronger" entered his mind.

Hearing Sensei clap twice, he lined up with the others to see what the next technique would be. Sensei looked at him with an expression somewhere between no emotion and disdain. He held out his hand. David realized that Sensei wanted to use him to demonstrate the next technique. Adrenaline shot through him and his mouth dried up. He got up as fast as he could, tripping and almost falling. He heard laughter from a couple of students.

Sensei spoke to him, loud enough for all to hear.

"So, you are eager to fall? I don't even have to throw you?"

More laughter. Sensei had a mischievous smile on his face. David stayed tight-lipped, not knowing how to respond. Jenna indicated to David to kneel while Sensei explained the next technique. She knelt with one knee on the mat and the other foot flat. He imitated her. Sensei spoke to the class.

"*Tenchi-nage. Tenchi* is heaven and earth."

He made an arc with his arm almost like a basketball slam dunk. Back, up and then down in front like a hook, palm out. He did it slowly, and then fast. Then, in the air, he did it at lightning speed. David tried to gulp, but could find no spit. He wanted out, but there was no out to be found.

Jenna whispered, "When he throws you, lift your rear leg and fall. Don't stay there!"

Sensei could hear this, but accepted it as helpful.

"So, *tenchi-nage*."

Sensei motioned to David to stand. He approached him. And then, in the time it takes to start the descent of an eyelid in the first half of a blink, the little man's arm came back and up, very high for a man of his stature. In that instant David thought he looked like an insane person miming a waiter with a tray. His arm then came down, hooking over David's shoulder and smashing on towards the ground. David and everyone in that room heard a horrible, loud "snap" emanate from somewhere in the lower leg of David Stein, would-be martial artist. He then hit the mat on his back as the air was knocked out of him. The class gasped at the snapping sound. David lay there as the pain started to flood his nervous system. He knew that he was injured. Sensei looked mildly upset. Simon and Jenna came over and knelt by his side. Jenna was close and despite the pain, he was entranced by her.

"I told you to lift your rear leg to fall."

"Is it too late to do it now?" said David, joking through gritted teeth.

"Um-hum. Too late."

Sensei motioned to more students to come over and help him up and off the mat. As they walked him, he hopped. They sat him down on a bench facing the mat. He wanted to hide. His first time working with Sensei and he'd made an idiot of himself. And it hurt like hell. Jenna examined his ankle. He was simultaneously turned on and in agony.

"Wiggle it up and down," she commanded.

He wiggled it. It hurt but it wiggled. She held the ankle again.

"I don't think it's broken, but I also don't think you're going to be taking class for awhile. You might want to see a doctor and have it x-rayed. We'll put you in a cab. When you go home you need to keep ice on it as much as possible and don't wait till tomorrow. The first forty-eight hours are crucial. Take some Advil, too.

CHAPTER
THIRTY-ONE

A few days later, after a trip to the doctor had diagnosed the injury as only a sprain (albeit a sprain with a mysterious "snapping" sound at the instant of its birth), he limped into the *dojo* with a cane. He was both shy about going in and excited by the attention that he would draw. It hadn't changed since childhood. In many ways we are fully formed early on. If "arrested development" includes the inability to make fundamentally necessary personality changes between childhood and adulthood, then he was arrested, developmentally.

He did not take class because of the injury, but stayed to watch and to let Sensei know that he was alive. He also came to enjoy attention from Jenna. Her smile however was cryptic enough that he couldn't deduce whether it was personal or collegial.

Today the *dojo* had another visitor. He was Sensei Matsui, a colleague of their own teacher, Sensei Hara. He was visiting Aikido schools throughout the U.S. to teach healing arts.

Jenna, who often spoke to the class upon Sensei's request, introduced Sensei Matsui.

"We are honored to have a special guest this evening. Matsui Sensei is a 7th *dan* Aikidoist who, in addition to being a powerful martial artist, is also a proponent of healing with the hands. If you study martial arts, sooner or later you're bound to have some kind of injury. Like dancers and professional athletes, we need to be able to get ourselves back on the mat as soon as possible. No matter what profession you are in, you need to have a healthy, resilient body that can bounce back from physical injury. Matsui Sensei is here to give us an introduction to techniques that will benefit us on or off the mat. Please, let's give a warm welcome to Matsui Sensei!"

She bowed low to Matsui Sensei. The class stood up and clapped as he stepped to the front of the mat to speak. He was tall and thin and looked to be about thirty-five. His skin seemed radiant and his general appearance was like that of a young willow tree or a bow made of bamboo. Matsui Sensei laughed and bowed repeatedly as they clapped. His smile was infectious, and his laughter only made the class want to applaud more. Many of them found themselves laughing in delight at his informality.

"Thank you very much," he said haltingly.

"I don't speak English well. But, I do Aikido pretty well." He nodded and they laughed in response. "Human being is like a tree. We have roots and limbs and vessels to bring blood and food to all parts of our body. As you understand from studying with Hara Sensei, stiff body is like old tree and is knocked over by storm. Soft body is full of energy like young willow tree that bends in the wind but does not break. When you are injured, energy is blocked and injured part of your body is like smelly old rotten tree." As Matsui Sensei mimed smelling a bad odor, the class laughed. "So, how to unblock natural energy flow so that body can heal and become young again? This is what I teach. When energy flows naturally through the human body, you stay young. I feel very well because I practice Aikido and healing arts, and I am person of fifty years."

The class gasped. The man in front of them looked like a very athletic thirty-five-year-old man. David, who was sitting on a bench off the mat, found himself standing up in shock. How could this man really be fifty? Was it a con? He remembered Sam Jaffe as the two-hundred-year-old priest in the Frank Capra film version of "Lost Horizon", revealing his age to Ronald Colman. And though this was not as extreme an age, it also wasn't a movie. It was a real man standing in front of him who just didn't look fifty. The class clapped in awe and David sat down again.

"Perhaps you know of acupuncture. Healing arts use the same lines of energy centers in the body. Instead of needles we use hands. We use fingers to stimulate energy centers to increase energy flow. In this way we can heal." Matsui Sensei paused to let the class digest this, and also to summon up his limited English. "Is there injured person in this class? Someone who is hurt in body?"

Every head turned towards David. His heart jumped. There he was with his cane, sitting on the sidelines in his street clothes. Matsui Sensei looked at him and crossed his arms.

"So," he said, smiling, "this person look like he got injured in Aikido class, and maybe he doesn't want to take any more now!"

Laughter from students. Gulp from David. He raised his hand to acknowledge his reluctant presence to the Sensei. His shoes were already off and he picked up his cane and limped onto the mat as they watched him. He bowed to Matsui Sensei. Out of the corner of his eye he could see Hara Sensei in kneeling position on the mat observing this quietly. Now he remembered Audrey Hepburn in "The Nun's Story", limping in pain and being admonished by the mother superior for attracting attention and pity to herself. He tried to keep a poker face, but every step hurt like hell and sent jolts of pain up his leg.

Matsui Sensei motioned for him to get down on the mat. Trying to go with the program, he went carefully down on one knee, but mercifully, Matsui told him to sit cross legged. He did so and slid the cane out of the way.

"Take off sock, please." David obliged. "Please tell what happened to you."

David cringed, not wanting to make Hara Sensei look bad.

"Sensei used me to demonstrate *tenchi-nage* on me and I guess I didn't practice my falls enough."

This was in fact, the truth.

Matsui Sensei now rolled David's pants leg up to his knee. His street clothes emphasized his hairy leg. If he had had his *gi* on he wouldn't have minded, but this made him feel as if he looked like an accident victim in the street. Matsui's brow grew furrowed and his eyes half closed as he took David's foot in one hand and his ankle in the other. He ran his finger over a large red swollen area where the foot met the ankle. David let out a quiet gasp of pain and his shoulders tensed up. The class leaned in to observe every detail. He felt like a cadaver in a Medical school class. Matsui Sensei held the foot and, bending his thumb, proceeded to exert pressure about an inch from the swelling. David found himself involuntarily breathing hard, nearly hyperventilating. The Sensei closed his eyes and continued to exert pressure. After a while he found another nearby spot surrounding the swelling and pressed. As he pressed he exhaled long slow breaths. David also did this. For about ten minutes, no one spoke. Matsui Sensei only occasionally opened his eyes. Now he slowly rotated the foot on the ankle. David had become calm and his self-consciousness had faded.

Matsui Sensei opened his eyes and looked at the class.

"Most important to wash feet every day."

From beneath his *gi* he took out a small hand towel and wiped his hands on the towel. David was horrified. Did his feet stink? Were they filthy? He was humiliated and ready to limp back to his bench.

"Stand up, please."

David reached for his cane.

Matsui Sensei put a gentle but remarkably firm hand on David's shoulder.

"Leave cane. Only need for mountain climbing."

"But Sensei..."

"Stand up."

David prepared to stand. His face started to contort in readiness for the pain he expected to come when he pushed off the mat to stand without the cane. Surprisingly, he felt nothing. His foot seemed almost numb, and certainly devoid of the electric- like shocks that he'd had a few minutes before. He stood up.

"Walk."

Now knowing better not to contradict any direct orders from Matsui Sensei in front of the class, David walked. The pain was gone. He tried to find the pain again, making sure that he completely bent the foot in his stride. He walked up and down the mat a few steps.

"How is foot?"

"It's great!" he yelled, and the class burst out cheering. David could not believe what he was experiencing.

When the cheering had subsided a bit, Matsui Sensei said, "Stand only on injured foot."

David stood like a crane on the injured foot alone.

"Hop like bird."

David hesitated for a moment. He didn't want to press his luck. Then he hopped. He hopped up and down the mat and the class went wild again. He returned to Matsui Sensei, who had by now stood up. David bowed to him.

"Thank you very much, Sensei!"

Matsui Sensei bowed in return.

CHAPTER
THIRTY-TWO

"**D**avid?"

"Yeah."

"This is Sal Lucci. We met on that Staten Island wedding last week."

"Oh, yeah, you're the bass player!"

"Right."

"How you doin'?"

"Good, man. Listen, you working tonight?"

"Nah. Unfortunately not. What cha got?"

"Jam session at a loft on Twenty-sixth Street. Good jazz players, piano's there. We're starting around 11 p.m. Wanna come?"

"Absolutely. Sounds like fun."

David had admired Sal's playing on the wedding gig and was flattered to be thought of as a jazz player rather than just as a wedding musician. Coming from Sal, it had particular meaning.

That night the shy/ham David Stein showed up at exactly 11 p.m. His ankle was almost completely healed and he found that

he no longer needed the cane. Standing outside the lonely building, he rang the bell. He was buzzed in and he took a rickety,
claustrophobic little elevator to the seventh floor. It let him off
at the entrance to a dimly lit live-in loft that had probably once
been a garment center warehouse. Nobody was there but the
drummer who owned the loft. His name was Alf Davies but as
he told David, people just called him "Bread" because like most
musicians, he was always looking for bread (money). David
knew that while "Bread" was a perfectly good nickname for a
jazz drummer, he'd have a hard time actually calling the guy by
that moniker.

Bread had put out some chips and soda, but no bread. David
felt foolish for being the first one there. It showed that he wasn't
cool and that he didn't have better things to do. Musicians
arriving later came from playing in Broadway pit bands and
other more "important" gigs. As others arrived David felt even
more self-conscious. If no other pianist arrived he'd have to
play and see how he matched up against these players. If other
pianists did show, he'd have to decide whether to take the piano
position from another player or give it up to somebody else. No
matter what, his stomach was fluttering in a situation that was
supposed to be about unbridled joy. Well, for some jazz players, jamming is joy and for others it's deadly serious. Maybe
too serious.

The old "cutting contests" in Harlem and on Fifty-second
Street during the bebop days of the 1940's and 50's consisted
of players trying to outplay each other and embarrass the other
guy off of the bandstand. Gunslingers with saxes instead of
six-shooters. And just like gunslingers, no matter how fast and
fancy you were on your instrument, there was always somebody
else out there looking to take the crown. Where was teamwork

and musical conversation in all this? It was still there in bands that worked together in clubs and concert halls, but here in the wee hours of a loft, nobody knew what the vibe or intent might be.

People started arriving. Bread sat down at the drum kit.

"Come on, David, let's play some music."

David sat down at the piano as an older man named Earl asked him for notes to tune his upright bass. Then Earl looked at him.

"What are we playing?"

David Stein, uncomfortable person, tried to think quickly. If he picked a tune that he didn't play well, he'd look stupid. If he picked too easy a tune, one that was overplayed, he'd look equally stupid. He'd look like a poseur. If he told Earl to pick the song, Earl might pick one that David couldn't play and he'd really lose face in a big way.

There was an uncomfortable silence for a moment, mercifully interrupted by a sax playing the head to Thelonious Monk's "Straight, No Chaser." The sax player was a squarely built black man with dreadlocks and a striped wool cap. His name was Malik. David was instantly relieved because no matter who came into that room at that moment, he was safe. He knew the tune. It was basically a blues. The thing about Monk's music was that even if the harmonic structure of the composition was relatively simple, playing Monk seemed to make a lot of players want to play in his style. Monk's playing style hadn't been simple blues. It was angular, intentionally dissonant, playful, and unexpected. As Monk used to say, "Wrong is right."

David was instantly able to play his part. He hadn't spoken with Malik, and letting each other hear their respective styles was like handing each other their business cards. As David listened to what came out of the sax, he made adjustments in his playing to relate to it. As Malik hit some big bluesy honks, David dug in and answered them with gravelly blues licks. Malik smiled and David felt validated as a human being. Malik played for a long time and then stopped. This was the understood cue for David to start his own solo over Monk's bluesy chord changes.

David loved this medium tempo. Playing too fast could cause his time to rush, or even fall apart, but here, he was deep in the groove and he had time to think. His solo was a combination of licks that everyone's heard before combined with an exploration of the piano. Jazz wasn't always about coming up with the never-before-played. All you had to do was look at a transcription of "Giant Steps" to see that even Coltrane repeated himself often. And for that matter, the blueprint for "Giant Steps" was clearly visible to those who bothered to look in Nicholas Slonimsky's "Thesaurus of Scales", a much-practiced tome. But no matter how many precedents you could dig up, clearly Coltrane practiced, expanded and codified his musical dialect in the ever-changing living language of jazz. And no matter what musical wells he might have drawn on, Coltrane explored and expanded to the end of his life on this plane. So for David, the idea of a good solo on this simple chord progression meant combining the familiar and the unfamiliar. Always play the expected and the listener gets bored and leaves. Always play the unexpected and the listener gets lost and leaves. But combine the expected with the unexpected and a journey is created that the listener will want to join.

That's what David tried to do on this solo. And yet, it's not about thinking. You don't improvise on a jazz-blues and think in words. The heart, the mind, the ear and the fingers all operate together. "Team Jazz", a good musical infield. As David reached his third chorus solo and created a melody that jumped up and down between the bass and treble registers, he heard Malik laugh and say

"I hear you."

That was a validation. Somebody bothered to hear his tree fall in the forest.

Other players had arrived. Recognizing fellow piano players and feeling good about himself for once, David got up from the piano bench at the end of "Straight, No Chaser" to let somebody else take over. Pizza arrived and David wandered over to the table. A Latino conga player set up next to Bread's drum kit and they played Chick Corea's fusion Samba, "Spain".

David was finishing his pizza when Eddie Clovis walked in. Seeing Clovis, the hairs on the back of David's neck stood up. Clovis radiated bad will. Same crew cut, leather jacket, big shoulders, sunglasses (come on, night time in a loft, what was *that* about?). He felt as if he'd been singing around the campfire and Hitler had suddenly shown up. He was fascinated though. It took the wind out of his sails as far as wanting to play. He couldn't imagine communing musically with this nasty *schmuck*. So, he decided to watch the proceedings.

After a number of trumpet and sax players had soloed, the band finished "Spain". Clovis, who had his horn out, started to play... something. He didn't discuss it with anyone first. He just started in, and as he played he walked up to Bread and blew in his face.

Once again David heard something that made him shiver. It was like a burn from dry ice. It made his stomach grip the pizza he'd just eaten. Clovis' playing got various reactions from the others. Bread looked at him and then started bashing away on the drums while staring Eddie back in the face. It looked like a challenge from both men. They were playing together but it sure wasn't love. The musical combination of the two of them seemed to insert itself into the spaces between light and dark. Between the antecedent and consequent beats of a heart. Whatever flow occurred disobeyed the laws of musical physics.

Bread held his own as Earl looked on, unsure what to play. And these were guys who had heard Ornette Coleman's free jazz and Cecil Taylor's illusion-shattering piano storms. Nothing that could happen should have intimidated them.

Bread looked mad. Finally he stopped playing. He threw down the sticks and walked off. The room was filled with emotional ice. Clovis smirked and went right on howling through the sax. His sound swirled around the room like a hit from a medieval mace. David tasted something foul in his mouth.

At the end of a long gnarled phrase, Clovis paused and took a breath. At that moment Jack Sanders, an Australian trombone transplant to New York, started to play "Blue Bossa." In terms of protocol, he had interrupted Eddie Clovis, but Clovis had already shown bad manners. People seemed glad to hear Sanders. Earl immediately joined in on bass and so did the percussionist, the pianist, and another drummer. David watched Eddie Clovis stare at Sanders with deep disdain in his eyes. Sanders had a beautiful full-throated sound and his musical entrance had changed the mood in the room as if a window had been opened on a stuffy summer day.

David watched his colleagues enjoying themselves and felt something wonderful well up inside himself. He watched Jack Sanders show mastery of his instrument. His tone was as warm as a singing human voice could ever be.

5769

David could see the inverted funhouse-like reflection of the room in the bell of Sanders' trombone. So bright. David looked up at the ceiling. There was no overhead light fixture within fifty feet of the area where the musicians were playing. A few scattered lamps around the loft were the only light sources. Where was the light coming from that reflected in the trombone? Mervyn! Mervyn's bass had that glow, in the photos and in the wood itself. He remembered Amanda Lewis' words, *It is the light of God that Mervyn instilled in the instrument. It's his spirit shining outward. The light in that instrument is just a symptom, an outward manifestation of the spirit within the man.*

David found himself involuntarily breathing in short fast breaths. Sanders' trombone was glowing as he played. Didn't anyone else see this? How could he ask anybody without sounding like a nut? But he was a nut! He was an abnormal person and he knew it. He accepted it. But, he had learned how to function in the world without getting locked up for it. He knew how to play "Normal Person". Sometimes, anyway. He was debating with himself whether or not to ask Malik if he could see the glow, when Sanders finished playing and a trumpet player took over. When Sanders put down the horn, the glow seemed to no longer exist. It didn't exactly stop, or fade, or get switched off. It just seemed to no longer be. David shook his head over and over. He knew that there were two musicians in that room that had something going outside conventional understanding. Eddie Clovis and Jack Sanders. And he needed to talk to them both. He waited till the tail end of Blue Bossa, knowing that Sanders would repeat the melody. The bone lit up again when he played and ceased to glow when he stopped. He meandered over to Sanders.

"You're Jack Sanders. I've seen you play. Somewhere, years ago."

"Yeh, right mate. How you doin'?" he said, extending his hand.

"David Stein, and I'm doin' fine. That was a glowing solo."

David waited and hoped for a knowing reaction from Sanders to his pun. He saw the slightest smile on Jack's face but wasn't sure if he was acknowledging what had happened.

"Well, it's a fun tune to blow on," said Sanders.

David decided to push his luck and abandon his fear of being ridiculed.

"Are you...aware...that your instrument gives off light when you play?"

Jack smiled. "Can you see that?" he said.

"Yeah, I saw it."

"Well then, I must be doing something right."

"I'd say so. Doesn't everybody who sees you play report this to you?"

"Nah. Most people don't seem to notice it."

"Really?" said David, fascinated.

"So are you telling me that I'm standing here in this room and I see your horn glowing and the guy standing next to me could be staring at it and he doesn't see it?"

Jack gave a small nod.

"Can you tell me how you learned to make to your horn do that?"

"I'm just trying to play music, mate. It just happens as a by-product. It ain't about the glow, it's about the music. After that, it's just a question of what you think playing music's all about, know what I mean?"

"I think I've started to know."

"It's good that you see that light. It says something good about you. But don't get all hung up about the light. I mean, don't let it get in the way of hearing."

"I get it. Still, I'm wondering if you studied any special technique that enables that to happen. Like maybe you studied with a particular teacher."

"Yeah, I did."

Jack stopped right there and just looked at David, poker-faced. He was only going to give as much information as asked.

"Could I ask you the name of that person?"

"First let me say that I didn't study with somebody to learn how to turn my horn into a friggin' Christmas tree. I studied various things with somebody that happened to result in a little visual sideshow. It's not the main event."

"Okay." said David.

"So what is it you want to learn?" Obviously, Jack was protecting someone from musical interlopers.

"I heard some music on a tape that changed me...profoundly. I want to understand what I heard. I'd...like to be able to play like that, I guess."

Jack Sanders listened and nodded. He seemed to be making a decision.

"Okay, Mate. I'm gonna take a chance on you, 'cause I have a feeling that you're an honest guy. I studied outside the States, but there's a guy in town who teaches what you want to know. He's good. He'll take your playing to a different level."

Jack took out a pen and his own business card. On the back of the card he wrote a phone number and the name "Billy Kovac."

"Give him a call tomorrow and tell him that we talked. It's up to him if he wants to take you on."

"Thanks, I really appreciate it."

"Just don't fuck it up. What he teaches is not something you want to take lightly."

David nodded. He shook Jack's hand. Jack started to talk with some other people and David looked around for Eddie Clovis. He was beginning to sense that Clovis was a piece of a puzzle that involved Mervyn, Jack, Billy Kovac, the tape, and God knew what else. He walked around the loft, wondering how to approach Clovis. He didn't see him. He even looked in the bathroom. No luck. Eddie Clovis was gone.

CHAPTER
THIRTY-THREE

A few days later David walked up three rickety flights and rang Billy Kovac's doorbell. No answer. He rang again. Nothing. He waited a minute and then knocked. Nobody answered. Frustrated, he was about to leave when he heard a yell from the apartment.

"What!?" The voice sounded pissed off.

"Uh, Billy Kovac?"

"What? Who wants Billy Kovac?" The voice had a strong, nasal Brooklyn accent.

"It's David Stein. We spoke the other day on the phone. I got your name from Jack Sanders."

"Jack who?"

"Jack Sanders. Trombone player." Silence. "Australian guy."

"Oh, Jack, yeah! Good player."

"Definitely."

David had pronounced the password. The door opened. And inside was a short, squat man of non-descript age with long hair and glasses. He was wearing a very brightly colored bathrobe and probably nothing else.

"Come on in."

David entered. The apartment was tiny and it was a mess. Papers all over, music scores in piles. A raggedy old cat sitting on the raggedy old sofa. But the walls were covered with framed posters from European jazz festivals. This gave a touch of class to the chaos. The living room was almost completely filled by what appeared to be a very long piano-shaped tent of cloth. The apartment smelled of cigarette smoke, foul cat litter, and some other unidentifiable pungent odor. Incense? Pot? Leftover Indian food? David wasn't sure.

"I'm sorry, man, I got in really late and I totally blew it" said Kovac. "Forgot we had a lesson today. I'm so wasted. I don't think I can do it."

David wondered what he'd gotten himself into.

"Look David, I'm really sorry about this. Tell you what. Please come back tomorrow at the same time. The lesson'll be free."

Kovacs' price was high and David was reasonably broke. But he had hoped to get on the path to wherever he was going today, not tomorrow. What could he do though?

"Okay."

"So sorry man. Same time tomorrow. I'm gonna write it down on my calendar on the fridge. I never miss that."

Exactly twenty-four hours later, David rang. The door opened and a blue jeaned, t-shirted Billy Kovac welcomed him in.

"Would you like some tea, David?"

"Oh, thanks. I'm okay." David didn't want to waste time.

"Have some tea, David." Billy sounded a little like a hipster Joe Pesce. Something in his voice made David give in.

"Sure."

"Sorry 'bout yesterday, this one's on me," said Billy, pouring tea in his tiny, messy kitchenette. David was relieved that Billy had remembered that this lesson was going to be free.

"That's a big piano you have," said David, not entirely comfortable calling him by his first name yet.

"Yeah, it's a wonderful instrument. Thirteen-foot Steinway grand."

"How'd you get it in here?" asked David, as Billy handed him a mug that said *merde* on it in large red script.

"Window," Billy said, sipping his tea.

David took a taste. It was horribly bitter and probably could have used an entire jar of honey to make it palatable.

"Interesting tea, what is it?"

"Panax. Specially strong ginseng."

David eyed the cup suspiciously, scanning it for any insects or any other form of *merde*.

"Is that supposed to be good for you?"

"You'll get a better lesson if you drink it."

"Is that because it makes you alert or something?"

"That's because if you drink my tea, I'm happy, and then I give you a better piano lesson." Billy eyed David, who was taken aback by this remark. Then he laughed at David. He slapped David on the arm and almost made him spill his tea. The friendly slap was from a powerful person. "Lighten up, man, I'm just kidding with you."

David could dish out the jokes, but he never seemed to know when he was being taken.

"Are these all festivals you've played?" said David, eyeing the posters.

"Um-hum," Billy said as he sipped. "I'm usually on the road. So if you decide you want to take lessons, we'll have to do it when I'm in town."

David had heard of Billy Kovac before. He had a great reputation as a monster of a player. He wasn't commercially famous, but his name had come to David's ears a few times. David had never actually heard him play, but the reputation, the posters, the grand piano and something about Billy all commingled to make him believe that he'd indeed want to study with him.

"Sounds good to me."

Billy finished his tea. Seeing this, David reluctantly gulped down his mug, which was almost full.

"Here, I'll take it. Why don't you sit down at the piano."

It wasn't a question. David walked over to the keyboard end of the piano and noticed that the piano was completely covered with large tapestry-like spreads. They were covered with pictures of mandalas and East Indian religious drawings. Even the legs were invisible to the eye because of the hanging spreads. The pedals themselves were wrapped in fabric. He'd never seen anything like this before. Only the keyboard could be seen. The keys were glossy white. The raised keyboard lid also had fabric with Indian patterns covering it.

"Interesting covering," said David, fishing for information.

"Lowers the decibel level. Keeps the neighbors from complaining... So David, play me something."

David froze up. He knew that he was in the presence of somebody who could do what he wanted to do. Somebody who could play in ways that he could not, even after a lifetime of playing the piano. He knew that he could not get away with sitting down and noodling recycled jazz runs sloppily, as he might upon sitting down at a piano on one of his gigs. Knowing that Billy would be capable of scrutinizing him to the core made him hyper-alert to whatever he was about to play.

"What would you like to hear?," he stalled.

"Anything. Play me some jazz."

David started to play "Autumn Leaves", a tune that had been played millions of times by everybody and their mother. It should have been simple. Harmonically it bounced back and forth between G major and E minor. Rhythmically, it should have played itself. He swung it of course, but like a pitcher who suddenly starts throwing wild when the bases are loaded, his lines fell apart. He was thinking so much and trying so hard to come up with perfection that what he played was stiff, square and sloppy. He stopped, dejectedly.

"Would you believe I played it better at home?" he said, trying to cover his bad playing with a bad joke.

"I'd believe it, but unfortunately, we can't tell that to an audience. They're not interested in our problems. They want to be moved by the music, and not moved to the exits. Try it again. Leave out the chords and bass, slow it down, and just play me right hand lines. And relax. You're not gonna play great if you think somebody's got a gun pointed at you. Go ahead."

This time he improvised on the chord changes without actually playing them. He played long lines of eighth notes, the way a sax might. Nothing to think about but melody. It sounded better than the previous effort.

"That's good, keep going," Billy said over David's playing. "More legato. Keep it clean but keep it swinging. Don't play the same thing twice. Don't rush. Slow down. Um-hum. Add some triplets. Do it again and this time I wanna hear each note

in the triplet cleanly. Good. Now give me some interesting unexpected rests in your lines. Think Miles."

David had never had guidance as he improvised. He hadn't
heard Billy play a note, yet he knew he was getting good advice.

"Okay, now finish your solo."

David completed the last thirty-two bar trip through "Autumn
Leaves" and stopped.

"Okay. Okay. Slide over."

Billy sat down on the left side of the bench. David sat on the
right with half his rear end over empty air.

"Now we're gonna play together. You solo, I'll accompany
you. Same tune, same tempo. One, two, three."

David started playing around the tune. Billy played chords
and bass lines. Instantly the piano started to speak with a different voice. It had become like a friendly rhinoceros who comes
over to say hello and you don't know if you're going to get
licked or gored.

David had never been in such close physical proximity
to somebody who could squeeze such sounds out of a piano.
The instrument was awake and frighteningly powerful. It was
a big piano and the sound tore through it, even with the cloth
coverings. And the chords and rhythms that Billy played were
unknown to David. They fit the song, but transformed it from
"Autumn Leaves" into "Forest Fire in the Fall." Just his tone
was like nothing David had heard before. It was fat and round
and rich and beyond his comprehension of what a piano could
produce. Each substitute chord Billy played completely changed
the meaning of "Autumn Leaves". The song meant something
else now. He'd heard it so many times on so many recordings.
Why did everybody record this song? What new information
could possibly come from one more version? And yet it did.

Then Billy started to solo and David knew instinctively to stop playing and just listen. That giant tone coming from what was ostensibly classified as a "percussion" instrument. Every note counted, nothing was wasted. The patterns were nothing he knew. The control was total, yet it swung like hell. Against this solo came dense chords and incredible bass lines that would frighten any good upright bassist. All of this at the same time. David wondered how one human could create all this spontaneously and simultaneously. Yet, he knew that people who watched him perform often had the same reaction. The more David knew about music, the more he was awed by Billy Kovac's playing.

Billy finished his titanic solo, and then out came that little nasal Brooklyn thing again.

"So that's what I mean, man. Dig in, make it count, reach into yourself and bring out the meaning of the music. You know, like Michelangelo with the block of marble."

David looked quizzical.

"Oh yeah, Michelangelo, I think it was him or one of those cats, he said that the statue was already in the block of marble. All he had to do was chip away the outside and the statue would come out. Same thing with music. You got this little thirty-two bar tune with its harmonic sequence. You chip away at the outside and inside is something beautiful and meaningful. Something holy."

Something holy? thought David. He'd never thought "holy" when playing jazz, but now he wasn't sure what to think. Ever since the tape, he felt as if he was being chipped away and letting something within himself show up. Something...holy? But who was doing the chipping?

At the end of the lesson, he thanked Billy.

"I'm glad I kept ringing your doorbell yesterday. Otherwise I wouldn't have had a chance to learn so much today."

"What happened yesterday was supposed to happen. Part of the first lesson was to send you home with no piano lesson."

"What? I don't get it."

"Old trick. Separates the pianists from the piano players. You got sent home by a half-asleep weirdo who said he couldn't teach you that day. Come back tomorrow. You came back. That was the test."

"The...test?"

"Yeah. I wanted to see if you'd come back today after being treated like that. You came back. You put up with the bullshit because you cared about learning. Good for you, man."

He patted David on the back at the door.

"Go home, practice. Call me when you're ready for another lesson."

CHAPTER THIRTY-FOUR

"**D**avid?"

"Yeah."

"This is Sal Lucci."

"Sal. What happened? You never showed up at the loft jam."

"I know. Sorry 'bout that. I fell sleep in the evening and woke up about midnight and I was too tired to make it. Too many gigs, I guess. I heard it was good, though."

"Well yeah, it was pretty cool. I heard some interesting people. Did some playing."

"Listen, I got a cool gig for you if you're interested."

"Hit me."

"I'm subbing in the Radio City Orchestra and the keyboard player told me he needed someone in two days for a couple of performances."

"Radio City? No shit!" Fear. "That's wild. But uh, I don't have a lot of orchestral experience."

"Come on man, you'll be great for this. Rockettes, five thousand tourists, easy charts, good bread. What's the problem?"

"Well, I appreciate it, Sal. I just don't know if I could cut it neatly. I'm not used to following conductors. I might fuck it up."

"David, I heard you play in Staten Island. You're good. You're better than most of these guys playing pit keyboards. You should do this."

The next day David picked up a free comp ticket and sat in the orchestra pit to watch the keyboard player play "The Radio City Music Hall Rockettes Summer Spectacular."

For David, there were a number of scary elements. First of all, you had to play the music as written. You couldn't go off and have a party and jazz it up. Second, you had to follow the conductor. Here he was totally off his turf. This formalist factor ran against his unruly grain. Third, the possibility of screwing up and the entire world hearing you ruin a show and having lines of beautiful, long legged, high kicking Rockettes fall off the stage and injure themselves because you couldn't get the music right was so anxiety-producing that whatever gain there was to be got from taking this job was nullified.

David showed up in black shirt and black pants as he was told to. Pit players in Broadway shows wore this outfit so that the audience wouldn't be distracted and notice them. God forbid that people paying big bucks for Broadway tickets should actually see the musicians who played the music that made the show what it was.

He introduced himself to Wolf Davis, the keyboard player, and sat down next to him on a chair to read the music over his shoulder. A sub needed to do this to get acquainted with the specifics of playing the show. He also was given a copy of the score to take home and practice, along with a recording of the show. That way at home he could listen to the music on headphones while he played through it at the piano. Actually, for this show, most of the playing was on old vintage synthesizers, and a good deal of the time, he'd be playing funky bass lines, the same notes that Sal would be playing next to him on bass guitar. He'd need to play it really neatly so that he and the bassist would sound as one.

He sat with the band, wondering where the audience was. He didn't see a curtain. The conductor cued the orchestra and they started to play a shimmering, Broadway, razzle dazzle fanfare. It was thrilling to be sitting in the midst of this group as they played. A second or two after they started to play, the earth shook. The walls surrounding the orchestra seemed to be sinking down. What was happening? Why didn't the players notice? Now five thousand cheering people in seats appeared above him and sank down around him 'til he was slightly above them.

The entire Radio City Music Hall Orchestra had come up from the basement on a giant elevator. The effect of being on that elevator and seeing the audience appear was breathtaking. It was a New York moment. As a boy he remembered sitting in the audience and watching in exhilaration as the orchestra rose up and appeared. It was exciting and magical then. Now he was riding with the magicians. Mandy Baskin, star of stage and screen was featured in the show, and besides the big splashy Rockettes numbers, she performed various show stoppers from various classic Broadway shows. David was thrilled when Mandy sang "I'm Flying" from "Peter Pan" in Act Two and flew out over the audience harnessed to a winch. It wasn't an easy stunt and David worried that the mechanism would fail and poor Mandy would crash down into the blue-haired ladies in the fourteenth row. Between that and trying to watch Wolf play the music, his adrenaline was pumping and thumping.

That night David sat at his piano reading the score while he listened to a tape of the performance. This was a good way to learn, except that it was late at night, he didn't want the neighbors knocking on the walls, and so he was barely touching the keys. Except for the mime's head sitting on one side of the piano smiling at him while drooling blood and one mouse in a tuxedo tap dancing on the other side, his work was uninterrupted.

Two days later the conductor gave the cue and the orchestra played its razzle dazzle music and the gigantic elevator rode up to meet the cheering crowd. David was at the keys and he tried to do some deep Aikido-style breathing to calm himself. He knew that the more he got excited, the faster he'd play. That was not an option here. He had to relax himself enough to take control of his hands. Watch the baton, listen to the band, hit the right buttons on your synthesizer. If it's supposed to sound like a bass, don't hit the button that makes it sound like a taxicab horn. Focus, focus, focus.

His playing was generally sloppy. If he'd had a longer period of time with the score he might have stood a chance, but forty-eight hours to learn a whole show authoritatively? Maybe there were players out there who were reading specialists. He was a good reader but his instinct was always to get away from the written page. Not here, though. As the show progressed he struggled to come in neatly on each musical cue. Just before intermission there was a funky R&B dance number where the Rockettes got a chance to show that they had more going for them than long legs. This is where David's synth played the same notes as Sal and he needed to match him perfectly note for note. The drums, the guitar, and the horn section were chugging away solidly and David loved hearing this big fat sound pounding around him. As he got to play those bass lines and pretend he was a bass player, he couldn't help but start to move. Pretty soon he was jumping up and down as he played.

Boom bupaDApa, buh buddahbimBOMP

Boom bupaDApa, buh buddahbimBOMP

What a kick! He could see the dancers up on stage and the audience going wild. What a great party! By the time the number and the act ended, David was in a sweat. The elevator took the orchestra down for their intermission break. David stood at the keyboard, smiling. A familiar figure with a violin approached him.

"Saul. Omigod! I totally forgot that this is your gig! I can't believe it!"

"David, what are you doing here?"

"I'm subbing for Wolf Davis. This is so great, man. You are so lucky to get to do this every day."

"David," said Saul, whispering harshly, "the musicians in the string section are very upset."

"Upset?" laughed David. "What about? Tired of playing whole notes?"

"They're upset with you."

David caught himself. "With me?... but... why?"

"David," said his older mentor, "you don't jump up and down in an orchestra."

"What?"

"You do not jump up and down in an orchestra."

And Saul gave him a very disapproving look and walked away. They hated him. All the string players. Just what he needed. They didn't even know him and they hated his jumping guts.

When Act Two commenced he was tenser than before. Now he had one more thing to worry about. Get the notes right but don't jump. Feel it but don't let your body show it. The audience shouldn't notice the musicians. The orchestra shouldn't notice David Stein. This was not the David Stein rock'n'roll Revue. Be a cog and do your job and do it well. His brain was going off in too many directions. Don't think about nervousness. Don't think about screwing up. Don't think about that look the conductor just gave you. Arrgh! Focus. Play it right.

Now came Mandy Baskin's flying number. There she was on stage in her green Peter Pan suit. Hmm, nice-looking woman in her Peter Pan suit. Focus! Don't blow this! Time for her to lift off. Reach for your music stand and turn the page. She's lifting off. Don't watch her, watch your music! Schmuck! He looked at her taking off while he turned the page. He pulled too hard on the page and the music score fell off the stand and hit his keyboard. It hit a button.

FLEEEEEEEMMMMM!

A horrible monstrous feedback fleem sound came fleeming out of the keyboard. Screaming melting metal instead of gentle piano arpeggios. David looked around in horror for the help that was not to come. The conductor covered his ears with his hands. The orchestra tried to keep playing but the conductor had missed a beat. David thought he was about to die. He looked up. Mandy Baskin's winch was clearly out of synch with the orchestra, and the whole audience of five thousand people, folks from Peoria to Tokyo, clamped their hands over their ears as the skin-scarring fleem fleemed them all.

FLEEEEEEEEEEMMMM!!!!

The winch operator clamped his hands over his ears and poor Mandy Baskin clamped her hands over her ears. The winch started to sway laterally and Mandy started to swing out too fast over the audience. She came down, almost hitting

Ms. Selma Carter from Huntsville, Alabama in row twelve. Mandy bounced back up and came down again and her leg knocked the hat off of Amelia Drinkwater from San Diego, California. The crowd screamed as they all were fleemed. Mandy screamed too, trying to put her arms in front of her to protect herself and cover her ears at the same time. Now she head butted Hans Meister from Munich, Germany in row eleven. He got it worse than she did, her brow to his nose.

And as the crowd screamed as they all got fleemed, David yelled

"I don't know what to do!!!" But no one could hear him.

Sal uncovered one ear and reached over and turned the synth off. The fleeming stopped. Silence (except for a horrible ringing in everybody's ears). The orchestra and the audience unclamped their ears slowly, like the munchkins coming out to meet Dorothy. The conductor looked straight down at the ground. He was sobbing. And there, up near the ceiling of Radio City Music Hall, hanging limply from the winch harness, was Ms. Mandy Baskin, star of stage and screen. She was not conscious. She looked just like Peter Pan after he eats the poison cake that Captain Hook has made for him. Actually, she looked worse.

The show was stopped while Mandy was lowered and a new keyboard player could be found. Needless to say, the conductor asked David to leave in a most unpleasant tone. In a hybrid of panic and shock, he left the building. His shirt was soaked with sweat, his ears rang so loudly that he could barely hear the evening summer traffic on Fifty-first Street. All his biological systems were in an uproar and were trying to go into damage control mode. He was humiliated and scared. He had blown the job. The world knew and all the musicians in town would know. He was responsible for Mandy Baskin's possible injuries (not to mention Hans Meister's nose) and the ruin of a perfectly good show. He would be the subject of discussion in the Rockettes' dressing rooms. Dozens of beautiful women mocking him! And that's only if they could hear each other after the fleeming! People returning to Tokyo, San Diego, Germany and New Jersey, all would soon be telling how David Stein "that asshole", "that dumbkopf", had destroyed the last vestiges of real civilization by not being professional. He'd be dismissed as an amateur. His entire cool quotient had been decimated to the nth degree. He was nothing now.

CHAPTER THIRTY-FIVE

*T*he next day David skulked down to the corner of Eighty-sixth and Central Park West and furtively bought both *The New York Post* and *The Daily News*. He read them standing up, in Central Park, across the street from his block. *The Post* headline read:

"Radio City Music Hell!"

and *The Daily News* headline read:

"Peter Pan Never Lands!"

He read the *Post* article first.

"Last night's Rockettes show at the Music Hall ended up looking like an outtake from 'King Kong'. Panicked, screaming crowds, deafening noise, out of control machines and dozens of lovely ladies running off the stage as fast as they could...."

The Daily News said:

"Who says Broadway is dead? Visitors to New York love a show, and last night they got the show of their lives."

His head throbbed as he read on. Mandy was okay in the bumps and bruises department, but she refused to fly on the winch anymore. From now on "I'm Flying" would be done standing on the stage, which, out of necessity would be rather less dramatic. The TV spots showing her flying would have to be pulled, of course, and it was questionable as to whether this unfortunate event would hurt the box office sales so badly that the show might close. Hundreds of musicians, dancers, actors and crew might lose their jobs in the middle of a sweltering New York summer. The incident was under investigation and the name of the musician was not given.

David dropped to his knees next to a park bench, hands clenched, and gave thanks to God for not identifying him. Yet, anyway. He bit his nails to the quick. He was a nail biter by nature. His piano teacher, Manfred Silver, who had taught him when he was a young man, would look at his bitten fingers and say "Man, how can you play with those globs of shit?"

Manfred was a pissed-off old jazz man and a great musician. His method was a bit unusual. While David would take a lesson, Manfred would smoke a joint. He'd have a TV next to the piano tuned to "Casper The Friendly Ghost" cartoons. When they'd work on Chopin and the music said *con fuoco*, Manfred would say, "You see that? That means you gotta play the music with FUCK!" It was not the traditional European Classical method of teaching piano.

There had been many off-beat characters who had had an influence on David's formation. Rarely did he get to know normal solid citizens in the music world like Saul. God, what would Saul think of him now? He cringed deeper than he had already cringed at this thought. Nobody whose respect he craved would tolerate him now. Maybe he should commit *hara kiri* with a wooden sword at the *dojo*. A slow, painful, splintery, and extremely difficult demise. How could he make things right? Unconsciously thumbing through *The Post*, he saw an ad that read:

> *"The inner depths of calm await you. Float in isolation and leave the outer world behind.*
> *Discover the inner you. Isolation tanks are the way to go.*
> *Come to: Tanks For The Memory."*

At Nineteenth Street and 5th Avenue, he headed upstairs to "Tanks." A young woman in shorts and (what else?) a tank top, showed him the tank. It looked like a coffin. She opened a lid on one end.

"Our tanks are full of sterilized water saturated with salt. It's completely antiseptic, of course. When you get in, you're going to lie on your back. The water is warm and you'll be very comfortable. It's only a few inches deep. Now, some people worry about falling asleep and drowning in a few inches of water, but in this water, because of the salt, you can't drown because it keeps you buoyant. You'll float in utter bliss."

"What if I fall asleep and turn over in my sleep? Then I might drown."

"You won't."

Thanks, lady, he thought. I won't. And if I do, she'll just tell them next year that 'last year we had only one drowned customer.' Great.

"If you become uncomfortable in any way, the lid has no lock and is easy to open with your hand, or more likely your foot."

"Why my foot?"

"Because the lid is on this end and you're going to float with your head at the other end."

"Do I have to?"

"Well," she said blissfully, "the stereo speakers are at the other end and it's designed so that you'll hear quiet music at the beginning of your session, and then quiet music at the end to wake you."

"When you say 'wake me', is that 'cause I'll be asleep?"

"You might be. People have different experiences with the mind when they float. Because of the total darkness, the warm water, the floating, and the soundproofed nature of the tank, you may experience discorporation."

"Discorporation? Like I'll cease to exist?"

"No, no. Just the bodily sensation of 'no body'."

This oxymoron was enough to make David feel as if he were discorporating already.

"Have you ever had anybody just, uh, freak out and go nuts?"

"No freak-outs. Whatever is in you is what may come up for you."

This is exactly what he didn't want to hear. David's psychological catch-22 was that he wanted to clean up his inner self, but he didn't want to meet his inner self in order to do it. He was afraid that his id was just itching to burst out and take over. He wanted to keep it in check and wash and dry it at the same time. Otherwise he thought that he might turn into a dog biting its own tail, so to speak. Was this tank really a good idea?

Too late. She handed him a towel, flip flops, and a key to a locker. It was recommended that he wear only the key on one ankle and his birthday suit. Blissful Betty left the room and David faced his coffin. Well, how was he going to get to the bottom of all the craziness that had transpired in the last few weeks if he chickened out on a little mind exploration? Come on! He was so pent up from the "Great Fleeming" that he needed to look deep. This was supposed to be relaxing. What could be bad about that?

He opened the lid and looked in. Lord, it was dark in there. No nitey-litey. He liked night lights. He didn't like total darkness. He never knew what he might run into in the dark. He was also claustrophobic. What if somehow, *somehow*, the tank got locked? What if somebody hated Blissful Betty and wanted to ruin her business, and burst in during his session (which he'd never hear in his discorporate state) and locked him in the tank? What would happen first? Would he drown, suffocate, or go insane trying to get out? Wasn't this like deliberately taking advice from Vincent Price to get into a coffin in one of those old Edgar Allen Poe B movies?

Now you are buried aliiive! HOO HOO HOO HA HA HAHHH!

Did Peter Lorre secretly run this joint? Why should he subject himself to the panicky proposition of profound relaxation? Why wasn't the idea of relaxing... relaxing?

He picked up one foot and placed it in the tank. The water felt perfectly warm. Now the other foot. The bottom of the tank was smooth. He sat down in the water. Slowly, he stretched out on his back so that his head was away from the lid. He could hear soft New Age muzak from the speakers. Hey, he was floating! Wow! Just like they said you could do in the Dead Sea.

Now came the toughest part. Closing the lid. He sat up and reached down to the end of the tank for the lid. He closed it slowly...wait! He opened it and looked at the outside of the tank. He needed to make sure that there was no way that this tank could get locked. He wasn't Harry Houdini. God, whenever he thought of Houdini in a straight jacket in a chained up box under an icy river, he shuddered. He closed the lid. Holy shit, it was dark! No visual reference point in this watery cave! Twice more he opened it and shut it. Even after he lay down in the water, he tried lifting the lid with his toe. Just in case! By now the music had stopped and he was alone with David Stein, whatever that might mean.

As his body relaxed, tension came up through various twitches. His legs shook, he stretched, he yawned, he splashed (careful not to get the salt water on his face). The less he felt external stimuli, the busier his body got shaking out internal tensions. He began to hum. A slight quick echo and sound carried by the water bounced around the tank. At least no Martians on the bottom of the tank here. Wait. None? Okay, none. But what was on the bottom of the tank in the dark? Maybe big chewy New York water bugs? They were the local dinosaurs and they took no shit from nobody, no how. But wouldn't the salt kill them? Sure. But, the ocean was full of salt and it supported eels and urchins and God knows what. Oh, come on, what crap. You're alone in a tank that no germ could even survive in. Stop whining. This is great... isn't it? He began to sing.

> *"Oh give me a home where the Buffalo roam*
> *And the deer and the antelope plaaay*
> *Where seldom is heard, a discouraging word... "*

Well, no discouraging words in here. This is a place for soul searching, internal therapy, mental research and lukewarm salty well-being.

He floated on. He began to hear his own heartbeat.

Bum BUM, bum BUM, bum BUM...

He heard his own breath as it slowed. Inhale, exhale.

Hmmmmmhhh, Foooowaaaahhhh,

Hmmmmmhhh, Foooowaaaahhhh,

He coughed.

AhhCHuuuuuh!

He became quiet. He felt something with his hand! AAAHH! It was the wall of the tank. He moved his arm away from the wall and slowed his breath again.

He thought that he heard his blood coursing through his body. It seemed to sound like a Grand Prix auto race.

He remembered Christmas morning as a kid. New race car set. An Eldon Race Car Set. The cars were orange. They raced around the figure-eight track on the dark green living room carpet. A car flew off and landed eight feet away. The carpet always looked like an airplane view of a lush jungle. Whenever he'd stare at that carpet his eyes would lose focus and he'd be almost in a trance. But now he was in a tank induced trance and he knew it. Or was he? Was he in the tank? He could reach out and touch the wall again. He could lift the lid with his toe again. But, he didn't want to anymore. He wanted to go in further.

He returned to Christmas. He looked at the tree. He scanned the room and to his right he saw the old 1940's radio cabinet. It was old when he was born. Full of lights and dials and wood. Striped patterns in the wood. He reached for the radio and turned it on. He heard "Oh What A Beautiful Morning" from "Oklahoma."

He saw his parents walk by, but he couldn't see their faces. He was little and didn't look up that high. He was involved with the gifts on the floor. He looked at his hand. It was so little and fat and round! The room was dark because the apartment looked out on a courtyard. His mother must have hated that view even though she never told him, because thick drapes shut out what little light might have come in. The tree was lit, though, and dominated the room. The lights on the tree grew larger and blurred as if he were squinting. He heard angels singing. He saw a flock of little angels balanced on the tree branches. Their hands were cupped and little candle-like flames rose from their cupped hands. They sang "Oh What A Beautiful Morning." They turned and smiled at him. He could see them from his perspective and simultaneously see himself from another angle sitting on the floor in those navy blue shorts with the button suspenders. Fat and round and blond. Rosy-cheeked. Rays of light streamed down on him from the angels. Why would he ever want to leave this room? Does everybody have a room like this, somewhere in their memory? A safe room where there's God and love and Christmas and music and toys and parents?

Now, the light grew bright and the ceiling peeled back and the desert sun burned down and he was in Africa. People were dying all around him. They starved. Flies covered their eyes. They were not fat and round except for their bloated empty stomachs. Animal carcasses lay on the ground. All bones. They had died almost meatless.

There was a sign on a post. His vision reached towards it. It read: "Here lies reality, cracked and gone." On the bottom of the sign was a signature. It was in script. He couldn't make it out. Was it in an African language?

An old man, a shaman, approached him. He was wrapped in robes that had once been bright, but that were now worn and dull. He used a walking stick to help him.

"Hello," said David. The shaman pointed at the sign with his stick. "I know, I'm trying to read it," said David.

"*Nafalazed atomo comanta*," said the shaman.

David smiled and shrugged. "I don't speak the language."

"*Nafalazed atomo comanta!*" argued the old man. Again he pointed at the sign. He hit the sign with his stick to make it perfectly clear that David needed to understand the writing. David got closer to the sign and stared at the signature. It shimmered in the heat. Still it was illegible.

"You know who wrote that sign?" asked the shaman.

"You speak English?" replied David.

"Did you write the sign?" said the shaman.

"Me? no, of course not. I'm just a visitor here."

"Tell me who wrote it," the shaman ordered.

"I don't know who wrote it."

"You know exactly who wrote it."

"I do?"

"Tell it to me."

"Bob Mahozada wrote it." David was shocked at his own words. He didn't feel as if he knew this to be the truth and yet the words had come out of his mouth naturally without his thinking about them.

The old man touched the sign again with his stick. This time he let the stick rest upon the sign. With his face he gestured to David to look again at the signature. David bent close and the shimmering ceased. As clear as could be, the signature read "Bob Mahozada."

David stepped back from the sign. The shaman's stick turned into a glowing trumpet. The shaman held the horn to his lips and blew. He played a Louis Armstrong-like Dixieland lick ending on a high note and the sign disintegrated, except for Mahozada's signature, which hung in the air. The shaman blew another lick and the signature flew away. The shaman turned to David, put one hand on his hip and smiled. David smiled back at him. The shaman looked up in the direction that the signature had flown. He sprouted large feathered wings. He held out his palm for David to slap it.

"Pastato mukumpa ohfonya!" he said.

David slapped his palm. David offered his palm and the shaman slapped it. Hard. The shaman flew off with his horn, chasing after Mahozada's signature.

David stood alone in the African heat. He heard music, but from where? Somebody was singing to him from far away. The skull of a cow lay in the desert. It opened its mouth and sang with the voice of Barbara Streisand.

> *"I remember every little thing that happened*
> *Like it happened yesterday*
> *The good times that we had*
> *And the time you went away*
> *You left me feeling empty*
> *When you took your love away*
> *But still I can remember*
> *Like it happened yesterday"*

He was in darkness in the flotation tank. Streisand was playing through the speakers. His body was totally, incredibly calm. The song ended. Reluctantly he opened the lid an inch with his toe. The light was very bright. He didn't want to leave, but he knew he had to.

CHAPTER
THIRTY-SIX

*T*he letter was from Florida. David knew that it was from Thossian before he saw his name on the envelope.

Dear David,

I had a dream last night that you should know about. My dreams these days seem to have more information in them than one expects in typically normal dreams.

In the dream I saw my grandfather playing the bass with a band in a nightclub. He was very happy and his joy affected everyone in that room. A figure of a man completely wrapped in an almost mummy-like veil stepped up to the microphone to take a sax solo. As he started to play (if you can call it that), everyone screamed and covered their ears. The musicians left the bandstand. Except for Grandpa Mervyn. Though he frowned, he kept playing, or trying to play, anyway. This veiled man played a horrid kind of series of sounds and blood started to spurt from Grandpa's ears. He collapsed. I saw him die in that club.

I then looked at the bandstand and saw you, David. You were sitting at the piano with your hands on your lap. You looked unsure of yourself and unsure what to play or do. I am telling you about this because I feel that, 1) the Mahozadans had something to do with Grandpa's death and, 2) I believe you are somehow necessary to the resolution of this problem.

There is something sinister about the Mahozadans that goes well beyond musical cultishness. Charlie Parker's fans may have written "Bird Lives" on the New York City subway walls, but they weren't out to hurt anybody (except themselves perhaps, with heroin).

I have told you before that since listening to the tape, I receive information in many different ways that I hadn't been able to utilize before. Believe me David, I know that I'm right about this. Stay away from the Mahozadans for now. The time may come when you will be instrumental in helping <u>con</u>struction to win out over <u>de</u>struction. Just be aware and watch for signs.

Thossian

David felt as if Thossian and he had been hanging out in the same dreams. Was he developing psychic powers like Thossian? He'd only heard a piece of the tape, and only once. Thossian had heard it twice. There was no "New England Journal of Medicine" study on this tape and its effects.

He had to put together his own information. Were musicians affected differently from non-musicians? Well, weren't they different from other people anyway? Were all the images of musicians as crazy or saintly or devilish or sensitive just hype? Which came first, the musician who was sensitive or the sensitive being who became a musician? How about his childhood pal Joey who seemed to be the most tone deaf person on the planet? He was a doctor now. To him, music was just "entertainment" and he seemed to be waiting for David to get a "real" job.

And just what did "entertainment" really signify? "Divert. To keep busy in a pleasant way. Amuse."

Amuse: *"To cause people to laugh or smile. Also, in connection with the muses."* The muses were the nine Greek goddesses of the arts: Calliope, Clio, Euterpe, Melpomene, Terpsichore, Erato, Polyhymnia, Urania, and Thalia.

Was this view of music and musicians just an academic self-congratulation or did it mean more? For David, music wasn't academic at all. To him, academic meant *"Having no practical application. Theoretical."* That wasn't what music was about.

Music at its best was about transformation from the earthly to the heavenly. He knew he was being transformed. Yet, on his jobs he forgot all this, frequently. The circumstances of the work were often so desperately mundane that all spirit was squeezed out. When people asked him if he enjoyed his work he'd reply "Every other note." He meant it. Some gigs were such a thrill that he might joke with the client that he should have paid *them*. But more often, he skulked through the job, bitter and nearly despondent.

He was confused now, because so much had happened lately that disproved the lie that music didn't matter. Nevertheless, he knew that if tomorrow he were to play a wedding or a smoky restaurant, there was a good chance he'd be miserable. He knew that it all depended in the end on what he thought about what he was doing.

He had always wondered about people who seemed to have the most menial, thankless jobs and yet smiled and seemed to be genuinely happy doing them. If he were playing piano at a party at The Plaza Hotel and he hated it, and he went into the bathroom and the bathroom attendant seemed to be enjoying himself, what the hell was going on? Who's right? No, it wasn't at all about being right. It wasn't really even about the work. It was how you felt about what you were doing. If he could play the piano and feel as if he were communing with God, it wouldn't be an issue that the room was full of obnoxious drunks. But if he felt like a high-priced slave, that slave mentality would poison the best gigs in the world.

He had slid into the musician's life when he joined a band in college. He had no understanding of any other life choice. It wasn't about the money when he started. There was none. It was about playing music for fun, meeting girls, attention, a sense of being significant. Wanting to feel different. Now, all these years later, what was it about? He never had much money. What was he doing, playing the piano all this time? What was it? He wished he could ask every person who had ever heard him play. Do I matter? Did I do something that moved you? Did I change your life in any way? Did I improve it?

Recent experiences were forcing him to confront himself. He was in the middle of change, half tadpole and half frog. Neither fully formed. Neither meeting its full potential. He was ambivalent about his half amphibian state. Above all, he hated the inertia, the downtime between transformative moments. How could he know if he'd get where he wanted to go?

David knew that if he went on as he always had, he'd end up a dead man posing as a live musician.

CHAPTER
THIRTY-SEVEN

For the next two weeks David worked out at the *dojo*. He
was starting to feel as if he belonged. There was a sense
of camaraderie on the mat. Whether you were a banker or a
butcher, out on the mat it didn't matter. Aikido seemed to be an
economically classless society. There was a set of social strata
starting with the black belts and working its way down to the
beginners, but it didn't seem to impede people's friendliness.

Considering the potential deadliness of the art if applied on
the street or in a *dojo* accident, the general mood at the *dojo* combined that of a serious discipline with a certain lightheartedness
that made you want to keep coming back. Though Hara Sensei's
usual demeanor was quiet, and his default facial expression was
a frown, at times he was quite the cut up. In fact, because of his
somber appearance, his occasional joking comment when dem-
onstrating a technique always drew genuine laughter from the
class. Because this man (who could clearly tear any heads off
that he chose to), was shy and retiring, his humorous moments
stood out and brought the group together. Most of them felt

honored and very lucky to have such a teacher there in the flesh. And as we have noted, beyond watching him throw, you learned the most from him when he threw *you*. When he tossed you wherever he felt like tossing you, you knew instantaneously that this was the way to do Aikido.

David found himself seeking out Jenna as a partner in class. He liked the physical intimacy of working with her. It was like a choreographed dance routine. In fact, most practicing was preset. If Sensei decided that the class was going to work on a *kokyu-nage* throw for the next fifteen minutes, everybody worked on *kokyu-nage*. When he switched and demonstrated *kata-tori kote-gaeshi*, the class switched partners and worked on that throw.

In Aikido, you defended yourself without attacking. In fact, most Aikidoists neither punch nor kick except upon occasion. Let the other person attack if they choose to. They will end up on the ground. Aikido is a circular art and there is great power in the use of the circle. The attacker is drawn into the vortex created by the Aikidoist's movements. The attacker is controlled and subdued, ideally without injuring him.

In the street in a real situation the rules may change. Just as in music, you internalize the rules and then throw them out the window. Rules in music, martial arts, and life have a structuring function that tend to make things work, but there are times in all three areas when circumstances may make employing the rules an impossibility.

David was at a reasonably high level in jazz and a rote beginner's level in Aikido. He understood, though, that just as in jazz where the improviser must think on his feet when creating music in real time, so must the martial artist react to any possibility that arises in class or even in an altercation. He knew that both the jazz pianist and the Aikidoist needed to have absorbed an end-less arsenal of choices at the ready. In both areas he was trying to reach higher. Both areas of learning spurred him on in the opposite area. His piano practicing made him want to be a bet-ter Aikidoist and his *dojo* practice made him want to be a better musician. He now had two role models of great skill and stature to follow.

And so it was that he returned to Billy Kovac's cramped apartment. He was surprised to find that Billy taught classical music to his jazz students as part of their training.

"Look man," he said through his nose, "Mozart didn't get up in the morning and say 'Gee, I think I'll write some old fashioned shit today.' He heard some music in his head very clearly, the way you're hearing my voice and he wrote it down. It came into his head from somewhere and he just put it on paper. Now it's sitting on my piano in front of you hundreds of years later and it wants to be heard! So guess what? You're the man who can help Mozart out and play it so that the rest of the world can receive what Mozart received on the day he received it."

"Where do you think he received it from?" said David.

"Well, I never met the cat, but from what I know as a musician and from studying history, I'd say he got it from God. And he also got it from everybody he'd heard before, like Haydn. And Beethoven heard it from Mozart and down the line ad nauseum. So there's the apprentice aspect, where composers have listened to other composers and improvisers have listened to other improvisers and they repeat it and they add on something new and they reinvent the wheel. And then there's the gift."

"Um hum," said David, nodding in agreement.

"The gift is native musicality. I have it, you have it, lots of people have it. You know that you can help nonmusical people to improve, but you can't make them intuitively musical. That's why there's a two-year old kid out there who sings on pitch and standing next to him is his dad, who after a lifetime can't sing."

Billy then proceeded to play part of a Mozart sonata. David could play the notes but what he had trouble matching was the tone, the clarity, the confident evenness and flow. How did Billy make his clothed-over piano sound so clean and bright and warm?

As David listened, he looked at the piano. Completely clothed-over. Not a spot of visible wood or metal. Only the plastic keys could be seen. He thought of Mervyn's bass and Jack's trombone. Was Billy one of them? Did his piano shine with that incredible glow beneath the cloth? Is that why it was covered, so nobody would know? But why? He resolved to find out.

Billy stood up.

"Okay, now play me the first eight bars. I'm less interested in the notes than in the intent behind the playing. You want some O.J.? Sorry 'bout the AC not working."

"Sure, thanks," David said, as Billy walked toward the slightly-out-of-sight kitchenette.

"Gah 'head, play it," said Billy.

David was unfocused. He wanted to pry up the cloth covering that surrounded the periphery of the keyboard. If he could just see if it glowed....

"No, no! Come on, David, it's in four! Dum, Dadadada Dum, Dadadada Dadadada Dadadada Daaah, Da."

David listened to Billy's words as his hand crept over to pull at the cloth. He pulled and it gave way. He was going to find out. Oh shit! He'd ripped a layer of cloth and now it was hanging there torn. And, he hadn't even reached the wood. David played the passage again. He tried to watch the keys but he kept seeing the torn cloth. Here comes Billy with two glasses of orange juice. He felt like a kid caught with his hand in the cookie jar.

"Lighten up. It's not Wagner. This is a beautiful, light, lyrical piece. Don't be an elephant."

David tried desperately to flatten the exposed piece of cloth. He must have been nuts to do this. He was a dead man and Billy was going to hate him and excommunicate him.

"Let me show you again."

David morbidly got up and Billy sat down. The corner of the cloth stood curled out. He must see it!

Once again a gorgeous sound came out of the piano. This time Billy even interpolated a few jazz notes into the structure of the passage that were somehow in keeping with the spirit of the composition.

Come on. How could he not see the tear?

Billy stopped. His field of vision passed slowly over the tear. He looked David straight in the eye. David gulped dryly. Billy spoke slowly, attaching great import to every word.

"The music came through Mozart naturally. He heard it and he wrote it down. Or, he heard it and he played it as he heard it. Whether you call it composition, improvisation, musical dictation or inspiration, it was as much a natural process for him as stretching is for my cat."

Not a word about the torn cloth. David felt a combination of guilt, relief, gratefulness and transcendence. This man was going to teach him even if David acted like a juvenile jerk.

CHAPTER
THIRTY-EIGHT

*L*ittle Albert Amato was mesmerized by Marcel Marceau. Every time he saw the great mime on television he stood up in his living room and tried to imitate him. Marceau often relied on tried and true routines that went over well on TV. The man enclosed in an ever shrinking box. The man pulling and being pulled by a kite. The transformation from baby to adult to old man.

Albert was only six when he first saw Marceau. As he grew older, he learned to parallel Marceau's routines in front of the TV with great detail. He performed at family parties. Soon he had added his own twists to the routines. By the time he was ten he performed at parties for money. His mother would manage him, taking care of bookings, costumes, payment, and transportation.

After high school he attended NYU as a theater major. A charming and industrious young man, Albert took the initiative in trying out his busking skills on the tourist crowds around town in spring and summer.

And so it was on a lovely spring day that he put on his white face makeup and black leotard and hailed a cab at West Fourth Street and Sixth Avenue. When he reached Eighty-fifth Street and Central Park West the cab turned into the transverse and crossed the park to the east side. At Fifth Avenue the driver made a right. As the cab approached the Metropolitan Museum Of Art's main entrance at Eighty-second Street, Albert paid the driver. This way, when they pulled up he'd be ready to jump out quickly and go into action. On a beautiful day like today in such an excellent location, he could easily make a couple of hundred dollars.

Albert thanked the driver, threw open the door and jumped out. He moved like a Green Beret on a raid. He walked briskly towards the great staircase where tourists sat enjoying the weather.

Albert froze in the middle of his stride. He held the pose till a number of people noticed him. A two-year-old boy named Michael Rose approached him. Albert instantly and effortlessly mimicked the child. When seventy-nine year old William Jones hobbled by with his cane, Albert became his clone. Kenji Obata took pictures of Albert, who returned the gesture in mime. Emily Miller, who weighed three hundred and seventy-five pounds got the treatment as did glamorous Shawna Udell. Albert was a hit with the crowd.

Now, it was time to give them a thrill and bring the whole city into his sphere. He stepped off the curb. Miming a traffic cop he took over the traffic. The audience went nuts. He stopped a limousine. Albert relaxed inside when the driver obeyed. His eyes darted around looking for real cops to overrule his new position. Seeing none, he continued. Emboldened now, he went after an approaching bus. He'd done this before and he knew he could handle it. Before he jumped up on the bumper to eyeball the driver, he looked him over from the street. The driver looked reasonably good-natured. Albert climbed up and stared at the driver. The driver waved back. Albert knew he could enlist this man. He jumped to the street and mimed towing the bus with a rope. The bus driver played along and the bus moved by inches in response to Albert's mock tugs.

After allowing the bus to pass, Albert saw a taxi rolling up. The driver, who had a solemn expression on his face, hit his brakes when Albert jumped into his path. He cursed at Albert. Albert pretended to cry and the crowd laughed. Albert wagged his finger at the driver and then he started to pretend to tow the cab with a rope. At this point Albert was just a bit unnerved by the cabbie's angry look. He wasn't fully connecting with Albert's plan. The last thing Albert Amato saw through his earthly eyes was the faraway look in the driver's eyes. Then the screech of the taxi starting up at full speed. Albert felt his foot go under the wheel.

The next thing Albert could see through his brand new unearthly eyes was an aerial view of Fifth Avenue. It was as if he'd been catapulted up over the street. There were so many potential customers sitting on the museum steps. And now they were on their feet! Were they going to applaud him? At the top of the steps, Albert's flying head noticed a man in a tuxedo who was watching him. Albert wondered why he was wearing a tuxedo. Then Albert's head fell and hit the pavement. It didn't hurt, because he couldn't feel anything. He landed on his side, which made it difficult to look at the crowd.

Through his new unearthly ears he could hear the screams of horror as they all got up and ran away. Certainly not what he wanted. How was he going to pass the hat if they ran away?

He lay there alone until the police and the ambulance arrived. They put him in two body bags. He lay in the morgue for a day until his family came to bring him to a funeral home. The man who handled him at the funeral home did a sloppy job. He did put him in the casket with his body, but he neglected to face his head in the correct direction. It still lay on its side while the body lay on its back. When the lid was closed for the funeral, Albert was supremely pissed off. If only his parents and his brother Matty knew. They never would have paid the funeral home.

He heard Matty eulogize him at the funeral the next day. It was hard to hear through the closed coffin, but he got the gist of it. Then he heard them watching videos of him performing. That was nice. He heard his girlfriend, Tina, sobbing, but he also heard that piece of shit Tony Sykes moving in under the guise of comforting her. Ooh, if he could have opened that coffin he'd have kicked that asshole's face in. He'd have torn his head off...so to speak. He could only hear all of this with one ear, because his head lay on its side.

Later that day a bitter and lonely Albert Amato heard the priest speaking at his grave. He felt them lower him down. He wasn't actually uncomfortable in the traditional sense, because his head was severed from his body, and even more importantly, because he was dead.

After this, all went black. All had actually been black since he'd been in the coffin because there was no light, but now all went black in the sense that he became devoid of consciousness. Lights out.

CHAPTER
THIRTY-NINE

David was haunted by Thossian's dream. Thossian had warned him to stay away from the Mahozadans. Were they really dangerous, or was Thossian's grief getting the better of him? By day it all seemed silly. The sound of the city nullified any serious thinking about this. At night, he wasn't so sure.

If he didn't have a gig in the evening, he'd go to the *dojo*. He also put in many hours practicing at the piano. He worked on his touch, his evenness, phrasing, pedaling, fingering, sight-reading, and his ear. He wanted to play like Billy and throw like Sensei. He couldn't express it in words yet, but he wanted to integrate all the loose ends in his life and stand centered. He wanted, to be whole.

Everything he started seemed to fail to complete itself. He'd never married, didn't have kids. Musically he'd had his moments, but he felt as if he hadn't left a meaningful mark in the world. Though he could sometimes express himself at the piano, he still felt unexpressed as a soul. He kept hoping that there was something greater, something more significant within him than that which anyone had yet heard or seen from him. This something, if it indeed existed at all, needed to be able to come out. David saw himself as a flashlight with an old battery in it that has to be banged on to work for a moment or two before fading out again. Since the tape, he was convinced that a better and more substantial battery waited within him for its cue to shine. Somehow whatever potential resided in him could not seem to start itself up. Was enlightenment supposed to appear in a flash or evolve gradually? He obsessed about these things. He was driven to discover the truth about himself, but felt that he was running in circles, always just inches or moments away from the answer.

Billy called him to cancel their next lesson. He told David that he'd picked up some kind of bug while playing festivals in India. He was too sick to teach. David was distraught. This was the wrong time for Billy to shut him out. David was on a quest and he couldn't tolerate this information stoppage. Of course he didn't tell Billy. Billy said he'd call him when he felt better. Meanwhile, he should practice.

"Reality Cracked" read the small display ad in the back of the Village Voice on the Cafes and Clubs page. It grabbed his attention immediately. *"The Varton White Sextet. Varton White, trumpet; Eddie Clovis, sax; Olaf Kiel, bass; Fantastico Estrada, drums; Neumann Mandible, keyboards; Ernst Harriman, guitar."*

There's that fucker Clovis again, he thought. And stealing a phrase from his flotation tank vision! He knew he had to go. He had to see what Clovis played on his own turf. The gig was in Brooklyn.

David was lost in Brooklyn. He'd been born and raised in Manhattan. Manhattan, as important as its prestige might be, did not lend itself to rights of braggadocio as much as saying "I'm from Brooklyn." Movies all throughout the twentieth century were loaded with tough cool guys saying "I'm from Brooklyn." Saying you were from Manhattan didn't even make sense to most people in the world. People moved to Manhattan from all over the country and from all over the world, but unless you could fine tune it and say "I'm from Harlem", being a Manhattan native was usually disconcerting and surrealistic to other folks from other places. It spoke to them of no sense of community. But to say that you were from Brooklyn spoke of being macho, surviving the tough streets, a rakish thick-skinned attitude that was a symbol to the outside world of New York's peculiarly cool people. Every black and white World War Two movie had a guy from Brooklyn. Usually Italian, sometimes Jewish or Irish. In recent years that same cool Brooklyn movie guy was black or Hispanic.

David was severely lost in Brooklyn. Manhattan is the easiest place in the world through which to navigate. It's a simple graph for most of the island. You're either heading uptown or downtown, west or east, but Brooklyn is a whole other animal. It's bigger than Manhattan and everything isn't so graphable.

Arriving at the elevated subway station at night, he might as well have been in Katmandu. He had to repeatedly ask directions to the club, and nobody seemed to have heard of it. Nobody had heard of "Momphom." He had no idea what "Momphom" meant. On a dark sidestreet he found the address, but no club. He checked the Village Voice ad, which had been crumpled in his pocket, next to his crumpled money. It seemed to be correct. The band was supposed to play at 11 p.m. and it was now 10:35. Then he heard vibrations from a door one floor below the street behind a gate.

He walked down the suspended metal staircase past open overstuffed garbage cans (and one rather healthy rat) to the door. He pulled open the heavy metal door and he felt, rather than heard, it creak. That's because upon opening the door, the vibrations became much louder.

He entered a dimly-lit room. The walls were decorated by garish dayglo posters of scantily-clad mythological-looking characters. He was overwhelmed by the pungent aroma of cigarettes, pot, wine, urine, disinfectant and sweat. The place was pretty full of people, most of whom looked to be in their twenties. They sat transfixed at their tables, staring and slowly shaking their heads horizontally. Their eyes stayed fixed on the bandstand while their heads did this lateral swing. They looked as if their heads were saying "No" while their eyes were saying "Yes, Master."

There, on the small raised bandstand, was the Varton White Sextet. Varton White had a shaved head and a downward-facing mustache that made him look professionally unfriendly. He and Eddie were playing a jagged melody that they harmonized (if you could call it that) in dissonant intervals. The drummer was playing some sort of funk groove that sounded as if it had been recorded and then played backwards. Somehow, impossibly, the cymbal sizzles almost sounded backwards, too. The two men swung their horns laterally and the crowd followed with their own synchronized head motions.

David stared at the band and found that his head started to go into the lateral move. He closed his eyes and took out soft rubber ear plugs and stuffed them into his ears. He went to the back of the club as far away as he could from the band and then watched them. What the hell was going on here? And since when in the history of jazz did a band ever go on early?

The band switched into a 5/4 groove and the pianist started to play clusters of notes with his elbows. Ernst Harriman, the guitarist, also played tonal clusters while using a steak knife as a slide on his guitar strings. The effect was awful and bone-jarring.

David tried to keep his head still, but now noticed that something was wrong with his vision. Either that or some other paranormal phenomena was emerging. The air in front of Harriman seemed to be shimmering the way it does on a hot day as heat radiates up from the cement. Was the music causing this? The air-conditioning seemed to be working in the club, yet the audience had sweat on their faces. Nobody seemed to be eating or drinking. They were so attentive that they looked as if they were about to explode.

All David could think was that whatever the tape had done to him, this band was working the opposite possible effect on the audience. The combination of the thump of the drums with the tonal clusters and the disharmonic harmonization of the melody by Varton and Eddie was gripping. David felt as if he were trapped in a microwave oven and that his blood was boiling. He took out the earplugs in order to close his ears tightly with his index fingers. He closed his eyes again and tried to regain his composure. Nobody saw him. They were either in front of him looking at the stage or simply too entranced to see him. No waiters walked by.

Now Fantastico went into a fast chaotic cymbal-dominated drum solo. Olaf added a horrid-sounding looped bass line on his six string electric. Eddie and Varton started to chant unintelligibly, which sounded almost like organized dog howling.

David felt terrible pressure in his ears and had to take away his hands. Now he was forced to either listen or leave. He decided to leave. And then Fantastico hit a flurry of notes on his crash cymbal and the music stopped. Eddie and Varton kept conducting the crowd's lateral head movements with their instruments. This went on silently for about sixty seconds. Then Varton looked at Eddie and they stopped. Total silence. No applause, no comment, no nothing. Then the band walked off the stage. They walked out the door.

Gradually, the audience returned into normal activity and conversation. David felt his biological systems cool down. He decided to talk to the musicians. He exited the club. He climbed the stairs to the street. There stood the band, talking to one another. He approached Varton White, who was talking to Olaf Kiel.

"Interesting set," he said.

"Was it interesting?" answered Varton White in a slow southern drawl. His response betrayed no emotion of any kind.

"It was different from anything I've ever heard."

White stared at him. He wasn't going to chitchat.

"What do you call your music?"

"My music calls me," retorted White.

"And where does it call you to go?" tried David, trying hard to dig into this guy.

"It calls me out of this world and into a new one."

David was about to ask him about the new world when Eddie Clovis came over and interrupted them.

"Don't speak with this one, Varton," said Eddie gruffly.

David's adrenaline filled him. "Why shouldn't he..." he began.

"He's not one of us," said Eddie.

"What do you mean, not one of you?" said David, raising his voice.

Now the whole band came over to listen. David felt trapped.

"You're a fucking fake and a pussy cocktail player", said Eddie. "You've never played music in your too-long life. You don't know what matters and you never will."

With that, Eddie, who towered over David, pushed him. David went backwards. He was in total shock that this was happening. His words caught in his throat.

"Are you fucking insane? I just came over to talk to..."

"You came to erase us, Notelicker. You'll be gone very, very soon."

Eddie pushed David again with his left hand. This time David stepped back with his right shoulder as the hand came. It rendered Eddie's shove nearly ineffectual. Eddie got madder. David heard the others laugh derisively at him.

"I'm taking you out now, Notelicker."

Eddie grabbed David by the collar with his right hand. He started to lift David up off his feet. David realized that he was about to get beaten to death. Without thinking, David grabbed Eddie's hand with both of his in a twisting *shiho-nage* grip. He centered himself making himself heavier and stepped forward close to Eddie and then passed him, twisting Eddie's arm up. He passed under Eddie's arm at great speed and spun around in place a hundred and eighty degrees till he faced where he'd just been. Eddie was big, mean, and totally helpless. He could neither punch nor kick with his arm twisted and caught in David's grip. Finally, David finished the throw bringing the still-gripped Clovis hand towards the ground with the rest of Eddie following. All this took less than half of a second.

Eddie Clovis, six feet one inch and two hundred and fifteen pounds of muscle and hate, slammed down on the pavement on his back. Very luckily for him, he kept his head up, or he would have been brain dead. The others gasped in shock as Eddie groaned in a very unmusical way. David looked at Eddie lying there, then at the others, and then, not wanting to press his luck, ran like hell into the dark, cool-movie-guy Brooklyn night.

CHAPTER FORTY

*W*hen David got home that night, he was buzzed. He was scared that they'd come after him, but he was proud that he'd defended himself. He was shaking so hard that he didn't even get angry when he tripped over Albert's head.

He had developed a very interesting co-independent relationship with the head. Sometimes the head was there and sometimes it wasn't. David knew better than to talk to it, and it generally didn't address him directly.

Albert didn't know why he was supposed to haunt this guy, but he knew to do it. Albert had unresolved issues. He sometimes manifested this with excruciating groans. He'd roll and shake and scream and fly in and out of the window at all hours if it were open.

In some ways they were alike. They were both artists who felt unexpressed and there's nothing more pissy and whiny and unpredictable than an unexpressed artist. Creativity is meant to create, not to sit within. David could not seem to get the right music out and Albert's present ability to do mime was.... well... severely curtailed.

Both men were also going through deep changes. David was trying to solve a great mystery and reach perfection. Albert found himself thrust violently into a new "life" and had yet to discover whatever purpose if any there might be in it.

So, when David tripped over Albert, David only perfunctorily looked back and Albert tried hopelessly to give David the finger, but it was just a physio-kinetic-phantom-limb memory. To David, Albert looked just a tad defeated. Not his usual grotesque and horridly id-filled normal self. David felt just a twinge of pity for his spherical poltergeist-like roommate. Looking sad and still bloody as ever, Albert rolled off into the unlit kitchen and hid behind the stove, sulking.

David sat down and tore open his mail. He hadn't looked at it in a few days. Mostly the usual. Bills, bills, and also a few bills. Con Ed, telephone, cable TV, rent, medical insurance, credit cards, and so forth. Also a free trip to Florida if you call right now and agree to visit our new condos by the sea. There was also a flyer from the Aikido *dojo*. *"Come join us for Hara Sensei's birthday! We will have regular class, after which everyone is invited out to Bonsai Restaurant on 18th St. for dinner. (Please bring your own money). Let's make Sensei's birthday a memorable one. Dress is casual."* David realized that the date was for the next night.

After Brooklyn, David didn't know if he'd ever leave home again. Now he had to avoid anyone who'd been fleemed at Radio City Music Hall and the Varton White Sextet, too. It was getting just a little chancy out there. But if he hid at home he'd never be able to work and then he wouldn't be able to pay his rent and then he'd be out on the street and they'd get him for sure. So, he decided to go the birthday party.

At the *dojo*, the people on the mat must have wondered why David was working so hard and particularly they must have wondered why his *shiho-nage* throws were so determined. Though one could learn hundreds of throws in Aikido, it was important to know a few throws really well. Not only did this make it more usable on the street, but it also helped when learning the endless variations on the basic throws. This principle also held in Jiu-Jitsu and Karate. Know your basics well. Keep polishing and polishing, as they say in Zen. It wouldn't help to know a hundred throws half-assed. Better to have a few techniques that were confident and powerful and reflexive. From this would naturally come the ability to learn the many variations. David understood this concept at the piano as well. It's all well and good to have fantastic ideas as a jazz pianist, but without a commanding physical technique, the ideas remain necessarily unexpressed.

David didn't see anybody wish Sensei happy birthday during class. Class was class. Sensei, a quiet and private man, probably didn't like this brouhaha all about his birthday. The high-ranking belts in the *dojo* had decided to honor him even if he didn't care to be honored. To him it was an invasion of personal space, however well-intentioned. Because he knew that they meant it as a tribute to him, he permitted it. Nevertheless, the last thing he wanted or needed was to be in the social spotlight.

After class everyone changed into their civilian clothes. David was surprised to see Sensei change into nice slacks and a flashy Hawaiian shirt. It made David realize that whatever else he was on the mat, he was after all, a human being. Jenna was wearing a light blue summer dress that made David stare. Simon actually had a tie on. This struck David as funny. This nasty bad ass wearing a tie. Another human!

The class walked over to the restaurant. Bonsai was a Japanese eatery with a few small tables in front. The *dojo* had booked a room in the back. It was a *tatami* room, named for the woven straw mats that covered the floor, even as they covered the *dojo* floor, hidden beneath the canvas covering. There was no covering here. In the center of this large room was a low circular table with settings for twenty-five people. Everyone left their shoes outside the room in neat rows. Sensei kneeled down on the mat at the table. Simon kneeled down to his left. Then Howard Masters, Jose Manuel, Edgar Chen, Doris Keane and the other high-ranking students. Jenna was to his right. David, seeing his opportunity, kneeled down to her right.

Jenna turned to him and said, "Normally, David, we do this by rank."

"Whoops, sorry!" Embarrassed, he started to get up.

Jenna took his hand. "Stay."

Once she said that, even Sensei couldn't have moved him.

Hot flasks of sake, Japanese rice wine, were brought. Each flask came with a small shot-size ceramic cup.

"Do you drink Sake, David?" asked Jenna.

"Ask me in a few minutes," he answered.

"You know you're supposed to drink the first shot without sipping it."

Their conversation was interrupted by Edgar Chen, who stood up, cup in hand.

"First of all I'd like to say that you don't have to kneel!" Everyone laughed, and most of them switched to a cross legged, seated position. "This is a party for Hara Sensei, who continues to inspire us all, and who teaches us the true way to harmony of mind, body and spirit. He has taught for many years, and he has many students. Still, few people in the world have the chance to study their area of endeavor with someone who is a master at his art. We are all especially lucky to have Sensei at the *dojo* night after night and year after year to work with. We get to see him demonstrate Aikido, and we get to find out what it's like to be demonstrated on."

The crowd erupted in knowing laughter. They had all had the pleasure of being slammed down or thrown far across the room. *Sensei* smiled like a little boy and bowed.

"So, please raise your cups and wish Sensei a happy birthday!"

Two dozen sake cups went up and David tasted his first sake. It tasted like hot turpentine. David gasped and Jenna laughed. The crowd sang Happy Birthday to Hara Sensei. David thought that they were better martial artists than singers, but it didn't matter. Their joy was palpable and infectious.

David was surprised to learn from Jenna that she was an artist. She made her living in graphic design, but painting was her *raison d'etre*. When she found out that David was a musician, her smile went right through him. He suddenly felt as if he really were a musician and not a *poseur*.

It's amazing how one well-placed compliment or insult from a fellow human being can direct another person up or down in their life. So many people are not as centered as they might be, and their sense of self gets knocked about by the winds of social commentary. Jenna's genuine warmth and enthusiasm about David's musical life was entirely welcome and refreshing. Instead of the patronizing comments like "But what do you *do*?" or "Can you make a living doing that?", her interest seemed to transcend monetary concerns. David was absolutely ecstatic to be sitting next to this beautiful woman, especially on a night like this.

Spoons started clinking on sake cups and requests of "Speech!" rang out good naturedly. Sensei waved them off, embarrassed, but finally realized that he wasn't going to escape this. David remembered an article that he had once seen in the *New York Times* listing the activities that most frightened people. Topping the list were singing in public and public speaking. Sensei seemed to be as susceptible as anyone else. He stood up reluctantly. Though his stature was short, his effect on people was that of a very quiet and polite jaguar. The group became still and listened.

"Okay, so today is my birthday. Thank you for coming to my party." He bowed almost imperceptibly as they clapped. "I have lived for seventy years."

David was fooled again. He had been sure that Sensei couldn't be more than sixty. How could he move the way he did in class? Others at the table were similarly surprised.

"Here is my plan for good health and long life. Practice Aikido."

Laughter.

"Meditate. Do *misogi* breathing exercises. Stay away from bad drugs. Sometimes drink sake," Big laugh. "but not too much."

Smile from Sensei.

"I came to this country many years ago. People ask me why I live in New York City. I tell them, not so crowded, like Tokyo." The group broke up laughing at this point. "I have had many *dojo*s since I came here. Some students here have been with me many years. I don't have family here, but Aikido *dojo* has been my family." Applause. "I hope that you enjoy Aikido practice. If you want to become good Aikidoist, you come to class regularly and practice hard. Your practice becomes yourself. After many years of practice, there is no difference between your practice and you. Aikido at this time then is not something you do. Aikido then is something you are. So thank you for becoming Aikido."

Laughter and applause.

"This is party. Keep speeches short. I am not politician. Okay, thank you, that's all."

The group applauded wildly. They really felt wonderful sharing this moment with their teacher. They felt that they were deeply in the group.

The professorial-looking fellow who David had met on day one, spoke. His name was Howard.

"There is an old tradition in Japan. Each person at the table gets up and sings." Lots of noise from the group, much of it nervous. "You don't have to be a great singer. It's a way for everyone in the group to participate. Who'd like to go first?"

Total silence. David felt his heart pounding. A young man with a crewcut stood up. David didn't know his name. He sang an aria from an Italian opera. He wasn't a pro but he gave a full-throated, over-the-top performance from the heart. They loved it.

Next, a woman who had moved to New York from Paris to study with Sensei sang "La Vie En Rose" in French. Her pitch was questionable, but her French won everybody over. It didn't hurt that the sake was taking effect.

David was feeling pleasantly disembodied. An Irish song was sung. Also some '60's rock'n'roll, "What I Did For Love" from "Chorus Line" (sung horribly, but who cared?), and one frightened person sang "Happy Birthday To You" in Japanese. Jenna got up and sang the title song from "The Sound Of Music." She had a pretty little soprano and her pitch was good. Now David had one more reason to like her.

Instead of sitting down, she pulled David up, totally against his wishes. The sake was covering his fears about performing in such an intimate setting for friends. Friends who had never heard him play or sing. He was just another guy with a *gi* on at the school. Now that was about to change, and he didn't know if he wanted it to. He took a deep breath and let it out slowly with a "ha" sound as they had taught him. They laughed.

"This is a song that was popular during World War Two," he began.

> *"Your eyes lit up the darkness on the night that we met*
> *I could see them shining even through the fog*
> *You stumbled and I reached out and I grabbed your hand*
> *And we found ourselves engaged in a little dialogue"*

He tried not to look directly at anyone, but he could still see the group. They were listening intently. For once he was relaxing enough to enjoy the sound of his own voice instead of trying to hide it. He sang slowly and confidently.

> *"I stammered as I tried to keep the conversation going*
> *I didn't want to let the moment go*
> *You smiled as you stood there*
> *And I knew that you could see*
> *That I was hopelessly enchanted*
> *Though we hadn't said 'Hello'"*

He didn't think about intonation, or how he looked. He didn't even think ahead to remember the lyrics. He just let it out. He was changing the vibration in the room.

"What a funny way to meet
The person you most want to meet
What a strange and funny world this is
No one knows just how it goes
Or even what's in store
What a strange and funny world this is"

He could feel them staring at him but he didn't feel their judgement. All he felt was love and friendship. He was getting energy from them as he gave them the song.

"And now as I look fondly back
Upon that wondrous night
The thought of you, brings to me a smile
Because though many many years have passed
I still have you to love
That foggy night we met
Brought us to walking down the aisle
It led us both to walking down the aisle"

He held the high note effortlessly and let the silence ring out. He waited just a beat before finishing the song.

"What a funny way to meet
The person you most want to meet
What a strange and funny world this is
No one knows just how it goes
Or even what's in store
What a strange and funny world this is"

He finished. He stood there in the quiet. Then they went nuts and cheered him to death. He took a Japanese bow and sat down. When he sat down, Jenna gave him an incredible hug and kissed him on the cheek. The kiss reverberated throughout his body. Between the sake, the song, the applause, the moment, and the hug and the kiss, David Stein almost disappeared into paradise.

After that, Howard Masters sang the old Motown tune, "The Way You Do The Things You Do" and even Simon got up. He gave his most serious look, the look that could disable bad guys in a dark alley. Then he sang "Guantanamera" in Spanish. He wasn't great, but it was so disarming to see Steely Eyes Simon Purcell sing, that it might as well have been a great Mexican mariachi tenor.

Now everyone had sung. Well, almost everyone. Hara Sensei stood up. Many of them thought that he was going to speak again. They stopped chattering as they realized he was going to sing.

His voice was deep, but certainly not lyrical. He had a gravelly sound. David thought that if he could swing, he'd make a good blues singer. David couldn't understand the Japanese words. He recognized the use of the pentatonic scale, so common in Japanese music. Sensei looked more serious then he had all night. He sang as if it meant life or death. David could hear the sound split into two as Sensei's rusty voice gave off overtones. The song seemed mournful, perhaps a dark Japanese equivalent of "Danny Boy". He knew that it was a great honor for all of them that Sensei was willing to go this far for them. The song ended and Sensei made a small stiff bow with a still intensely serious face. They stood up and cheered. Jenna did not hug him, because it would have been unseemly for her to do so. He was not the huggy type, except out on the mat where he might do a bear hug on you that would crush the breath out of you and force you to the floor.

"Okay, everybody sing," said Sensei. "Now finished. Time to eat!"

David stuffed himself, which helped to modify the effects of the sake on an empty stomach. He still felt high, but more coherent. When the evening broke up, he held his breath and spoke to Jenna.

"Feel like being walked home?" His heart was bashing away in his ears.

"By you?" she said with a quizzical smile. He couldn't read it. Was this headed for a big put down?

"Uh, I think so," he managed weakly.

She paused for a moment to think. He was miserable.

"Yes. I feel like being walked home by you." She smiled.

Va va VOOM! said David's heart.

"Good," he said, and smiled back at her.

It was a nice night. It was too bad that he kept thinking that the evil Mahozadan minions of the Varton White Sextet were going to pop out of the shadows. He wondered how powerful a martial artist Jenna was and if the two of them could take them on. Other than in his mind, none of them showed up.

They talked about Aikido, music, art, and their respective backgrounds. She was from Colorado. In fact she was going out there the next day for a couple of weeks to visit her parents. When she asked him how he came to study Aikido at the *dojo* he had to restrain himself from telling her the truth. He was so strongly attracted to this woman that he didn't want to ruin it by announcing that he was in the grip of a mystical experience. Better to let her get to know him and then gradually allude to it.

When they reached her door, he really froze. He was dying to grab her and kiss her, but whatever radar he might have had had been short-circuited by his desire to not blow it. She sprang up the steps to her beat-up brownstone and turned around to face him.

"I'll be in Colorado till August fifteenth. Wanna get together and go out for dinner when I come back?"

"I'd like that a lot," he managed to say, even though what he really meant was *hommina-hommina-hommina, y-y-y-yessss*!

She blew him a kiss and went into her building. On his way home he whistled "Singin' In The Rain."

CHAPTER
FORTY-ONE

*T*hat night he lay awake for hours. He couldn't get Jenna out of his mind. He tossed and turned and tossed. He got up and did some stretching that he'd learned in class. He sat on the dirty old green carpet with his legs out in front of him and tried to relax. He tried hard not to try. This didn't work. When he gave up trying not to try he found himself relaxing. Luckily, observing his own body relaxing, he didn't try to stop it. If this sounds confusing, so be it. Many folks find Zen to be confusing. That's part of the game. Sometimes clarity only comes after much confusion. Maybe after a long lifetime of confusion. If you were to grab somebody on the street and tell them the correct answers to the most important questions of existence, why are we here, who are we, where are we going, that doesn't mean that they'd care or get it. As the saying goes: *When the student is ready, the teacher will appear*.

If the listener ain't ready for the answer, the truth will go past them noiselessly. Why do they say that you can't change people? They say that you can't change people for a good reason.

When you've changed, you want to communicate your change to others because you think that you've learned the truth. Now listen. Just because you know the truth, somebody else may not be ready to hear it.

Two people staring at a painting. The first person sees the universal beauty and presence of God in the painting and cries and laughs and jumps up and down. God is actually waving at him from the painting and saying "Hello, here I am!"

The second person stands next to the spiritual jumper and examines the painting carefully and with an open mind and a double doctorate from Harvard. This person however, only happens to see paint and shapes and a tableau of some sort. The second person looks at the painting, then looks at the jumper and raises an eyebrow disapprovingly. The eyebrow-raiser lowers his eyebrow and moves on to another painting. What's the point? The point is that had the jumper turned to the raiser and said "Look! There's God! Isn't it great?", he wouldn't have made a jumper out of the raiser. If the raiser is ever to jump, he'll have to jump when he sees God himself. And he won't see God until he's ready.

When the student is ready, the teacher will appear.

Mr. David Insomnia lay on the carpet on his back. This is a good way to relax the body during panic attacks, when listening to music, after a hard day at the office, or to facilitate a meditative moment. Eventually, he relaxed into dreamland, a land that's generally referred to in story and song as a nice place, but, in fact, for Mr. Insomnia was really not always a nice place.

He found himself onstage in a beat-up theater. It was a variation on the actor's nightmare. He dreamed brand new permutations on this theme frequently. The basic premise was that he was in a show of some sort and had a featured role, but that he didn't know his lines, his blocking, or the songs. The first thing that happened (if you can have a first thing in dreamland) is that he looked like Billy Kovac. There he was alone on this *farshtinkener* stage in this ratty old place. Up on the proscenium stage he stood dead center looking down at the audience. He was Billy but he was David. I can't explain, it's a dream.

He spoke, facing the audience. "Forsooth, my lord, 'tis a soggy night for this sorry knight."

The audience laughed. The wind machine blew and Billy-David's long, stringy hair blew. Had he just been David, there wouldn't have been much hair to blow, but Billy had a good messy head full.

He was afraid because he hadn't learned his lines and the damned director wouldn't let him read from the script. He'd have to make it make sense like a jazz improvisation. Yes, that's the way to approach any impossible situation, he thought.

"Bring me the young Vampiress that I might feast upon her with mine eyes."

That'll work, he thought. I'm on a roll, they'll love this line. On walked the young voluptuous blond Vampiress. She had on a 1960's hippie-esque peasant blouse, very tight jeans, and too-high stiletto heels. She also had a devil of a time walking in them and almost tripped as she waddled over to him. She had bloody fangs. She spoke badly through the false fangs.

"You may call me Rachel," she moaned.

"Rachel what?"

"RACHEL UNREST!" she cackled.

He cowered as she held out her hands at him in a clawing gesture. The audience went "oooh!" He went down on his knees and thumped his chest.

"Never have these eyes beheld such beauty in a woman, dead or alive!"

"Guess."

"Guess what?"

"Dead or alive!" she said, crossing her bloody arms impatiently.

"Guess if you're dead or alive?" he said in a cockney accent.

"Yessss," she hissed, dribbling spit out her fake fangs.

"What is your name again?"

"Rachel."

"Rachel what?"

"RACHEL UNREST!"

David hesitated for a moment. He didn't know the script. He didn't know what was going to happen. He was afraid that he'd disappoint the audience. He had not appointed the audience, but he didn't want to dis-appoint them either. He went for the only choice that he could handle.

"I judge thee to be alive!"

"I'm DEAAADDDD!" she shrieked in the most horrible tones, as the dream soundman turned up the reverb to create bouncing echoes of her shriek. Something about her manner frightened David, who had become almost transparent. Her scream was so real! Maybe she *was* dead! How could this be happening to him? Billy's face fell away and he became David. He was frozen with fear. He didn't know what to say, what to do, and he was stuck on stage in front of an audience in a crappy little theater with a shrieking bloody dead woman. Now what? No time to think. Act! He took a chance.

"Thy fangs are false."

"Whaatt!?"

"Thy bloody fangs are but a theatrical device. Wax and lipstick."

"H-H-How d-dare you?" She was terribly embarrassed at this effrontery.

"Thy fangs are false, Rachel Unrest. Thou hast no power!"

"Yes I hast... I have!" she corrected herself. "I am the undead spawn of a bat and a witch and I am powerful beyond your wildest dreams!"

This was actually a nonsensical statement of sorts, as this was indeed one of David's wildest dreams.

"You are no Vampiress, but merely a student thespian with wax fangs. Thy garb is unfitting, thy makeup unflattering, and thy speech unintelligible."

Rachel was boiling over. She jumped over his head and landed in a flying Aikido somersault. She then proceeded to somersault at incredible speed round and round the stage. The audience roared its approval. David stood still. Rachel rolled off from where she had entered stage right.

David instinctively stepped to the front of the stage. He now looked like Billy Kovac again. He began to sing, and as he sang, an invisible band accompanied him. It was a sort of medieval polka.

> *"Roll and roll and roll and roll around the stage of god*
> *Waxy fangs and dribbling spit are dripping from your bod*
> *Oh!*
> *Am I in a dream state, or have I lost my mind?*
> *I'm driving on the thruway and I just hit my behind!*
> *Oh!"*

And now the knights from the Metropolitan Museum of Art's Medieval Room marched onstage from both wings. The band got louder and David got prouder. They sang en masse, in a triumphant, slower, big time production marching verse.

THE DISHARMONIC MISADVENTURES OF DAVID STEIN

*"RRRoll (big English 'R") and roll and roll and
roll around the stage of God
Waxy fangs and dribbling spit are dripping from 'er
bod
Oh!
Are we in a dream state or 'as 'e lost 'is mind?
We're riding through the countryside for all of
humankind
Humankind, (humankind) humankind, (humankind)
We are riding now for all of humankind! Two, free,
four!*

*RRRolling rolling rolling, we're carrying our spears
Carrying neuroses and we're chewing up our fears,
OY!
Bill is Dave and Dave is Bill and Rachel's really
dead
Can we 'ave free cheers, for a certain flying
'ead?!"*

Now the music modulated up a step and Albert flew on.
He smiled his biggest grin. He flew out over the crowd, which
"oohed" and "aahed" at this wonderful special effect. He flew
up to the ceiling and kissed Ms. Mandy Baskin, star of stage and
screen, who was still stuck up there from the great fleeming at
Radio City. She returned the kiss and waved to the crowd.

Waitaminit, thought David. This doesn't make sense? This
isn't Radio City. How can Mandy Baskin be here? Is this a
dream?

As the knights passed David, he opened the armor helmet of
each one. Luis was in the first one, and he smiled and waved to

David. Simon was in the next. Then Thossian, Eddie Clovis, Mervyn, Abby, and Jenna, who blew him a kiss. Then Sensei, then Saul, then Stefan. David was amazed, if not a little afraid to see Eddie. They all turned and faced the audience, arms around each other's shoulders. Final verse:

> *"RRRoll and roll and roll and roll and sing this little song*
> *Hope we didn't bore you if our rolling was too long*
> *OY! (and they all threw a fist high in the air)*
> *Rachel really isn't dead, that's just an actor's scream*
> *Now it's time for David to wake up. It's just a dream!"*

Massive prolonged applause. David now looked like himself. He took a Japanese bow. He took an American bow. He waved to the crowd. He and Jenna blew kisses to the crowd. She turned to him onstage and looked into his eyes.

"David. Wake up. Go ahead. Wake up now."

He woke up.

CHAPTER FORTY-TWO

"**C**ome in, David."

David was shocked to see how pale and drawn Billy looked. He'd also lost weight, but not the good kind.

"How are you doing?" said David, knowing that to ignore Billy's appearance would have been more awkward than to acknowledge it. Billy shook his head and made a face as if to say "no big deal".

"What kind of bug did you pick up?"

"A heavy one, man. Nothing you've ever heard of."

"Well, what's it called?"

"Sit down, David. There's no charge for today's lesson." David sat down on the small sofa. "There are some peculiar things going on in the world today."

David felt right at home with this line of conversation. Billy took his time.

"As a musician, you know that there are many layers of understanding. Many levels of perception. Many dimensions, many realities, endless possibilities. Perhaps you've experienced some of these viewpoints lately."

"I have."

"Good. So what I'm going to tell you is not going to be incomprehensible to you."

David sat forward on the sofa and clasped his hands and listened.

"Sound has always been a creation tool in the universe. All matter is vibration. The universe resonates with sound. Sound can build or sound can destroy. It can expand the spirit or take down the walls of Jericho. It can be the word of God or ear-splitting feedback from an amplifier."

David winced at the thought of this. He had not shared with Billy his adventure at Radio City.

"Those of us who love music have spent our lives learning how to organize sounds in a way that expresses our souls, and that reaches out to other souls. But there are others, who use sound for malevolent purposes."

David knew where he was going. "Like the Mahozadans?"

"Exactly. Like the Mahozadans."

"And what are they trying to do?"

"The Mahozadans are using sound to create a master race."

"Say that again?"

"They are using sound to win converts, kill their adversaries, and in the final step, they want to shatter reality."

"I think I saw a bit of that the other night in a Brooklyn nightclub."

"Who'd you see?"

"The Varton White Sextet. They're Mahozadans."

"Punks, David. Poor imitations of the man whom they idolize."

"Bob Mahozada?"

"Um-hum. The big cheese. The big saxmaniac."

"What's his story?"

"Grew up on Long Island. Started sax as a kid. He had some talent. His parents moved to the city so he could attend Music and Art High School. When I went to college at Manhattan School Of Music, he was there too. He was caught selling drugs in his freshman year and they expelled him. He begged them to let him stay. When they refused, he threatened the school administration. He was ousted. It was devastating for him. In his mind, he was God's greatest gift to the world. When a hip school like Manhattan kicked him out, he became bitter, and dare I say, twisted. Bob started reading dark books. He hung out with like-minded players who'd been rejected in one way or another from the music scene. Revenge through his music became his *modus operandi*. He wanted to be an innovator, but he also wanted to hurt people. He channeled his hatred into his playing. The angrier he was, the more that music that healed people seemed weak and contemptible to him."

"How did you learn all this information?"

"Like I said, I knew Bob."

"And where does this guy live?"

"That I don't know."

"But the people that've studied with him, they must know."

"Maybe. There's lots of ways for him to pass instructional materials without showing up in the flesh."

"But my recent experiences have told me that there's something more powerful in human interactions when people are physically present with each other."

"That makes sense. Still, it doesn't discount the possibility that a recording of music might affect you deeply."

"Well... that's how I came to you."

David told Billy the tale of the tape. Billy listened intently. When David finished, Billy spoke.

"What you heard on the tape, your experiences with the Mahozadans and our meeting, are not by chance."

"So it would seem."

David had that out-of-body feeling again. He had become remarkably calm. Intuitively, he knew that this would aid in his receiving Billy's information.

"Very soon, David, I will go into battle with the Mahozadans, and you will be coming with me."

"Are you an alien?" David said, expecting the unexpected.

"Worse," said Billy, with a serious look. "I'm a jazz piano player."

They both laughed.

"Well, that's an alien of sorts," David said.

"Yes it is."

"What do you mean, 'go into battle'? Ray guns, or battle of the bands?"

"Battle of the bands."

"You mean like a festival, or a cutting contest?"

"More like each side sends forth its best players to decide whose musical ideology is more powerful."

"Like David and Goliath with saxophones?"

"Your analogy is getting closer."

"Sounds like fun."

"It's not going to be fun. People may die playing this gig."

"Go on."

"Bob's music hypnotizes. People either come over to it or it kills them. It boils their blood and physically kills them. The ones who come over to him don't die, but they're affected another way. This music creates genetic mutations. The children of Bob's listeners are sterile."

"Holy shit."

"Wait, it gets worse."

"How can it get worse?"

"Bob's final goal, after he creates a world of people who've been shaped by Mahozadan music, is to tear apart reality."

"This is getting to be a little bit much."

"Um hum. I know. Nevertheless, his sounds are so antithetical to the atomic structure of our world that he believes that he can disintegrate all matter. People, mountains. You name it."

David might have gotten up and walked out, had he not been to Momphom for the Varton White performance. If those guys could control the crowd, what could Mahozada himself do?

"Okay, so what do you mean I'm 'coming with you'?"

"I'll need a second person to back me up at the piano in case I'm unable to continue."

David was stupified. He still didn't feel fit to clean Billy's shoes when it came to the piano.

"I don't get it. Why don't you go get Keith Jarrett or Chick Corea? I'm just a *schmuck* trying to get a little bit better on the keys. You know I'm not in your league."

"You're better than you think, and when and if the time comes, the notes will come to you. You are the right man at the right time for this job. You're undergoing a spiritual transformation that, combined with your musical skills, makes you the man. Also, today I'm going to start giving you a fighting chance."

"Really?"

"Definitely."

David mulled for a moment. "Where does this gig take place?"

"New Hampshire."

"New Hampshire?! Like New Hampshire, the state?"

"Yeah."

"Where in New Hampshire?"

"More on that later. Right now, we need to work on helping you help us defeat Bob."

"Who's 'us' ?"

"There's a lot of good people out there working on this project."

"Hey, Billy?"

"Yeah?"

"This is some crazy shit you're telling me."

"Yeah."

CHAPTER FORTY-THREE

*T*eacher and student sat before the cloth-covered grand piano. The piano player from Brooklyn turned to the piano player from Manhattan.

"So here's the deal. All your playing life you've dealt with patterns. Compositional patterns, rhythmic patterns, chord patterns, scale patterns. As a performer you know that these patterns create reactions in the listener. You can make them laugh or cry. You can make them pensive, nostalgic, angry, you name it. You can give them an out-of-body experience. You can make them get up on the dance floor and shake their asses. You don't have to think this through when you're an artist. It's the natural way to proceed."

Billy demonstrated. He played music that David knew from Bugs Bunny cartoons. He played "As Time Goes By". He played blues, Scott Joplin, Chopin, Beethoven. Each piece created an immediate mood. David got the point. A point he already knew.

"There are patterns that you've probably never played," Billy continued. "Some of these patterns are right in front of you on the keyboard, just as Michelangelo said that the statue was already inside the block of marble and just needed to be released from its prison. Look at the keyboard. In a moment I'm going to show you something that was always there but you never realized it. Once I show it to you, you'll be totally amazed that you never saw it. And man, it's simple. It's a simple pattern. It's a scale. You've used major and minor scales. Blues scales, dominant scales, diminished scales, pentatonic, chromatic, ancient Greek modes, altered scales. Lots and lots of them. Now listen."

Billy started to play and almost instantaneously David knew that he knew nothing. The sound was inside him and speaking to him as clearly as if Billy were speaking words. David found himself inhaling and exhaling through his nose involuntarily in short fast repeated bursts. Billy stopped.

"Teach me," David gasped.

"Here's the scale. They don't teach this at Juilliard."

At first David thought that the scale had seven notes, but then he realized that it was structured differently then any pattern he had ever consciously used. It actually used different notes as it crossed through each octave. He thought and realized that he had used elements of it when improvising alone in his apartment, but had not known what he was doing. The power of the mood created by employing the scale to make melodies was incredible. How had the rest of the world missed it? How many great and innovative players had not found out this simple truth? Even more amazingly, the actual layout of the piano keyboard offered the scale to you. It reached out and said "Play me", but nobody seemed to notice. How had the great composers let this go by? It was like the old optical illusion where the picture of a young woman in a feathered hat became an old crone when you saw it a different way. We were all programmed to see the old crone and thus we missed the young woman. But here she was now, only in sound. And now that David had seen her, he could never go back. The scale had been embedded in the keyboard for centuries, waiting for enlightened mankind to spot it and use it.

"I want to write it out."

"Don't write it out. Just play it. Watch me again." Billy played the scale and then improvised a bit with it. "Go ahead."

David looked at the keys as if he had never seen them before. His mind flipped back to the living room of his childhood Christmas. Little David lifted his pudgy face and gazed across the room past the tree. There in the corner sat his parents' grand piano. He was too little to see the keyboard. He wanted to walk over to the piano to see the keys and to find out if the pattern was there. Had it been there all his life? It must have been! He stood up in his little shorts and suspenders. His mother didn't seem to notice. He walked over to the piano. He slowly and carefully climbed up on the stool and sat on it. The keyboard cover was closed. His tiny hands lifted the cover carefully and slowly. He looked at the keys. He looked at what should have been so familiar to him, yet he understood nothing. He was too young to understand the keyboard. How could he possibly find this pattern?

Now David looked at Billy's piano. Now he understood what he saw. He touched the keys without playing, lovingly. His oldest friend. Now it revealed new truths. He realized the power within the instrument. It had the whole universe inside it. He had always sensed that it might be a doorway to God and now the doorway was finally cracked open. He started to play a slow lyrical melody using the scale. Immediately he felt as if his position in the universe had been transformed. He knew why he was here.

He closed his eyes and bathed in the sound. He winced when he hit wrong notes, but quickly found his way back into the pattern.

"What is it called?"

"The scale?" asked Billy.

David nodded.

"The Gabriel scale."

"For the angel Gabriel?"

"That's correct."

"Can I mix it with other scales?"

"Go ahead."

This time David played a swinging line of jazz eighth notes using traditional bebop scales, but he interpolated the Gabriel scale into his improvisation. The result was a multidimensionally-enhanced version of his regular jazz style. He'd gone from black and white to color. From a photo to a hologram. A byproduct of the scale was that he seemed to have better physical control of the instrument. His frequent sloppiness seemed to clear up and settle into a groove. He sped up to see if he'd derail, but as long as he used elements of the scale, his technique remained confident; not through pride, but rather through the confidence that comes from knowing.

"David," said Billy, breaking into his reverie. "Did you bring your left hand today?"

"Yeah."

"We have new chords to learn."

"There are Gabriel chords?"

"Chords imply scales and scales imply chords."

Billy now began to play and added chords in his left hand.

"Whoa!" said David involuntarily.

It sounded like a carousel floating in the sky. The clouds parted and the sun came out and Niagara fell and the green grass sang in a thousand-part harmony. Incredibly, the chords looked familiar to David, but in conjunction with the Gabriel scale they had taken on totally new meaning.

"Billy, I feel like I've fallen into Dr. Seuss's 'On Beyond Zebra'."

"Interesting analogy. I'd say a closer one might be that you knew the alphabet but never realized the available syntaxes that it could form."

They played for hours. Nothing was written down, nothing was recorded. The knowledge was transferred viscerally from teacher to student. The student absorbed the information as if he'd been waiting all his life for this day. When they both sensed that the lesson was at an end, David spoke.

"Can I ask you something about your piano?"

"Shoot."

"Underneath the cloth covering..." Billy smiled. "It glows, doesn't it?"

"For some people. Some people see it and some never will."

"I thought so."

"It's not just from the scale. It's from the individual who's playing, or rather, through that individual. You could make it glow with a funky old blues. It's about you. And listen, the scale? Some people are gonna hear it and be affected. Others are never gonna notice it. And then there's others who can't stand to hear it. It's like a flashlight shining in their cave."

"The Mahozadans?"

"The Mahozadans."

"And you're gonna shine a flashlight in their cave?"

"We're gonna shine a flashlight in their cave my friend. We're gonna do it."

CHAPTER
FORTY-FOUR

A few days later, David showed up at a prearranged midtown location. He had decided to follow this madness through to the end, because he believed that he'd be able to solve his mystery once and for all. What was the tape and who had played on it? Now he was beginning to wonder if it had been Billy, but he decided not to ask. He trusted Billy's intentions.

Waiting on a quiet street corner early on a Sunday morning in August, David was surprised to see Sal Lucci show up.

"Sal, you doing this gig?"

"Hey, David," laughed Sal. "Yeah, I'm going but I didn't know you were on it!"

"Different kind of gig, huh?"

"Different, yeah. Good cause though."

Jack Sanders showed up. Then Bread Davies, the drummer from the loft jam showed up in a beat-up woody station wagon with Billy. Billy looked even worse. David had the distinct feeling that he'd be drafted at the piano to play for Billy. In some ways he felt ready. Even after a few days, the Gabriel scale and its chords had opened up his playing completely. Maybe he was better than he had thought. He had to see himself in a new way in order to even consider success on this adventure. That had always been difficult for him.

This whole idea was so screwy that he had to suspend his disbelief to be willing to go. Somehow it seemed as if he might be risking his life in a musical contest. Why were they all told not to bring instruments? Not only that, but he'd been carefully instructed by Billy to go to Eastern Mountain Sports, an outdoor clothing store, to purchase certain articles. Topping the list was a good pair of hiking boots and a backpack. This gave him a clue. The most significant hiking in New Hampshire was in the White Mountains up in the northern part of the state. The same summer that he swam the lake at camp, he'd gone on a backpacking trip with a few counselors and campers. He had climbed Mt. Washington and a few other smaller peaks. It was an incomparable thrill and he'd never forgotten it. It was one of the few really triumphant moments in his life that he could remember. Now he was forty-two and the thought of trying to get up any mountain seemed daunting.

Bread drove. Bread was a real road warrior of a musician. He had worked with James Brown, Wilson Pickett, and many other great soul acts. He was just as adept at R&B as he was at jazz. David was still fascinated by people who could drive distances as easily as David could watch long hours of television. Billy refused to discuss the gig. He told them that all questions would be answered when they arrived. The AC was ineffective enough that Bread opened the windows. The outside air was hot, and eventually David dozed off.

In David's dream he was walking through the woods. A large walrus blocked his path.

"Uhh, hi," said David.

"Hello, David Stein," harrumphed the walrus.

"You know my name?"

"I know your name and your playing abilities. You're in the right place at the right time."

"And just who are you?"

"My name is Hugh."

"Hugh who?"

"Hugh Manatee."

"Hugh Manatee?"

"That's me."

"That's a whale of a name!"

"Does it get your seal of approval?" shot back Hugh.

"I'd be a blubbering idiot not to approve, but there's something fishy about that name."

"Finny you should mention that," said the great beast.

"I'll bet you go to the dentist in Alabama."

"Of course," said Hugh, and they both said, "because the Tuscaloosa."

"Are you a symbol of something, Hugh Manatee?"

"I am. I represent humanity. Humanity is blocking your path."

"And what must I do about it?"

"You must shake hands with humanity, and then stay on your path."

"That seems simple enough."

David approached Hugh and extended his hand to shake. Hugh extended his flipper to shake. They shook. The weight of Hugh's flipper pulled David down to the ground hard.

"I'm sorry about that, David, but humanity can weigh you down sometimes."

"So I see," said David, getting up and brushing the mud off. This time he stood with one leg forward with his knees slightly bent as he'd been taught at the *dojo*. He mentally grounded himself and extended two hands to Hugh. This time he was able to shake hand with Hugh Manatee successfully. "Now what?"

"Now stay on your path."

"Stay on this road, man!" David heard Sal say to Bread as he woke up.

"You sure? This is kind of off the beaten path."

Sal had the map.

"This is what Billy said to do. I'm just telling you what he said."

Billy was asleep. Sal was up front with Bread. Jack and David were in back with Billy.

David was confused. Hadn't they just left New York? How could they be up in New Hampshire? He didn't remember much of the drive through Connecticut and Massachusetts. Maybe they'd been abducted by aliens, or even Mahozadans. Or maybe Mahozadans were aliens. Was there jazz on other planets? Was there music on other planets? Was it like that silly watered-down glop that he used to hear on "Star Trek" when an alien would play a harp and Spock would sing? Did aliens have ears? And if they didn't, was there no music? Did you need to have ears to have music? Were there snobby musical cliques on other planets? Jazzers and classical snobs and rockers and folkies? Did they have chromatic and diatonic music or not? Even on earth there was a wide and wild variety of music. One didn't need to stay programmed with the same old western styles. But people felt safe with their chosen musical styles as much as they felt safe with their chosen foods or baseball team or sitcoms or fashion styles. David was trying to master styles he knew about and simultaneously stretch out of the box into somewhere else.

It was late in the afternoon when they pulled into North Conway, New Hampshire. The highway led directly through town, a combination of strip malls, touristy shops and outdoor supply stores. At the far end of town they pulled over. While David and Jack and Sal got out to stretch their legs, Bread took Billy to a pharmacy.

"What's with Billy?" David asked Jack.

"He's been ill a long time, man."

"I thought that he picked up some bug in India."

"That's right mate, but it happened about twenty years ago."

"Twenty years ago? What is it?"

"I dunno exactly. I think it's killing him though."

"Jesus. Nothing can be done?"

"I heard he's not big on doctors," said Sal.

"So what's he doing at the pharmacy?"

"I guess he'll take painkillers for an important gig."

A few minutes later Billy and Bread came back. Billy was walking slowly and Bread slowed down to accompany him. Nobody mentioned Billy's illness.

They got back in the car and headed up Route 16. Almost immediately, everything changed. They were entering the White Mountains and the station wagon started to climb. David felt intimidated by the topography. Everything here was God-made instead of man-made. The air was different, the trees were taller, and the clouds had come down to visit. As they slid into the fog on that August afternoon, David distinctly saw snowflakes outside the window. Snow in August. What was left of his old world? If he could tell his old self about the things that he'd experienced lately, his old self would tell him to fuck off. With such new information coming at him all the time now, David had trouble drawing on old experiences to compare them to. It was hard to react in this new world. All he could do was observe strange events and try to remain detached enough to handle them as they occurred.

David craned his neck to see the mountains looming up alongside the road. They were dark green where they weren't covered by the clouds. After a little while they made a left and pulled into a parking lot at a place called "Pinkham Notch Camp, AMC."

David looked at his watch. It was just before 5 p.m. They got out of the car. As he stepped across the gravel-covered ground he felt and smelled the air that took him instantly back to camp at age thirteen again. A couple of weeks after he swam the lake, he had heard that there was to be a backpacking trip. Feeling powerful after his watery success, he decided to go on the trip. They climbed Mt. Washington, the highest peak in the northeastern United States. They had hiked up the Tuckerman Ravine trail and climbed the narrow path up the ravine. Above the treeline they had scrambled through the moon landscape of boulders up to the top of the mountain. Once there they stayed overnight in a barracks-like room of an old hotel. Almost thirty years later, he could still remember the revelatory sensations of being on the mountain. It had been the transcendent antithesis of life in New York City, where he had spent most of his time on cement.

After camper David returned from the mountain trip, something subtle within him had changed. At the time he could not have possibly put it into words. His sense of the world had been opened mightily. Too much time in the city would eventually reseal it.

Mt. Washington is understood by climbers as unique. In terms of height, it's a mere pebble next to the great peaks of the world. It's six thousand, two hundred and eighty-eight feet high. Everest, for instance, is twenty-seven thousand. However, little Mt. Washington is a mountain that one minute may afford a lovely woodland hike and another minute may turn into a snarling deathtrap. Well over a hundred people have died on the mountain from falls, ice slides, and hypothermic exposure. At its barefaced rocky top, the highest winds ever clocked on the planet have reached two hundred and thirty-one miles per hour.

Somewhere within David Stein, the transformational power of the mountain lay dormant. Now, rather unaware of this internal sleeping giant, he arrived at its base. Pinkham Notch Camp, run by the Appalachian Mountain Club, served hikers in warmer weather and skiers in the cold. While Bread went in to the main building to see about their rooms, the rest of them stayed outside.

"I don't get it," said David to Sal. "Where's the mountain?"

A hiker walking by heard them.

"If you want to see the mountain from here, you're too close. Walk across the highway and look back in this direction. You'll see it."

David walked out of the camp's main entrance and crossed Route 16. Then he turned around and looked back. What David saw shook him to the core. The mountain loomed impossibly up into the sky. Great clouds covered parts of it and their shadows raced across its giant ravines. At that moment he understood the depths of mythology and the reality of history. Life and death and nature yawned before him. He felt afraid that the mountain might notice him and smother him. He almost had to look away. Was this the same mountain that he had climbed as a boy? Who was that boy? How had that boy become this sniveling, sarcastic, frightened little man? Confused, he returned to the base camp.

They were to stay in the hostel a few dozen yards from the main building. David and Bread were in one room and the others next door. David was surprised to find two sets of bunk beds in the room and backpacks on the two top bunks. He had expected at least a motel. Instead, it looked like grownup summer camp.

The five of them left their packs in their rooms and went over to the main building. They entered a cafeteria. Hikers of all ages were eating. David overheard French, German, and Japanese.

"I seem to be the only black man in the state of New Hampshire," said Bread.

He walked over to some Japanese hikers and to David's surprise engaged them in conversation in their own language. There were benefits to frequent long international jazz tours that went beyond music and money. Once they had obtained trays and food, the five of them sat together, away from prying ears.

"So Billy," said David, "what's the story? Why all the mystery here? Is this gig gonna happen in a club?"

"So to speak," Billy responded.

Billy said nothing more. Now David was totally confused. He looked around. Bread and Jack looked as if they knew all they needed to know. Sal seemed a bit more quizzically inclined.

"I'm sorry," said David, embarrassed. "I just don't get it. Where are we playing?"

Billy looked at David and smiled. He then pointed up towards the ceiling, diagonally.

"On the roof? There's a nightclub on the roof?"

Jack spoke. "We're playing on the mountain, David."

Nervous energy raced through David.

"On the mountain? There's a nightclub on the mountain?"

"So to speak," said Jack.

"'So to speak'? I'm sorry, I'm having a stupid attack. Please help me to understand."

"Here's what I can tell you for now," said Billy slowly. "Tomorrow morning we're going up the mountain. Tomorrow night we'll be playing on the mountain."

"We're driving up the mountain?"

David felt vertigo, claustrophobia, and agoraphobia all at once.

"We're climbing the mountain."

David leaned in and whispered to Billy. "W-we're climbing the mountain? Up the mountain? Mt. Washington?" His voice shook.

Billy smiled and nodded. "Yeah."

CHAPTER
FORTY-FIVE

David lay all night on the lower bunk in a nonstop clockwise, lengthwise rotation. His head always on the pillow, he looked like a pig being slow-roasted on a spit. What the hell was he doing here? He heard some damned music and he wanted to find out who the hell it was. That's all! He never meant to get mixed up in cults, murder, crazy people and death gigs, and he certainly hadn't planned on climbing a mountain!

He was a piano player, not a Sherpa guide. Could a Sherpa do what he could? Could Sir Edmund Hillary have played some of the funky lowdown bars that he had survived? Could the Donner Party have emceed the Shapiro Bar Mitzvah in Syosset? Could the soccer team that crashed in the Andes have worked with some of the crummy out-of-tune singers he'd played for? Could Lewis and Clark have *schlepped* a Hammond B3 organ and a Leslie amp up three flights of stairs to play in a smelly firetrap of a club in the middle of a hundred-degree heat? He was a piano player! A musical warrior. A *mensch*. A hardworking keyboard artiste who really didn't want to go up this monster of a mountain to be in a "play-to-the-death jazz jam" with some thuggish zombie music maniacs. He wanted Chinese food, take-out. He wanted the *New York Times* and the sound of police sirens and screaming neighbors to calm his soul.

He got up. He opened the door and walked down the hall in his pajamas. What kind of place was this anyway? No soda machines, no ice machines. This was no motel. This was the Pinkham Notch AMC hostel and he was a hostile hostel hostage. He didn't know how to drive, so he couldn't escape. He'd get lost on the road anyway. He opened the door to the outside and stepped out. It was freezing! He was amazed. This wasn't August anymore. In New York it was August. What was wrong with these people? Where was summer? He stepped across the gravel in his bare feet. He walked toward the entrance to the camp slowly and carefully, because the only light was a small bulb on the main building. He looked up. There it was again. That BIG... NIGHT...SKY.

It wasn't a skyscraper or a helicopter or a passing jet. It was this thing that had always been there. It wasn't going to change or go away for little David. It was cold and dark and bright and marvelous and terrible. It was God and aliens and meteors and it was right up there conversing with that gigantic dark mass that he was supposed to hike up in a few hours. He knew that he was going to die on the mountain. Then he'd be part of that sky and he could lord it over the mountain.

His teeth started to chatter uncontrollably. Something small ran by his feet and he jumped. Maybe it was a chipmunk that might bite his toes off! Maybe there were rattle snakes in New Hampshire. Who the hell knew what kind of weird batty night-crawling things scurried about at night in these Godforsaken places? He started to walk back to the hostel, lifting his frozen bare feet high whenever they touched the ground to avoid ...whatever. He made his way back to his bed and when he put his heavy wool blankets on, he shivered for a while. You don't even want to know about the dreams he had. Forget it.

He awoke to the sound of people walking down the halls, taking showers, repacking their backpacks. The bright sun streamed in the window and right there in his room two Australian hikers named Barney and Clyde were lacing up their boots.

"G'wan up today, mate?" said Barney to David, who barely peeked from beneath his warm blankets.

"Uh, yeah, I think so."

"Better get up now, mate, if you wanna eat. They don't wait here with breakfast. It's eat or be eaten!"

Well now, Clyde thought that that was the funniest thing that he had ever heard and he guffawed, nice and loud. David wasn't quite ready for this loud noise breaking his reverie (the reverie that all insomniacs get when they finally fall into a deep sleep around 4:15 in the morning).

The door opened and in walked Jack.

"I thought I heard some familiar proper English! What the fuck. Where you boys from?"

"We're from Perth," said Clyde. "And you?"

"I'm from New York City now. Once I was from Sydney. Hey, you boys wouldn't by any chance have some extra Vegemite, would ya?"

"Whaddya think Barney?" said Clyde. "Can we spare some Vegemite for a guy who left Sydney to move to New York City?"

"Well I guess we can, Clyde. We've got more than our fare share. Just makes our packs a bit lighter. Here ya go, brother."

Barney threw Jack a small jar. Jack caught it with one hand.

"Thanks. That's mighty fine of you."

David watched this gratis transaction with great interest. He had no idea what was in the jar, but he made a mental note to find out.

The band of musicians stumbled into the cafeteria. David couldn't seem to get warm. He had on jeans and a heavy hooded New York Mets sweatshirt. The hood was up and his hands were in the pockets. He sat next to Jack while the others drank coffee.

"What's up with that jar they gave you?" he asked Jack.

"That's Vegemite, mate."

"Whaddya do with it?"

"Bring me some bread, I'll show you."

David got up and brought a basket of bread over to the table. Jack took out the Vegemite and spread it on the bread. It was a foul-looking spread.

"Here ya go, David, knock yourself out."

David picked up the Vegemite-ed bread and looked at as if it were the ugliest bread mold school science project. He closed his eyes and took a bite. It was indeed the bread mold school science project. He gagged and made such a loud noise of disapproval that half the hikers in the room turned to look.

"Come on now, be a man and eat your Vegemite. S'good for you. Lots of vitamin B."

Billy, Bread, and Sal were all laughing now.

"Finish it, man!" said Bread.

"Let's see *you* eat it," said David to Bread.

"Uh uh, man, I ain't no fool. Oatmeal for me."

David suffered his way through the Vegemite sandwich and longed even more strongly for some Chinese fried rice with soy sauce.

When they'd finished eating, they walked out of the cafeteria portion of the building into the adjoining store. The store sold hiking supplies. Clothing, food, maps, books, compasses and such. David walked around and looked at the books. Some of the books were mountain survival stories. Then he saw a table with a large model of the Presidential Range of the White Mountains with Mt. Washington in the center. It looked big even at two feet tall. Billy wandered over.

"You see this hump here? We'll be hiking up through the woods for a couple of hours. Then we get to the base of Tuckerman Ravine and we go up alongside the headwall here."

Tuckerman Ravine! The name lit a match inside him. He had climbed it as a boy. He should be able to do it now. He had vague memories of scrambling along a path on the edge of the ravine and looking down, many hundreds of feet below to the base of the ravine. He had seen a large boulder the size of a house. On it was the name of a climber who had died years before, crushed under the falling boulder. What kind of place was this? Could he climb it now? When had he become so phobic about heights? He didn't remember it being an issue when he was thirteen. Behind the table he saw a chart listing all the deaths on the mountain since 1849. Hypothermia, falls, avalanches. Who needed this? Let some other poor *schmuck* go up the mountain and fight Bob "Music Nazi" Mahozada! He was going to get out of this gig even if he had to hitchhike all the way back to New York City.

"Billy, I gotta talk to you."

"Okay, I'm listening."

"Not here, outside."

They walked outside. To David's amazement, the temperature had climbed fifteen or twenty degrees during breakfast. The morning fog had lifted, literally. The clouds were moving up the mountain and the air at the base camp had become clear. The air smelled wonderful.

"Billy, I can't do this."

"Can't do what, David?"

"This gig. This mountain. The whole thing."

"Sure you can."

"No, no, I can't. I can't get up this mountain. I don't like heights. I don't like nature. I didn't sign up for this. I just wanted you to teach me to play piano better."

"And I have. You play piano better than when we first met. In a short time you've made miraculous changes in your playing. I need you here to do this. This is for everybody, not just for me and you. These people need to be stopped before they become a larger movement."

David nodded his head nervously. He didn't want to debate, he just wanted to get out. He wanted to be told that it was alright for him to quit. He wanted to get out of the summer camp lake and back into the rowboat again.

"I just can't. I can't."

"Listen to me, David. I don't want to coddle you. You're a big boy."

That was painful. That really smarted and humiliated him.

"If you don't face your fears, you'll die anyway. You'll die a slow death. Maybe not a physical death, but a death of the soul. That's no way to live. This has to be done."

"I don't want to die on that fucking mountain, Billy."

"David, listen to my words. I am dying, David."

"What do you mean?"

"David, look at me. I'm ill. I've got the chops to beat this bastard, but my physical body is in bad shape. I may not be able to play. If that happens I'm gonna need you to take over the keys, man."

"If you're ill, why the hell are you climbing a mountain? You should be home taking care of yourself. Couldn't this war happen in New York? In a club? I saw these guys play in a club. Can't you just jump up on the bandstand wherever they play?"

David was speaking faster and faster, desperate to avoid what he had been brought there to do.

"What is about to take place has been agreed to on a level that Carl Jung called 'The Collective Unconscious'. The challenge, the terms, the location, the significance of all of this has been determined by those involved. This battle involves entering a state that we haven't discussed. A state that's right up your alley."

"You don't mean a state like New Hampshire, do you? You mean something else."

"Correct. Not a state like New Hampshire. More on that later. Meanwhile, let's get your pack ready. Everybody's gonna leave their extra shit in the car."

"But I'm not going."

"You are going, man."

"I am?"

"Of course. Everything that's happened to you has brought you to this point. This is the ninth inning. The Mets are down two-zip with men on first and second and you're on deck."

"How many outs?"

"Hey, you're stretching my metaphor, pal."

Billy had appealed to David's sense of humor to charm him into doing what he did not want to do. David knew this, but as much as he didn't want to go, he wanted to be told that it was all right to go. A little while later he found himself entering the Tuckerman Ravine trail. He knew that it was about two and a half miles up through the wooded path to the base of the ravine. He felt the weight of the pack on his back. He was out of breath almost immediately and then admitted to himself that it was about stress rather than the cardiovascular shape he was in. He started to breath long slow breaths as he'd learned at the *dojo*. His torso relaxed as soon as he started. He centered himself mentally and walked. He was at the back of the group. He started to hear music in his head. It was the whistled theme from "The Bridge Over The River Kwai." He slowed the song down a bit and sped his step up a bit until they interlocked rhythmically.

He had to admit that it was a magical place. How could anything be this big? How could you march on up the hill and still be in the woods and not at the top of the hill? Could the mountain fall over? Could it blow its top like Mount St. Helens? That would be painful. Nah, come on, it's not a volcano for Christ's sake. What about lyme disease from ticks? He stopped and pulled up his thick woolen socks. What about murderous insane deathcult noisemakers like Eddie Clovis? Was that dick somewhere on the mountain? What was going to happen when the Varton White boys showed up? How did Billy know that they'd make this a music battle instead of a street fight? Billy said that people could die on this gig! Did he mean himself? What about Mervyn? *They must have killed Mervyn.* How could such a beautiful place give him such a feeling of impending horror?

After awhile they turned left to cross over a footbridge. The bridge was a little wooden plank job over cascading water. Bread and Jack stopped to let Billy, David, and Sal catch up. From this point they could also see across the highway to another mountain. Something about the combination of wind, sun and water translated in David's mind as music. It wasn't a reproducible tune but rather an essence of music. He imagined that this was what the "Waters of Life" referred to in the Bible might be.

David noticed Billy staring down at the water. His look of grim determination seemed to ease for a moment.

"Are you okay?" asked Jack.

"How can you not be okay in this place?" Billy answered.

"Let's press on, gentlemen," said Bread.

Soon they came to a lookout point. David tried unsuccessfully to approach the edge of the viewing platform to look down into the gorge. While the others stood at the edge of a low wall, David held back. Every time he tried to get closer to the edge he felt vertigo in the most visceral way.

The air over the gorge was different. Lush, thick, the way he imagined a rainforest would be. This mountain was a big living thing and he was on its turf.

He was back in summer camp heading up the mountain. The fat kid, Steven Bird, couldn't keep up. The counselors taunted him to move his butt. The other kids were so tired that they were oblivious to it. The kid cried and waddled his way up the mountain slowly. Finally one of the counselors agreed to stay back with him and move at Bird's pace.

Now David kept walking behind Sal. The trail became a giant escalator. He rode it higher up the mountain. The escalator was packed with morning subway riders trying to get to work in midtown Manhattan. Lots of working class folks in cheap imitation black leather jackets. It was winter on the escalator. Ice formed on the handrails. Fire broke out in the machinery. People screamed and jumped off. David stayed on. Then the melting ice and the fire stopped the gears and the escalator ground to a halt. It dissipated and he kept hiking up the trail with the musicians. A giant boulder rolled down the path and killed all of them. The boulder hit a tree and cracked open and out came Eddie with giant dark wings, flying around playing the sax. Fire came out of his horn.

He spat in David's face. David gave him the finger and kept walking. David's backpack grew arms that reached around his eyes and covered them. He pried the fingers off and kept walking. Two eight-foot tall chipmunks stood up on either side of the trail with their paws crossed. They jabbered angrily at each other in cartoon chipmunk talk. One of them stared at David and when he passed them, made a mock lunge at his toes as if it were going to bite them off. David pulled his foot back reflexively and then moved on. Suddenly a crowd of horrid-looking mangled people came running down the trail towards him wailing awful banshee wails. They were people who had died on the mountain in the 1800's. They were bloody and green and crushed and scared. They blew past him on either side. He was frozen inside but kept looking forward. He kept on going. His mother came down the trail.

"Be a doctor!" she said, and smacked him in the face. He kept going. Then his Dad.

"Be a lawyer!" he said, and smacked him.

Then his brother and sister. Smack smack smack. Cousins that he'd only heard about came down to smack him. He'd had enough. He spun around and ducked and threw the cousins one by one. *Shiho-nage, kokyu-nage, tenchi-nage, kaiten-nage.* Instead of being tested in the *dojo* wearing a *gi* and *hakama*, he was being tested on the trail, wearing a backpack, boots, a sweatshirt, and shorts. The cousins went flying all over the mountain landing in heaps. He loved it.

Billy stopped for water. They all took swigs from their plastic water bottles. Sal was going to sit down.

"Don't do it, man, it only makes it harder to get up again." said Jack, who was flushed.

Sal stood up again, reluctantly.

"Better to lean against a tree, mate."

And so they leaned, these creatures of the night, who weren't so used to seeing the day. The trees were getting shorter up here. The treeline was the altitude at which vegetation disappeared.

"Hey, Billy, I'm glad I didn't have to lug my bass up here."

"Yeah, Billy," said Bread, "tell me that there's a drum kit at this gig."

"Everything you guys'll need will be there. Instruments, sound system, everything."

"Food?" said Jack.

"Everything that you'll need."

They pressed on. As hikers went, they were a slow bunch. From time to time more seasoned hikers passed them in both directions.

Late in the morning they reached the base of the ravine. David couldn't believe his eyes. Instead of seeming smaller than when he was a kid, the ravine appeared monstrously large and terrifyingly high. His throat became dry. Everything seemed different up here. It was silent but for a breeze.

An old wooden building with restrooms and a porch served as a gathering point for those were planning to assault the ravine wall. They took off their packs and ate. Energy bars, oranges, peanut butter sandwiches. "Silly" food, thought David. He could see that it was a great distance from the base of the ravine to the headwall. He knew he'd either lose his balance and fall to his death or get killed by the Varton White boys and their diabolical megalomaniacal vile leader, Bob.

It didn't bode well for booking those nice cushy autumn gigs. Those fancy private parties he'd play when the rich got back from their summer homes and greeted their blue blood friends in their Park Avenue homes. All signs portended an aborted relationship with Jenna, something he really would have enjoyed deeply. At least he was in the right place to solve the biggest mystery of his life.

They wrapped up their garbage and stowed it in their packs. Mountain culture meant carrying out at least as much as (if not more than) you brought in. The sanitation trucks that he heard growling through the morning streets even from his courtyard window were not coming up here today.

They put on their packs and started walking towards the ravine wall, about a half mile away. To David it seemed as if they were on a raised path in the center of a great valley. As the trees became more like miniature bonsai trees, they seemed more exposed. He stepped gingerly on the rocks that made up the trail here.

Seeing the wall was like seeing the Red Sea parting, a magnificent tsunami frozen in motion. And wasn't that really what it was? It was a glacial cirque formed long ago and though it seemed to be solid, to God it must look like a moving wave. A wave one thousand feet high. You could just about put the Empire State Building next to that headwall and it would barely reach the top of the wall. Well, hell, if he wouldn't climb the Empire State by stairs, why should he go up a trail onto loose avalanche debris with a pack on his back?

And then he came to the sign. A simple yellow sign on a post. It read:

STOP

THE AREA AHEAD HAS THE WORST WEATHER IN AMERICA.

MANY HAVE DIED THERE FROM EXPOSURE, EVEN IN THE SUMMER.

TURN BACK NOW IF THE WEATHER IS BAD.

WHITE MOUNTAIN NATIONAL FOREST

"Oh shit," said Sal.

He was a big gentle man of few words and many notes. David was glad that Sal said this, because David needed everyone to mutiny and declare the mission cancelled. Billy smiled.

"Nah, that's nothing. There's signs all over the White Mountains like that. Let's keep going."

"But Billy," said David, "I think that considering all the people who've died on the mountain, there are reasons for those signs. Don't you think?"

"Mathematically speaking, you're probably not going to be one of those people," said Billy.

David wanted to say "Can you guarantee that?" but for once he kept his mouth shut. They kept walking past the sign and he realized he was in a world which had just left its orbit and that was tumbling away into space.

As they climbed higher David looked at the sky and saw a cloud pass right over the lip of the ravine. It was moving very fast. Rather than going straight up the middle of the wall, the trail turned right. Soon it became completely free of all vegetation. They were walking over large boulders left from innumerable rockslides.

Why doesn't somebody clean this mess up? he thought.

The diversity of boulder size meant walking one moment and scrambling on all fours the next, all the while moving higher and higher up the right side of the ravine. He could barely follow the trail if there was one. How did Billy know where to go? Soon they were all spread out laterally. Where was the trail? What if somebody dislodged a boulder above him? What if he screwed up and knocked one down on some poor *schmuck* below him? He looked back. Whoaaa! Bad idea! The base of the ravine was getting smaller. He looked back towards the entrance to the ravine. He could now see a valley beyond it, probably where they had started. It all looked the same to him. Green, beautiful, and big. Too big. He wasn't used to open space. When he was in the city he longed to experience it, but now that he'd arrived, he realized that open space can be very open.

Up ahead of the boulder field the trail reappeared as a rocky ledge. He could see Billy and Jack talking to hikers who had just come down from above them. The two musicians waited for Bread, David, and Sal.

"What did those guys say?" asked Bread, who was panting and sweating.

Jack looked at Bread.

"No big deal, man. Bit windy up above the top of the wall. Clouds coming in. You know what they say in New England about the weather."

"Nah, man, tell me what they say," said Bread.

"'If you don't like the weather, wait a minute.'"

Bread laughed. David smiled and nodded, thinking *Yeah. That's funny. Very funny.*

They started to traverse the ledge trail. This is where David remembered hiking as a kid. Now it was more than all he could do to walk upright. The trail was thin and the drop already hundreds of feet. In order not to fall off the trail to the ravine on his left he found himself leaning to the right as he walked. No one else did this. It really wasn't necessary, except to David, who decided that rather than take a chance of becoming a statistic, he'd make a fool of himself. So there he was, exhausted, leaning to the right, pack on his back, looking like a hunchbacked mountain troll.

His head started to hurt from fear. His heart beat fast. He returned to his long slow breaths. He re-centered himself again mentally and his body followed. Briefly he thought that he was actually enjoying himself. The wind picked up. He was afraid that he'd be blown off and he ducked down again.

This was the biggest goddamned place he'd ever been. Was the world filled with places this big? Bigger? Onward and upward rose the quintet. They were almost at the lip of the ravine. The wind became faster and louder. Movie wind. Movie storm wind. Horror movie storm wind. The hikers at the base of the ravine looked like ants with backpacks.

At last they reached the top of the ravine. David was shocked at himself. He'd climbed up this humongous mountain past the most difficult part. It was breathtakingly glorious to look down the ravine and over to the valley in the distance. He now could see other mountain ranges in the far distance.

Well, they couldn't take this away from him, anyway. He looked around at the area he had arrived at. It was the moon. Rock, rock, and more rocks. As far as the legs could possibly walk. The air was incredible. Powerful. Bracing. Like a dive into a cold lake. A cloud came in on the ground. It wasted no time. They became invisible to each other. David was soaked.

He got out his rain jacket from his pack. The cloud passed and he could see again.

Billy had that faraway look in his eyes. David wondered how Billy had made it this far. The wind picked up. David felt as if it were lifting him off his feet. He was glad for the weight of the backpack. From this point they hiked a vaguely level route over the rocks. Nothing could be a problem after the ravine. David was tired, but relieved to be over the lip of Tuckerman.

After fifteen minutes, off in the distance David could see what appeared to be a house. They were heading straight for it. This was Lakes Of The Clouds hut, run by the Appalachian Mountain Club. It did, in fact, have two ponds in its vicinity. As they approached it, there seemed to be a thin layer of moss-like grass mixed in with the rocks. Still, no bushes or trees. They were on the shoulder of Mt. Washington.

"How come we're not heading for the top?" said David. "Is the gig in this building?"

"The gig's on top," said Billy, shouting above the wind. "We're playing tonight. Rest of the day we spend at the hut."

"So how do we get to the top tonight?" Bread wondered.

"We climb, my friend, we climb."

"In the dark?" said Sal.

"Flashlights."

Lakes Of The Clouds hut was built in 1915. It had since been expanded. It slept 90 people. It was a refuge with hot meals and a warm bed for many a hiker over the years before they took off on the next leg of their journey. By staying in the huts that the AMC provided throughout the mountains, hikers could make day trips from hut to hut and leave tents and sleeping bags at home.

David was surprised to find dozens of people at the hut. Not everyone looked like an athlete either. There were people in their sixties and children of ten or eleven, who somehow seemed to have had no problem getting up the mountain. David knew that he was the problem. He had a tendency to occasionally over-dramatize, just a wee bit. Other folks just seemed to go about their business in life and not make a big deal about it. He invested meaning in activities and events that others would have called "luck", "drudgery", "same old same old", or "the rat race".

There were Barney and Clyde, leaving as he arrived.

"So you made it, did you? Well done," said Barney.

"You're leaving already?" said David.

"We had our lunch," said Clyde, "so we're heading along the ridge to Mt. Madison."

"Did you eat all your Vegemite, mate?" said Barney.

"Every drop, thank you very much," answered David, with as much civility as he could muster under the circumstances.

"Tastes like monkey shit, eh?" said Barney.

"Only monkey shit's much better," added Clyde.

So they knew this all along and didn't admit it? David nodded in agreement.

Later, after they ate, the musicians sat around in a circle in the common room talking. Billy spoke.

"Tonight we'll be leaving our packs here. We dress as warm as possible. Besides your warm clothing you'll each need to bring a wool blanket from the bunks here. Other than that we bring water and flashlights and ourselves. That's all. You're probably wondering about the venue. This is an outdoor gig of sorts."

David frowned. What the hell could he be up to? It would be freezing on the top of the mountain at night with no protection from the wind. There couldn't be an audience.

"This gig will have elements of other gigs you've played. You'll have instruments and you'll play jazz. Other than that it's gonna be a bit different, and the stakes'll be higher than usual. As I mentioned to you, David, the gig has been agreed to by all parties involved in their collective unconscious. In other words, you might think of it as a telepathic conference call between Bob, myself, and various other concerned parties. The actual venue is not a physical venue at all."

Everyone looked at each other for support. Things were getting stranger and scarier.

"I will help you to induce yourself into a higher state. An out-of-body state. As a group, we, meaning you and I and the Mahozadans, will mentally construct a jazz club. We will enter that jazz club and we will play there."

"Um-hum," said Bread, disparagingly.

"'Scuse me," said David, raising his hand to speak. "Why am I on a mountain? Couldn't we have worked this out in Central Park at noon?"

Billy went on in his nasal Brooklyn twang, which was totally alien to this part of the world.

"There are certain climatic and geographic factors that make this event possible in this location, but not in others. Storm systems from all over the continent tend to merge in this area. As a result you get the unique, fast changing weather of New England. Throw in the highest spot in the northeast and you get a location that radiates with power. People have known intuitively about the power of this mountain for centuries. People climb it and never forget it for the rest of their lives. And yet, in the whole world, only Mt. Everest has killed more people. It's a mighty place. And unlike, let's say, an improvised jazz solo, it sits here year after year, century after century. Solid. Unchanging. Eternal. Beautiful, and terrible."

"So?" said Bread.

"So," Billy went on, unfazed by Bread's interruption of his elucidation, "because of this confluence of weather and geography, a distinct effect is placed on the mind and the body. What you might erroneously call an 'O.B.E' or 'Out-Of-Body Experience' is possible."

"You mean like astral projection?" said Jack.

"That would be more about leaving the physical body and traveling and experiencing in a so-called 'astral body'. We won't be using our astral bodies. We will be using the same natural skills we use when we make music. There's nothing 'occult' or 'magical' about what we're gonna do. When you play jazz, what do you do?"

"You make choices," said Jack.

"Uh huh, you make choices. What you do with those choices?"

"You chain them together in sequences," said Sal.

"Okay, choices in sequences. What's the result?"

"Music that moves people," said David.

"That's right. While we're not addressing the heart and soul here, and they need to be addressed, we're making music that moves people. Choices in sequence. And from those choices, come Charlie Parker, Miles Davis, Monk, Ella Fitzgerald. From other choices come Coltrane, McCoy Tyner, Herbie Hancock and everybody else, including everybody sitting here. So what we're gonna do is make some choices up on the summit of this mountain tonight, that will help us construct something beyond just a solo. We're gonna make musical choices that will connect us to some other people, and together we'll all construct, using sound, a sphere wherein we can meet and play jazz."

Bread leaned in from his chair.

"Are you telling me that we're going to play a nightclub into existence?"

"Basically. Sound created the world. Many cultures talk about it. The Judeo-Christian idea of the 'word of God'." (David remembered Luis talking about that.) "In the East, the idea that the world was created using sound is no secret. Transcendent states can be reached using sound mantras. Sacred instruments give off frequencies that alter matter. Quantum physics sees the world as a wave of energy. We're gonna do a little energy shaping tonight."

"Let me ask you something," said Jack. "How is it that the Mahozadans can participate in what would seem to be such a high use of the human mind and yet they're still such fucking tyrannical assholes?"

Billy smiled. "How is it that one person uses the advanced evolutionary solution called the human hand to embrace, and someone else uses it to kill? We have been given tools. Most tools by themselves are neutral. We make choices with those tools, as we make choices with notes. Same chromatic universe for Mozart and Stravinsky but they took it to different places. The Mahozadans have made bad choices. Choices that are hurting other people. Choices that are enslaving people. They are creating music that is taking away all choices for those who hear it. We're gonna take back what they've done."

By the end of the conversation, David had become uncharacteristically calm. On one hand he was resigned to the possibility of death from the mountain or death from the Mahozadans. On the other hand he knew that he was vaguely prepared for this.

That afternoon David looked at some of the books on the shelf in the common room. He was fascinated to find guestbooks dating back to the 1930's. All those souls that had passed through here. They had lived and died and the mountain beneath their feet had just.....been. He skimmed through the World War Two years. Forward and forward through the '50's and the 60's until he came to the year when he had climbed the mountain at thirteen. And then he remembered that on the way down the mountain, the campers had stopped at the hut for lunch. He had been here before. Had he signed the book? He thumbed through the yellowed pages. So many groups had been there that summer. Just about every camp in New England. And there, on today's date, twenty-nine years ago, were the guest signatures from Camp Fairwood in Maine. His camp.

There were the signatures and comments of his counselors. Notes from his old buddies. Where had they all gone to? Did that world ever really exist? If there was nobody that he still knew from Fairwood, did it ever really happen? He was transported and transfixed as he read the entries. One by one the names and faces came back to him as if they were sitting there with him now. Halfway through the group's entries he came to his own. The illegible left-handed scrawl was unmistakable:

We just came down from the summit. Slept on the mountain in the old hotel last night, but nobody slept! This is the coolest place in the world! This mountain is biggg! Someday I'm coming back here again! Hello and so long, Mount Washington!

Signed,
Davey Stein

He felt a whirling of time and then timelessness settling in. What did it matter if he were adult or child? The mountain removed all petty human distinctions. It eliminated all references to nationality or economic class. Like the *dojo*, the mountain equalized all humanity. As illusory divisions fell away, real connections appeared. Everyone in that hut knew this, whether or not they knew that they knew. Once again he had a sense of music within him without sound.

Outside the hut he stood in the wind watching the sunset. It was the only event that existed at that moment. He knew that it would become dark in a way that he was not accustomed to. There was darkness in the city, but more in the heart than in the sky. Here, it was different. From moment to moment the spectrum was changing from pink clouds to blue air. The temperature was dropping fast and he could see clouds' shadows far below race across the western side of the mountain, the side that remained unexplored to him.

As he had packed on detached auto-pilot that morning, this evening he silently put on his warmest layers of sweatshirts with sweatpants under his jeans. He took his little EMS mini-maglite flashlight (small but rather dependable, and more importantly, lightweight), his water bottle, and a thick wool blanket from his bunk, a bunk in a room with fifteen other bunks. Billy said to bring nothing else, and at this point, David was boldly determined to go with the program or die trying. Or, go with the program and die trying. Either way. It almost didn't seem to make a difference in this Halloween Twilight Zone world he seemed to now travel in.

He had glanced up earlier towards the summit. He could see the top of a radio tower and not much else. The summit lay about a mile away, up the steep rocks. They'd be on the moon at night with flashlights. No 7-Elevens or gas stations on this trip. Not only that, but Billy had told them that the Mahozadans were on the mountain somewhere. That they would be up there. He had told them that there'd be no physical contact with them, but why did Billy trust them? Up those rocks in the dark in the freezing cold knowing that Eddie Clovis was looking for you. That Bob Mahozada wanted to make your ears spurt blood or turn you into a jazz zombie. And this knowledge was supposed to make you feel like playing better piano than you'd ever played in your life? In an other-dimensional night club? Sure.

"Couldn't be worse than the rush hour subway, now could it?" said David outloud to no one but himself. Now he was getting into quite a state. Well, maybe Billy would play and he could just watch from the safety of a dream bar, drinking dream scotch with a dream babe.

At 10 p.m. they set out. He would have been gratified not having to bring his pack, had he not been frightened to death. They went single file with Billy leading. He looked bloodless and weak. This was ludicrous.

Let's all go to a movie, guys! Let's go bowling in New Hampshire, huh? Let's skip this! Behind Billy, came Bread, Jack, Sal, and David. Hooded figures all, they started walking in the dark, but soon had to scramble, using their hands. They had their flashlights fixed in their belts to aim forward and down. The moon was nowhere to be found. How could it be, thought David, we're on it! He was already sore from the morning's climb. His legs, shoulders and back were stiff. Aikido or not, he was only partially prepared for this.

As they moved in the pitch black, he had no sense of distance or space. Even in the daylight this part of the climb confused hikers, because there was nothing but endless rock by which to try to judge distance. In the dark it was totally useless. Perhaps he was in the universal uterus, floating in the dark, waiting to be thrust into the world. But the uterus would have been warm. This was raw. The only sound was the wind and the occasional bumping of boots on boulders.

He looked up and the stars almost kissed him. A meteor flew completely across the horizon with no light pollution to interfere. Up on the mountain, for the first time in his life he saw stars not only above him, but surrounding him down below to the horizon. The air was clear enough that night that the stars appeared rounder than the skimpy few that hung mournfully unnoticed around the city skies.

Because other land features were invisible, it seemed as if he were floating in the midst of the stars. And weren't they? Aren't we just rolling around on this little pebble out in space, just like everybody else in the galaxy? We tend to think of space as "out there", but really we're smack in the middle of it, riding this sphere for dear life. And now, he realized how dear it was.

He followed Sal's gigantic frame as well as he could, but mostly he followed Sal's light. Occasionally it created an eclipse of Sal in front of him. It seemed as if he were following a giant Sasquatch back to its lair. He hoped that it wouldn't notice him.

The Bigfoot picked David up and twirled him above its hairy head. It howled relentless ranting riffs of raging rancor at its new possession. David tried to whistle Brahms' Lullaby to calm it down, but the wind made it impossible. The Sasquatch brought David to its nest at the top of the mountain and chained him to an out-of-tune upright piano where it forced him to stay fifty years, playing children's music for its horrid little monster progeny. Finally, after the fifty years it released him on Neil Diamond's birthday. Ancient David hobbled down the mountain in his ragged old tuxedo 'til he came to a town. He told them that he had been kidnapped fifty years before and that he needed work. Was there somewhere in town where he could get a job playing piano? They laughed in sorrowful shock and proceeded to tell him that all music had been outlawed and had been replaced by government-controlled newspapers. Anyone who had the urge to make or hear music was forced to read the government newspapers till they couldn't stay awake. David hobbled back up the mountain towards the Sasquatch family.

David hobbled up the mountain behind Sal. He was cold and he was tired. He took a swig from his bottle but it only made him colder. He felt as if the inside of his body and the world outside were one and the same. In between stood his feeble little ego and his rather large id. Well, they'd better get their shit straight tonight and reach out to each other fast or they'd be listening to Varton White music for all eternity.

Stars started to appear directly in front of him where the mountain's darkness had been. He realized that they were arriving at the summit. The wind burned his face. The path became flat and clear. Billy had stopped and they stood around him, hands in pockets, bouncing up and down on their toes for warmth.

"Take out your blankets and sit down in a circle crosslegged. Wrap the blankets around your shoulders. Drink some water. This will increase your body's ability to maintain a chemical balance while you're otherwise occupied."

"Aren't we gonna freeze to death, sitting here?" said David, looking around for Sasquatches.

"No," said Billy. "you'll be okay. The energy we use to mentally construct our temporary habitation will also keep our body systems in tip top shape. In fact, we'll be generating heat. You study martial arts. Martial artists, yogis, and anyone who knows how to meditate are able to slow their hearts, move into alpha wave brain patterns, generate heat, all sorts of good things. What does the word 'Aikido' mean, David?"

"Union with *ki*."

"And what is '*ki*'?"

"The life force of the universe coursing through your body when you focus your mind."

"Sounds good to me," said Billy. "Let's do it. There's really very little to explain to you all about what will happen when we arrive. Things will happen naturally. You will know exactly what to do throughout, barring unforeseen circumstances."

"Whoa man, what's that about 'unforeseen circumstances'?" said Bread, above the wind. "I signed on for an organized little jaunt here. Be specific."

"Well," said Billy, "You know... shit happens."

"That's reassuring," said Bread.

"Basically, it's gonna be like the first time you had sex... with somebody. You'll figure out what to do."

"Too bad," said Jack. "Then I guess these guys'll have to leave on account of no former experience."

"Yeah, well, that's about the last thing on my mind right now," laughed Bread. "I just hope I get another chance. After this, who knows what's gonna happen?"

"Relax gentlemen," said their leader. "You're in my hands now. We're going to use sound to launch this little party. We start with long slow breaths in the nose, out the mouth."

David knew this one, and he realized that he was right for this job. He'd been on the mountain before, he'd taken a giant leap in his playing abilities, he was in spiritual transformation, and he'd been able to throw Eddie Clovis down on the ground. He was confused as to whether God, fate, or Billy Kovac had led him to this moment, but he knew that he had to be here now to complete his journey.

"The perfect jazz club," said Billy slowly as they kept up the breathing. "See it clearly. The instruments you'd like to play. The sound system, the built-in acoustical properties. The lighting system. Audience sightlines. Tables or booths? Familiar smells? A bar. Make it perfect. Make it specific. Art on the walls? Photos of players you admire. Smokey air like the Village Vanguard or a modern soundproofed wonder? It's your club. Make it the best possible venue for you to perform in. Keep breathing."

Billy now started to lead them through vocalizations, call-and-response style. Their eyes were closed and their lungs were open. Starting with long mantra-like tones, Billy moved on into elaborate polymetrical rhythms and scale usages that David recognized but couldn't quite place. He heard blues riffs mixed with the Gabriel scale, which was no easy feat to sing with your eyes closed sitting around in the frozen darkness. He recognized snatches of Bulgarian melody and quarter-tone scales that he didn't think he could even repro-duce. But reproduce them he did, echoing Billy's musical pronouncements.

Now he heard Billy emit syllables from a language he knew to not be of this earth. Was it angel-speak or Venusian or gob-bledy-gook? No matter. He mimicked it. He'd failed French all through high school because he couldn't master the grammar, but he had nevertheless learned the language by imitating its sound. Now he was smiling in the dark as they sang. It was the best scat singing class he'd ever been to.

After a few minutes the wind seemed to be quieter and he felt light in his eyes. Gradually, his vision cleared, even though it was night and he thought he hadn't opened his eyes. He saw Sal sitting across from him. Or almost Sal. More like essence of Sal. The feeling of Sal's personality. White light covered them both. Now he saw the others, still singing, but eyes open, smiling at him. He knew that they were wherever Billy said they were going. That, somehow their bodies were still sitting on the mountain, while here he was.

What he saw was white, everywhere. It was like being in a Matisse drawing. A few simple lines creating an outline of something greater. The resolution of this reality floated in and out of focus. David was at a table. Other tables were adjacent and had drinks with little parasols in them. Beautiful young women with old fat men sat at each table. He couldn't determine if they were real, or just imagined decor. A young buxom blonde in a low-cut outfit brought him a drink and smiled at him, piercing him. Up on the raised bandstand was a gorgeous white grand piano. A spotlight shone on it.

The emcee walked out onto the stage. He was a short fat man, balding in front and with long unruly brown hair in back. He had on spectacles and a florid waistcoat. He wore white tights. He was quite the dandy. It was Benjamin Franklin. David could not believe his eyes. He pulled out his wallet which was packed with one-hundred-dollar bills to compare the picture of Franklin to this apparition. The bills were blank in the area that should have contained Franklin's picture.

"What a wonderful evening this is! The finest use of electricity, don't you think?"

The crowd murmured, "Ahhh!"

"You know, in my day, besides all my other fantastic contributions to society, I enjoyed composing string quartets. Tonight you'll hear the best improvisers making new music on the spot. Swinging music that will set your feet to tapping and your knuckles to rapping."

"Ha ha ha," laughed the audience, good-naturedly.

"I have the duty (if not the honor)," said Franklin in dark tones, "to introduce something new and developing in music. Tonight I take great pains, uh...pleasure in exposing you to the... existence-morphing sounds of Bob Mahozada."

The audience was silent. You couldn't have heard a pin drop, but it was rather quiet for a jazz club. Only the hum of the air-conditioning.

"On bass, Olaf Kiel!"

Olaf charged onstage and picked up his bass and started bowing it, making a screeching low sound.

"On drums, Fantastico Estrada!"

Fantastico walked on from the other side. He put his hands on his hips and gave his most pissed-off stare to David, who sank down in his seat. Then he sat down at the kit and started bashing away. David heard the now familiar "reverse-recorded cymbals" effect that had unnerved him in Brooklyn. But this was definitely not Brooklyn.

"On guitar... electric guitar I might add," preened the proud father of domesticated electricity, "Ernest Harriman."

Harriman charged on and went straight to Franklin. He grabbed the microphone.

"It's Ernst Harriman, not Er-nest!"

He shoved the mic back in Franklin's face, picked up his axe and jammed it up against the amplifier, bringing forth feedback clusters that sounded as if a lost rocket from Neptune had decided to crash the club without paying.

Franklin went on, but David could only read his lips, what with the music so rudely rude. Franklin was miffed and ready to give up.

"On keyboards," he quickly spat out, "Neumann Mandible, on tenor sax, Eddie Clovis, on trumpet, Varton White."

The three remaining men of the White Sextet walked on and situated themselves at their instruments. Mandible scraped his elbows all over the piano keys, producing violent *glissandi*. To David, it looked like a rape of a perfectly good piano. It ruined any thoughts of playing it. Clovis and White turned their horns around and held the open bells against their faces with the mouthpieces facing the audience. Above the din David could see their lips moving as they spoke into the apertures where the music normally came out:

"The world shakes and claws in pain and tears its entrails out
because we will it so, and so you will when he appears.
His mother a hyena and his father mighty viper
gave this trembling globe a doer who'll undo your sorry
sounds."

Billy leaned over to David and cupped his hands in front of
his mouth so David could hear.

"Just remember, this is all bullshit. His parents aren't a hyena
and a viper. They're Phil and Judy Mahozada from Syosset,
Long Island. His father's a retired postal worker and his mom's
a guidance counselor at Syosset Elementary school. Don't fall
for the bullshit!"

This temporarily broke the spell for David, and he calmed
down in his mentally constructed chair in the mentally constructed nightclub. He sat up. Clovis and White went on:

"He'll lead you to your graves and you will thank him with
your ears
as you are brought to truth your blood will boil with bridled
joy."

They spun their horns around to normal position and started
to play. It was an *ugglyy* tune, if you could even call it that.
Some scale patterns David didn't know. His mentally constructed shoulders began to twitch. They took down their horns
and shouted in dissonant harmony:

"The master of aghast-er, the leader of no meter, the disharmonic monarch of universeless song. His deadly swing
will take you out and carve you up for take-out food. He'll
put you in the mood for love where no love will be found....

336

please give a warm welcome to our favorite bad guy, Bob Ma-ho-za-daaaa!"

The Varton White Sextet stopped playing and applauded wildly. The audience watched in silence. The Whites were angry and applauded even louder. No audience response.

On came Bob.

Robert Herman Mahozada (or "Old B.M." as many of his detractors called him) was about five feet four inches tall. He weighed about one hundred and eighty pounds, and could have benefited from an occasional visit to the gym. He was nearly bald except for some curly brown tufts growing out of the sides of his head, which resembled earmuffs. He had on an old brown suit that looked like he'd slept in it for a week. He wore a spotted yellow tie, the kind office workers who are never going to make it up the corporate ladder wear. His button-down white shirt had a distinctly dingy appearance. His eyebrows were in dire need of trimming. In fact, had there been a Hollywood agent in the house that night casting for an overweight, over the hill leprechaun, Old B.M. would have been their man for sure.

Bob looked nervous. Well, why not? Even for the little Hitlers of the world, insecurity at the moment of a power grab is not out of the question. But Bob was here to rock the universal boat and make it up end like the Titanic if he could. He was an angry little man who had learned to manipulate sound to satisfy his really nasty needs. If people didn't really like Bob for his good qualities (good with numbers, a near-perfect memorization of the entire script of "Godfather III", and the ability to consume heart stopping amounts of cooked cabbage at a sitting), then by God (well, not God, but by whatever is unholy), he would use that tenor sax of his to obliterate them all.

And he could.

Total silence in the room. David held onto the table. Bob brought his sax to his lips. With sax in mouth he slurred out a "one-two-three-four" in his gravelly voice, and the band kicked in.

"FWAAACCHH!" was the name of the piece, and it did sound fwaaacchhish. It sounded like you were stuck inside a soon-to-die washing machine with Bob's dirty laundry. Bob was exceedingly not graceful in the way his body attempted to move with the music that they made. His jerky spastic little dance was out of sync with the band. They'd hit the down-beat and then sometime later B.M. would stomp his foot. David was incredulous. Was Mahozada unable to count, or was there method in his musical madness?

The timbre of his horn was like nothing David had ever heard. He immediately realized what a poor imitation of his mas-ter Clovis had been. Eddie had tried to imitate what David was now hearing. It didn't sound like a sax. It sounded like what an elephant in pain sounds like when you are the elephant. David had a headache that was panning from left to right in his skull and back again. Wherever Bob pointed his sax, David felt the pain.

Ben Franklin, who had been standing by the door smoking a cigar, spat in disgust and walked out to...whatever was outside that door. Two tables away, one of the mentally constructed old men with the young babes had a problem. His head exploded. Blood and guts spattered David's table. He jumped up in horror, but fortunately the gore disappeared almost as fast as it hit the table. At another table, a lovely young lady's ears spurt blood all over the floor.

It looked like it was going to be an unanswered rout of all good things, when out of the blue (in the white) David heard the most beautiful sound. It was a very fast, unaccompanied version of "When The Saints Go Marching In" played on the trombone.

Jack came walking from the back of the room, his brightly glowing trombone slide moving so fast that the spaces within it looked like solid gold. It was "When The Saints", but Jack was taking off into bebop Milky Way territory. The Fwaacchers stopped for a second. They heard Jack and then tried to resume their demolition derby. Jack jumped up on stage (careful to remove his trombone from his mouth at the moment of being airborne) and pointed his bell at Varton White. Varton aimed his trumpet back at Jack and they went at it.

White spat granite lines of rusty notes at Jack who made a disgusted face and pitched them back at White as perfectly rounded sequences of pristine tone. Now the stage started to grow in width and David did a double-take as Bread appeared at a second spontaneously-present drum kit, along with Sal standing next to him. They locked in their groove under Jack's lines and it sounded like a really well-oiled commando squad landing under cover of night in fast 4/4 time. Next Billy showed up onstage and sat down on the piano bench next to Neuman Mandible who, let's face it, wasn't much of a player to start with.

Billy sat there next to him, watching him play, completely unnerving Neumann, who got up and sulkily slunk off the stage altogether. Billy now dug in and David recognized the Gabriel scale mixed in with some altered Lydian lines. The tone was so deliberate. Nothing was wasted, nothing without purpose. Bob was pissed, and he blew harder. He pointed his horn at Billy and Billy bobbed and weaved his head to avoid Bob's brain bombs. As Billy shot back bitonal chord hits at Bob, Bob bobbed, too. As they both bopped, both Bob bobbed and Billy bobbed, but Bob's bobs were better than Billy's bobs, and Billy got hit a few times.

David could see that his teacher was in pain. David's hands started to shake. This was as close as he wanted to get to the action. He did not want to get up on that stage. Still, he'd climbed the ravine. He'd already been drafted. He now had a feeling that he was about to be volunteered.

Behind Billy, Ernst Harriman was flailing away at his frets. He was doing a Pete Townshend windmill on the strings, only incredibly, he was using his leg instead of his arm. Like an out-ake from "The Exorcist", it was an impossible contortion realized to diabolical sonic perfection.

Billy stopped playing and grabbed his head in agony. He fell off the bench and his body lay on the stage, rapidly becoming transparent. The audience had become enslaved and was in the grips of the Brooklyn Momphom Mahozadan lateral head swing (except for the guy whose head had exploded).

Enough, thought David, charging the stage. Better to die like a man than live like a musician. He jumped over Billy's transparent body and got to the piano bench. AARRRGH! The bench was too low. It was like those horrible gigs at hotels where the pianos were raised up on wheels so that the staff could move them from room to room. This left the piano player seated too low, and it left the short guys like David seated way too low. This was the wrong time to have this happen. Well, hell, if Jerry Lee Lewis, Little Richard, Elton John, and Keith Jarrett could do it, so could he. He stood up. He'd play standing if he had to.

Bob took one look at this upstart who stood before him replacing the great master, Billy Kovac. He aimed his sax at David's face and let loose a pachydermous proliferation of histrionic honks, and David evaporated.

David opened his eyes. He was in total blackness. The wind howled. He was back on the mountain! Bob had honked him completely out of the mental construct like Bluto knocking

Popeye out of a window before he can eat his spinach. His breaths were fast. The blanket was still wrapped around him. He could see nothing but stars. Was Billy still in the circle? Now what? How could he get back in?

He heard Billy's voice, very faintly, almost whispering. So he was still alive! He was reinitiating the vocal sequence. David tried to catch his breath and slow it down. He echoed Billy's feeble chants. Billy slipped into the mystery language. David mimicked it perfectly and soon the white light returned. He was back in the club. But there was Ben Franklin introducing the Varton White band again! He'd landed in the wrong time! Wait! Now he could warn Billy to avoid Bob's blasts.

He ran toward the stage. As he did, time fast forwarded and he saw himself at the piano being hit by Bob's honks. As he reached the piano bench he ducked in time to miss getting hit. He quickly grabbed the height adjusters on the bench and turned them up. Now he'd be high enough. Ernst Harriman tried to distract him by screaming obscenities at him.

David looked back at Harriman and said, "Fuck you, Ernestine."

Harriman turned red.

"It's ERNST! ERNST! ERNST! ERNST!!!" he screamed, almost foaming at the mouth.

Eddie and Varton stood on either side of Sal, blowing nasty vomitous disharmonies in his ears. Sal was a big, easy target. He picked up his upright bass, and held it sideways like a guitar and tore off a machine-gun-like run of thirty-second notes interspersed with super funky, thumb-popping pizzicatos but it was too late. He looked like Davy Crockett going down to Santa Ana's forces at the Alamo. He dropped the bass and ran off stage holding his ears.

David was afraid that he'd be overwhelmed, too. Clovis approached him amid the din and looked him in the eyes. Triumphantly, like a gladiator who has been given the thumbs down sign by the emperor to execute his vanquished rival, he looked at David and said one word.

"Stella."

Eddie was going to kill David by defeating him in a duel playing "Stella By Starlight", the tune that had humiliated him in Florida. Eddie launched into the song as he had in Florida at breakneck speed. He knew David would fall apart on his solo. Then he'd be eliminated by B.M.

Seeing Eddie's scheme in action, the rest of the Mahozadans jumped into the musical assassination plot. They must have heard from Eddie about Florida. What they didn't know is that David had been practicing "Stella" since that torturous tropical night.

First of all, in the calm of his apartment, David had realized that "Stella" was not an especially difficult tune at all. In fact, it was a very basic circle of fifths standard. Only in its many momentary modulations could the chord sequence get confusing. So, he had made a point of memorizing those chords inside out and outside in (which, by the way, are not opposites. They are in fact the same thing. The opposite of "inside out" would in fact be "inside in". Try this with your shirt.)

Secondly, working with Billy, he had learned how to interpolate the Gabriel scale and its attendant chords into the mix. His physical control of the instrument had improved, and at this point, David was beyond fear, and too tired to be nervous anymore.

Eddie ripped through two choruses of grungy ashcan runs that made you want to puke nails at your pet gerbils. David's aesthetic distaste for Eddie's solo made him want to say something musically that *meant* something. He wanted to construct the world instead of just tearing it down. He was sick of Eddie Clovis and his demeaning demeanor, which got more demeaning, the meaner he got. And now it was time for David to solo over "Stella", and if it was the last thing he played on this earth (though really, he wasn't on this earth at the moment), then so be it.

Yet, how could he solo on "Stella By Starlight" with Olaf Kiel on bass sure to sabotage him? Eight fast bars to go and he'd somehow have to make it work through the harmonic gauntlet that Olaf would throw at him. Four bars, two, then...another man appeared on stage. David's jaw did not drop, but he felt like dropping it. It was Mervyn Lewis.

Not only was it Mervyn Lewis, but he looked perfectly healthy. He wore a dapper three-piece suit and he had on the world's warmest smile. He held in his hands a glowing bass. It wasn't the same bass David had seen in Indiana. No physical instruments made the trip from mind to jazz club, but it was a beautiful bass. He stood next to Bread and they locked in on the groove to "Stella".

At the shock of seeing Mervyn appear, Olaf stepped back and fell onto Fantastico's drum kit, knocking half of it over. David, in joyful amazement, launched into his solo.

"Stella By Starlight" was no longer an obstacle course to David. A chain of conventional minor seventh to dominant seventh chords, sometimes resolving, sometimes not, it flitted through various keys. Rather than being lost in this chain, David rode it like a really adept surfer rides a wave. He opened with pentatonic lines in a McCoy Tyner fashion. Where the song expanded into longer phrases on a single chord, he dashed off lightning fast Art Tatum-inflected whole tone runs. Then, on his second chorus he moved into the Gabriel scale.

He made every note count as he had been taught to do. He thought about every time music had affected him throughout his life. He thought about all the people in the world who've ever been moved by music, and all the people in the world who weren't allowed to listen to it. He dug in deeper and felt energy move through him. He knew that something greater than himself was coming through him.

Bob started to blow his horn and the first blast hit David on the shoulder. When the next one came he thought of the *randori* four-man attack in the Aikido black belt test and he dodged it. As Bob blew, David kept dodging.

Then, he fused his Aikido understanding and his jazz understanding. Every time Bob began a line of negative music, David, in the great tradition of jazz, finished the line and turned it into a thing of beauty. No matter what darkness Bob came up with, David answered and completed it with a turning on of light. In Aikido, it was like taking an attack, spinning and joining with your adversary, and letting him use his negative energy against himself.

And now, something else was happening. This incredible white grand piano, started to give off another light. It started to glow. David's brain wanted to stop and look but his hands kept playing. Jack stepped over to him and reprised the melody to the song. There they were, David and Jack with their glowing instruments, and Bread swinging away on the drums with Mervyn smiling as he laid down a fat walking bass line.

The Mahozadans looked less corporeal and more like wraiths. They stated to fade. Olaf, Fantastico, Varton, Ernst, Eddie, Neumann, who was seated dejectedly at a table, and Bob.

Bob was yelling, "I'll be back, Notelickers!"

And Ernst Harriman, looked at David and said, "Remember my name, Ernst Harriman."

The Mahozadans were gone, and the quartet came to the end of the tune. Bread played a roll and a fill to signify an ending and Jack blew a cadenza. They hit what would seem to be the last note, and then David, not wanting to let this incredible feeling go, decided to add a musical ribbon to this package and to celebrate the triumph of good over evil. He played a series of chords that he had never combined before and immediately recognized them. He played a glorious melody up high on the keyboard that seemed to bring forth spirit over mind as the day's events had been mind over matter.

He gasped as he realized what he was playing. He had heard no other music like this in his life, except once. Once, when he had pressed that radio button in his apartment. It was him.

Somehow, some way, out of time like a one-sided mobius strip that turns in on itself and never ends, he was playing the music from the tape. *He was the player on the tape.* It had been him all along. He had made the journey from artifice to art and found that it was a circle.

CHAPTER
FORTY-SIX

*T*he audience had evaporated. A shaken Sal lay on the floor resting with one bloody ear. Billy was gone. Bread, Jack, and David sat at a table with Mervyn Lewis. The room was already becoming less distinct.

"How is it that you came to be here, Mervyn?" said David.

"My friends let me know that there was a need," said the older man.

"And who are your friends?"

"There are many people in the world dedicated to keeping the 'civil' in civilization, young man."

"I noticed our emcee tonight," said Bread.

"Yes," said Mervyn, "Ben Franklin is one of those cats. Guys like him pop up when they're needed. Tonight you needed a bass player, and very quickly I might add, so I took this job."

"If you hadn't shown up exactly when you did," said David, "I would have blown the gig."

"Well, maybe you would have and maybe not. You reach down far enough into yourself and you find what you need. You'd have worked it out with or without me."

"Well, we're glad you showed up," said Jack. "It was a pleasure playing with you."

"Oh, anytime, Jack, anytime!" laughed Mervyn. "Right about now I have to be going. I have a gig in Chicago. Blues club. Two a.m. set. Should be fun. Oh, by the way David, love what you played at the end of 'Stella'! That was extremely beautiful. Sort of sums up the whole meaning of the evening. I recorded it." Mervyn held up a little portable cassette recorder. "Hope you won't mind if I play it for my grandson, Thossian. Young people don't hear enough really good music these days."

"Not at all," said David, beginning to understand the idiosyncrasies of time.

There was no time. Only time in music. All the prophetic visions by people who had heard the tape. They didn't necessarily portend linear events. And they weren't necessarily correct visions either. Thossian had gotten it wrong. Mervyn didn't bleed on stage the way Thossian had dreamt it. No man in veils, unless it was Bob Mahozada. Still, it was pretty close.

"How'd you manage to bring a tape recorder into this place? I thought that physical objects couldn't accompany us?" asked David.

"Same way I got this suit in here, David. I willed it into existence. This tape recorder wasn't made in Japan, China, or Kansas City. I made it with my mind. The harder part will be transporting it back out, if you know what I mean."

"Can you do that?"

"If I can take my mind and my memory with me, I believe that I can take this damn little machine! Heck, I don't even need the machine, just the tape!"

Mervyn stood up. He took out a white pen. He removed the cassette tape from the machine and wrote upon the label.

"What did you write?" asked Jack.

Mervyn held up the tape. He had written the number "7" on the label.

David had always assumed it meant that there'd been at least seven copies of the tape. Maybe there had been only one.

"Why '7', Mervyn?" said Bread.

"You know, like the Miles tune, 'Seven Steps To Heaven'? That's what this young man played tonight. We all did. Seven steps to heaven. Um hum."

Mervyn waved.

"*I'm gonna take a little trip*," he sang with a mighty voice, "*Got my suitcase in my hand*" and walked out the door.

Quite a man, thought David. The kind of man who'd show up to sing at his own funeral.

CHAPTER FORTY-SEVEN

*T*he four men walked out the door. It was white out. They sat down on the white ground and found themselves back on the mountain. It was sunrise and the air was clear. Four men and five blankets.

"Is Billy dead?" asked David.

"It seems so, whatever that means," said Bread.

"What about the Mahozadans?"

"They're pretty resilient bastards," said Jack. "They may show up again someday. Or maybe not. Old B.M. will stay out of sight for a long time. We hurt his pride and his movement."

"Yes," said Bread. "Old B.M.'s movement has been eliminated."

They all laughed, even Sal. Sal was in pretty bad shape. It was decided that Sal would be taken down the mountain via the cog railway. The cog railway, built in the 1800's, was the steepest railroad in the world. An impossible "little engine that could"- style engine that pushed a passenger car up an elevated track from the west side of the mountain.

Jack and Bread agreed to take Sal down. David would hike down so that he could stop and pick up their valuables at Lakes Of The Clouds. Besides, it was a beautiful day. David decided that if he could get up the mountain and defeat the "Satanic anti-music hordes", he could certainly walk down the mountain.

At Lakes Of The Clouds he retrieved only their wallets and a few other articles and put them in his pack. The hutmasters agreed to keep most of their clothing and the other packs for autumn hikers in need.

As he maneuvered across the rocks toward the lip of Tuckerman Ravine, he thought about Mervyn. Somehow, Mervyn had brought through the recording of David playing piano. Somewhere in time he had given the tape to Thossian, who had passed it to Alex, who gave it to Simon, who played it on the radio before destroying it. And then, Mervyn was murdered, no doubt by Mahozadans. Why? Because with his music he spent his whole life standing up against people like them? Or because he had the tape and the tape was powerful?

The tape showed what music could be at its best. That music had come through David Stein's hands, from within him and from beyond him. Could he have prevented Mervyn's murder by warning him? Did Mervyn already know what would happen to him? Was he prescient, as Thossian had become, by hearing the tape? And did Mervyn "come back" to sing that last note of the blues at his own funeral?

He descended into the top of the ravine. When they had discussed the club, David mentioned that he had experienced a low resolution all-white environment. Jack had seen bright colors. Bread had seen everything with crystal clarity and high definition. Sal didn't remember what he'd seen. He still had a monster headache from Varton and Eddie's sounds.

The ravine was his now. He knew not to trifle with it, but felt blessed to be walking in it. The wind blew but the sun shone down, and the visibility up ahead was spectacular. He knew he was seeing fifty to a hundred miles on the horizon. The only clouds were behind him, but they were closing in fast.

He thought about God, and Jenna, and Sensei, and poor crazy Alex. He thought about who he really was beneath all the crap that he'd accumulated over the years. He remembered Sensei once saying that it's easy to meditate on the mountain, but when you come down from the mountain and go back to the city can you keep that feeling? There he was on the mountain, and he couldn't believe that he'd ever be the old David again, even in the lowliest of bars playing for drunks at three in the morning. He knew that he had profoundly changed.

He hiked along the ravine ledge, this time without leaning over in fear of falling. It was a narrow ledge, though. No point being stupid. Now the clouds blew in and caught up with him. Their speed was incredible. The old New England weather adage was true. He was on the ledge with only about fifty feet visibility in front and a drop of many hundreds of feet to his immediate right. Maybe he should have taken the cog railway? No. He had made peace with this mountain at last. He hiked on slowly and carefully. Ahead he saw a form in the fog. Was it a lost hiker? Or was he the lost hiker that they'd found?

"Hi," he shouted. "Nice day for a long walk, huh?" He waited for the laugh. No laugh. "Hello?"

Maybe they were German, or French. Still, "hello" was pretty universal.

He froze in his tracks. He knew that bulky figure. He thought that he'd never see it again. It was Eddie.

Eddie was supposed to be dead. Well, actually, Jack said they'd be back. But David didn't want to hear that. He thought they were gone to music hell, but maybe it was just wishful thinking.

There stood Edward Arthur Clovis III. High school bad boy gone worse. Too much time on his hands and not enough structure in his home life. Needed a soccer mom, got a gambler-turned-hooker instead. Absent father. Sister in jail for God knows what. Angry, bitter, futureless outlook. Big guy. Vindictive. Vituperative. Looking to avenge his master's humiliation. Took a chance and waited on the trail for David Stein to pass by.

Eddie spat on the ground. He was the troll under the bridge that David needed to trip-trap by. He was the anti-Friar Tuck that David needed to Robin Hood by.

David took his pack off as fast as he could (Carlos Castaneda's first rule: keep your hands free.) He didn't know if he should put the pack behind him, closing him in to Eddie, or in front of him, between himself and Eddie. There was nowhere else unless he dumped it over the edge. He opted to put it in front of him. Wrong.

Eddie walked over like a slow-moving freight train and stomped on it. Then he stood it up and kicked it over the edge. It disappeared in the fog.

"Shit! Are you fucking crazy?" said David, expertly trying to diffuse his adversary's anger. "You could kill somebody that way! What the fuck's the matter with you, you, you.....*PUTZ*!"

Unsuccessfully mollified, Eddie snarled. "I could kill somebody that way, Notelicker. I could kill you!"

David wondered if Eddie was afraid of him after David threw him in Brooklyn. For a nanosecond he felt pride. And as we all know, pride comes before a fall.

Eddie seemed loath to touch David, perhaps fearful. Instead, he picked up a rock the size of a teenage tortoise and held it over his head with two hands, a la Frankenstein's monster. David spun around and ran, except that you can't run on a boulder-strewn ledge in dense fog. The rock caught his heel and he yelped in pain as he kept moving.

Eddie was coming after him. He grabbed David and pinned him against the mountain side of the ledge. He towered over David, and held him by his sweatshirt collar. He open hand slapped him in the face. It was painful and degrading. He did it again. David's eyes watered and Eddie did it a third time. As his hand passed after the third slap, David spearhanded him in the throat. (He had not learned this at the *dojo*, but rather, he'd seen it in a movie).

While David felt as if he'd broken his middle finger, Eddie clutched his own neck and gasped and gurgled. David took the opportunity to duck and started running down the trail in the direction of the bottom of the ravine. His heel hurt and his eyes were so filled with water that he could barely see. Eddie was right behind him, still holding his throat.

David was running out of wind. The trail was slippery from the soaking wet fog. He turned to face Eddie. Eddie was barreling straight at him. He was going to get hit by a guy the size of a pro-football player. And this guy was going to murder him.

David stood with his right foot about ten inches behind his left. He stared straight into Eddie's raging eyes, and he made sure Eddie saw it. At the very last instant, David executed a perfect *sudori*, bringing his right foot in front of his left and jumping down on his right knee and his palms so that his very low-down right hip faced the charging bull. The bull tripped on David and went flying over him. He went over the side.

David heard an injured throat gurgle yell that lowered in pitch as gravity enabled the doppler effect. It lasted long enough for David to know that Eddie was gone. He didn't catch on a ledge, or hang on with one angry hand. He was off the gig.

A packless David Stein spent the morning leisurely hiking down Mt. Washington. The sun came out again and it was really quite a pleasant walk.

EPILOGARHYTHM

Whoever said that the spiritual path was an easy one was surely drunk.

It's not like David suddenly became an enlightened being. After all, he had to come back off the mountain figuratively, as well as literally, and go back to the city. Yes, he was somewhat different, but he was also just as much the same. He still had to play some pretty disgusting gigs to pay the rent. Not every note that he played was a gem, but you could certainly argue that he was capable of a new awareness, a new approach to playing the piano. It wasn't just about the Gabriel scale or his newly-glowing piano. It was more about the significance of being a musician and the meaning of music. But, he had to work at it. If he didn't keep his mind and heart open, they sometimes shriveled a bit. They sometimes returned to that cynical skeptical attitude that had always been his default template for being. Now though, there was always that potential for seeing things a new way, or putting his soul into his music.

He started to compose. He didn't play any of his compositions for anyone, but that didn't matter. He found notes that he cared enough to keep. Perhaps one day he'd share them with other people. Right now it was enough to make the musical choices and to write them down.

David also found himself becoming more patient with other people. He started to overlook their faults and he also didn't really have much left in the way of buttons that they might push to anger him. His zest for life increased but his fight or flight mechanism left town. He just wasn't all that pissed off anymore. He still made jokes, but they weren't as cruel as they might have been in the old days.

On August 16th, David went out to dinner with Jenna. He took her to a nice Japanese place on Columbus Avenue, not far from his apartment. They stared at each other and held hands. He got a feeling from being with her that was like hearing the Gabriel scale, and she glowed as much as any instrument might, but in a different way, of course.

This was a magical night, and he couldn't help but feel that his recent experiences had made him into a much better man. A man capable of loving and being loved by this wonderful woman. He wanted to take his time with this relationship. Still, part of him, the "good old David" part, thought how nice it would be to get her up to his apartment. God, that would be bliss. Just the two of them finally alone. Except, of course, for a certain flying head named Albert.

THAT'S ALL.

Made in the USA
Charleston, SC
28 February 2012